An Eternity of Mirrors:

Best Short Stories of Johnny Townsend

From over 500 short stories published over three decades, author Johnny Townsend presents several of his favorites.

A gay couple steals from the rich to support their favorite charities.

Two young women vie for the affection of the same missionary.

A father with a speech impediment is forced into the spotlight after his daughter survives a school shooting.

A reporter seeks the identity of Salt Lake's new superhero—a masked man wearing temples clothes who mysteriously shows up at crime scenes.

Two young missionaries in the Pacific Northwest sneak out on a date.

An uncle awaits word on his niece caught up in the 2004 tsunami.

Missionaries in Rome try to prevent a terrorist bombing.

Townsend's favorite stories celebrate life and love in an often-troubled world.

Praise for Johnny Townsend

In *Zombies for Jesus*, "Townsend isn't writing satire, but deeply emotional and revealing portraits of people who are, with a few exceptions, quite lovable."

Kel Munger, *Sacramento News and Review*

In *Sex among the Saints,* "Townsend writes with a deadpan wit and a supple, realistic prose that's full of psychological empathy….he takes his protagonists' moral struggles seriously and invests them with real emotional resonance."

Kirkus Reviews

Inferno in the French Quarter: The Upstairs Lounge Fire is "a gripping account of all the horrors that transpired that night, as well as a respectful remembrance of the victims."

Terry Firma, Patheos

"Johnny Townsend's 'Partying with St. Roch' [in the anthology *Latter-Gay Saints*] tells a beautiful, haunting tale."

Kent Brintnall, Out in Print: Queer Book Reviews

Selling the City of Enoch is "sharply intelligent…pleasingly complex…The stories are full of…doubters, but there's no vindictiveness in these pages; the characters continuously poke holes in Mormonism's more extravagant absurdities, but they take very little pleasure in doing so….Many of Townsend's stories…have a provocative edge to them, but this [book] displays a great deal of insight as well…a playful, biting and surprisingly warm collection."

Kirkus Reviews

Gayrabian Nights is "an allegorical tour de force…a hard-core emotional punch."

Gay. Guy. Reading and Friends

The Washing of Brains has "A lovely writing style, and each story [is] full of unique, engaging characters….immensely entertaining."

Rainbow Awards

In *Dead Mankind Walking*, "Townsend writes in an energetic prose that balances crankiness and humor….A rambunctious volume of short, well-crafted essays…"

Kirkus Reviews

An Eternity of Mirrors

Best Short Stories of Johnny Townsend

Johnny Townsend

Contents

Personal Favorites 9

The Italian 11

A Life of Horror 26

Elder Peterson's Penis 38

Best Christian Example 65

Temple Man 76

Woman on the Wharf 93

Life in the Dungeon 108

Kugel Exercises for Men 129

The Sunday After 142

Sneaking in the Carpenters 154

Ronnie and Clyde 164

The Date 185

Spirit Prison Blues 199

The Removal of Debra 219

Splitting with the Sister Missionaries 249

Partying with St. Roch 258

An Eternity of Mirrors 269

Books by Johnny Townsend 317

What Readers Have Said 336

Personal Favorites

Shortly after I returned to the U.S. from my two years as a Mormon missionary in Italy, I found a cassette tape at a local New Orleans music store. *Personale di Claudio Baglioni.* It seemed to be a Greatest Hits tape, and I fell in love with every song on it. Only later did I realize that while the cassette did indeed consist of "grandi successi," the most important consideration was that the songs were among Baglioni's personal favorites.

I lost track ages ago of how many short stories I've published. Probably over 500. No doubt many of them are clunkers. Some I liked were panned. Others I thought were so-so received more praise. Authors, readers, and critics have different needs and interests and are never going to agree on everything.

In deciding which stories to include in this "Best of" collection, I at first wanted to gather a wide variety to show my "range," hoping to appeal to different tastes.

Ultimately, though, it's a failing strategy. I can't possibly know what most readers or literary authorities will or won't like.

So I decided to simply choose stories that have stuck with me over the years, stories that make me smile when I flip through an old collection and start reading.

I wrote my first story when I was eight. I completed my first novel when I was sixteen. Fortunately, neither still exists. While I knew from an early age I wanted to "be a writer," it's been a skill requiring many years of study and far more effort than I could have imagined.

But it's the only job I've ever truly enjoyed. And when I get something right, I feel more satisfaction than I do for almost anything else in my life.

I hope to share some of that pleasure with you now.

The Italian

I first met Sandro three months after I moved out of my family's apartment in Vomero. I didn't want to be one of those Italian men who lived with his parents until he turned forty. Nineteen and ready to face the world, I found a dingy place in downtown Napoli but of course could rarely afford to eat out. One day, however, I stepped into a tiny pizzeria and ordered two etti of pizza bianca—their cheapest pizza. I could see on the scale that the young man behind the counter had placed almost three etti on my paper.

Just as I was about to protest, he put a finger to his lips and announced, "Due etti," and told me what I owed him. He winked as I walked out the door with my free etto of pizza, and I knew I had to go back. To see him, of course, not for another free bit of food, though I had to admit that possibility was tempting as well.

Two weeks passed before I could afford another such extravagance. When I walked into the pizzeria, Sandro was behind the counter, singing "Biancaneve," every bit as animated as I'd seen Rino Martinez on RAI. "I'm paying you to work," a middle-aged man thundered from the rear of the store, "not to sing." But Sandro continued to mouth the words as he greeted me with a smile. He stopped just long enough to ask if I wanted two more etti of pizza bianca.

He remembered me.

I wanted to order something more expensive this time, but even the pizza bianca was stretching my budget. After he handed me my slice and I turned over my lire, I decided to be bolder this time and not immediately walk out the door. I took a bite, savoring the rosemary, and tried to think of something clever to say.

Sandro looked to be about my age, perhaps a couple of years older. He was tall, a good 1.75 or 1.78 meters. His dark brown hair partially covered his ears, and his half-filled moustache wiggled like a caterpillar when he continued to mouth the words to the next song.

I wondered what his moustache would feel like against my lips.

"I'm Gaetano De Luca," I said. I wanted to reach out and offer my hand, but the glass counter was too high to make that practical.

"Alessandro Rizzi," he replied. "My friends call me Sandro."

"I'm not paying you to make friends," the middle-aged man shouted from the back.

I grabbed a pen from my pocket and tore a piece off the back page of a book I was carrying. "Here's my number," I said. "Maybe we can hang out sometime."

Sandro smiled and began singing, "Lisa se n'é andata via."

"Try selling some pizza," the man shouted from the rear.

I let my fingers touch Sandro's just a tad longer than necessary as I handed him my number. He called two days later, and we decided to meet at Piazza Nazionale, just a couple of blocks from the pizzeria. I wore a pair of American jeans and a T-shirt that said, "The Cars," with a photo on front of a girl smiling behind a steering wheel. Sandro also wore jeans, his T-shirt plain white. I was mesmerized by his nipples and flat stomach. Clearly, his boss didn't let him take home much leftover pizza.

"Want to get some coffee?" I asked.

Sandro shook his head. "I'm too poor to do anything that fun," he said. "I even had to call you from a pay phone since I don't have a line myself. You mind just sitting for a bit?"

I shrugged, unsure if I wanted to admit my own poverty this early. At the same time, I didn't want him to worry I considered him beneath me. "Do you like working in the pizzeria?" I asked. "Any plans to do something else?"

Now it was his turn to shrug. "I'm a zingaro," he said. "No birth certificate. No ID. I'll never be able to get a good job."

"A zingaro?" I repeated. "You look awfully pale for a gypsy." Almost no one used the term "Roma" in a country whose capital bore the same name.

"There was probably an American serviceman somewhere in my family tree." He grinned.

"Where're you from? Your accent's different."

"Up north," he replied, his smile fading. "I don't want to talk about that."

I nodded. "My father works for *Il Mattino*," I said after a moment. "I've got a job in the newspaper's mailroom. You have to know someone to get even a low-level position anywhere in this town. It's a start."

"Sounds a little stuffy." Sandro wrinkled his nose. "I just want to be free."

"It's easier to be free when you have money." I was thinking more about my own situation than his and didn't realize how my comment might sound until after I said it.

He shook his head. "I feel free every day of my life. Even with Cerasuolo breathing down my neck at work."

I took a deep breath and blurted out what I'd been thinking since the first moment I'd met him. "Do you feel free enough to spend the night with me?"

Sandro's face first registered surprise, but he followed that expression with a big smile. "Does tonight work for you?"

We walked to my apartment on Via Parma, Sandro explaining that he lived just a few blocks away on Vico Tutti Santi. I hoped he was hinting we could continue seeing each other. Scaffolding covered the building next to mine. Empty cardboard boxes and dog feces dotted the sidewalk. A rat so unfazed by our presence someone had probably already named him sauntered by.

Still, the neighborhood wasn't as grungy as the ghetto on the other side of Via Roma. I showed Sandro into my apartment. Not even any cockroaches in here, thankfully. I couldn't give the man much of a tour, of course, as I only had the one bedroom, and a kitchen even smaller than my tiny bathroom. Sandro trembled as I took his hand.

"What's wrong?" I asked.

"I-I've never done this before."

"But you sounded so smooth back in the piazza."

"Well, it's all about putting on a show, isn't it?" He smiled nervously. "I've *wanted* to do this for a long time. I've thought about it." His cheeks reddened. "Way too much. It's just scarier now that it's happening." He paused for a moment. "Have you…?"

I nodded. I'd had sex with a cousin when I was fourteen and later that year with a boy in my liceo. And then with a teacher in my liceo. But it was hard to do much while still living with my parents. That only gave me a few months in my own apartment without supervision, and I didn't have enough money to go to any clubs where I might meet men. Since I'd never done anything sexual as an adult, either, I was almost as nervous as Sandro.

I pulled off his T-shirt and he pulled off mine. We took our own shoes off, and while I wanted to be the one to pull his pants down, I let him finish disrobing on his own. We stood staring at each other by the foot of the bed.

"You're not a zingaro," I said, pointing. Sandro was circumcised. His brow furrowed at my statement and he started to protest. "You're a Jew," I concluded. "But that's okay. I have nothing against Christ-killers."

Sandro's mouth fell open.

"Cretino." I laughed. "I'm kidding. As many hang-ups as Catholics have, I'm glad you're Jewish."

Sandro looked at the floor with a weary expression, and I vowed to learn more about Jews so that even my jokes wouldn't be so prejudiced. But I had something more pressing on my mind at the moment. I pulled Sandro close and hugged him loosely, rubbing my hairy chest softly against his bare chest. He closed his eyes and shuddered.

We climbed into bed together and began kissing. Knowing this was Sandro's first time, I made sure to go slow and make the event memorable. After such a long wait myself, I wanted to go slow for my own benefit as well. Two hours passed before we finished. "I feel like I should offer you a cigarette," I said, "but I don't smoke."

"I don't smoke, either. You have any music you can play?"

I slipped a cassette into my player, and soon Al Bano and Romina Power were singing "Felicità," low so as not to disturb the neighbors. "Kind of sappy, I know," I said, "but I've liked Romina Power ever since I learned her father was gay."

"Gay," Sandro repeated, looking at the ceiling. Then he turned to me. "Can I see you again sometime?"

I smiled and reached over to give him a kiss.

We began dating regularly, calling each other boyfriend right from the beginning. One afternoon we walked through Capodimonte park. Another afternoon we caught the funicolare up into the ghetto. On yet another occasion, we strolled around Piazza Carlo Terzo, memorable not because Sandro let his arm touch mine as we sat on a bench but because we witnessed a Camorra killing not five meters away.

We walked along the waterfront one evening in the rain. Sandro showed me the spot on Castel dell'Ovo where he worked his first job as a fisherman, a job he loathed but which gave him enough money to move from a rented room to his own apartment. As much as I enjoyed our strolls, Sandro's hours at the pizzeria were awful and we couldn't see each other nearly as often as I wished.

He slept over two nights a week, even if we didn't have much chance to do anything other than talk about pizza or office mail and then have sex. He invited me to his place once, but the one time was enough. The place was so damaged from the earthquake a couple of years before that I was surprised it hadn't been condemned. We spent the rest of our nights together at my apartment.

"Maybe you *are* a gypsy," I said one evening after we'd been talking about movies for a while. "You know so little about Totò and Nino Manfredi and Claudia Cardinale. A Jew would be better educated."

He smiled but didn't answer.

We went to a neighborhood bar for some acqua Ferrarelle, a real luxury, and Sandro put a coin in the jukebox, singing "Sarà Perché Ti Amo" as he danced across the floor. He finished on his knees, taking my hand in his and giving it a kiss. I looked about nervously. Napoletani weren't the most progressive of people. A young woman drinking an aranciata hissed "Finocchi!" loudly and then walked up as if she might hit us.

"Valeria," she said, her hands on her hips, jutting her chin upward in a challenge. When her frown turned into a mischievous smile, we introduced ourselves as well. "My brother Gennaro's gay," she went on. "Dad beats him every time he stays out all night." She shrugged. "But what's a guy gonna do?" She lifted her hands upward in frustrated supplication. "Dad would absolutely murder me if I stayed out, and that's no exaggeration."

Sandro hugged himself at the words.

"What time do you have to be home?" I asked her.

"10:00. Enough time to have a little fun, but not much. Gotta be heading back now."

"You and your brother should come over to our place some night and dance," Sandro suggested. It was the first time he'd referred to my apartment as ours. I found I liked the sound of it. That night after we made love, I asked if he wanted to move in.

"We've only been dating six weeks," he said.

"Seven."

"Seven," he conceded.

"Do you love me?" I asked.

He smiled. "It's just that getting married so soon seems like something people in my family would do."

"Your gypsy family?" I asked. "Or your Jewish one?"

The following Sunday, Sandro moved his few clothes and other belongings into my apartment. Perhaps with our combined income, we could now eat out in a real restaurant once in a while or go see a movie. There were posters for a new Fellini film plastered all about the neighborhood next to the various death notices. I wanted to go with Sandro to Sorrento and Castellammare. I wanted to take him to Capri to see how beautiful it was, though I wasn't sure anything was more beautiful than looking at him across the table from me in the kitchen first thing in the morning.

About a week after we officially became a couple, two Jehovah's Witnesses knocked on our door. Sandro came up to see who I was talking to and grew even paler than usual. "Non ci interesse," he said curtly and shut the door. Later that night, he awoke from a nightmare, sitting bolt upright in bed. "You okay?" I asked, taking his hand.

"Y-yes," he replied. "I am now."

"What does 'el dair' mean?" I asked. "You kept saying it in your sleep. Are you Spanish?" Maybe that accent he had wasn't even from another region of Italy.

"Non ne voglio parlare."

"But why, sweetie? Why don't you want to talk about it?"

"Non ne voglio parlare," he said again. He put his head back down on the pillow, and I let my arm drape across him as we both fell back to sleep.

We had Gennaro and Valeria over most Saturday nights for the next little while. Sandro could mimic any singer he wanted, entertaining us with "Una Notte Che Vola Via," "Una Sporca Poesia," "Romantici," and "Maledetta Primavera." How he could sound just like Loretta Goggi was beyond me.

One night, Gennaro asked if he could stay overnight with us. I kissed him on one cheek while Sandro kissed him on the other as we said no.

Things were getting worse at the pizzeria. Cerasuolo yelled at Sandro more and more and once slapped him across the face. "You've got to find another job," I told him as we undressed that night, looking at the mark the man had left.

"I can't," Sandro replied. "I'm a gypsy. I don't have any papers. No one will hire me."

He started tapping the side of his head with the butt of one hand, groaning softly.

"I talked to my father. He knows someone who can get you a job as a door-to-door salesman."

"*No!*" Sandro squeezed his eyes shut and began swaying slightly side to side.

"Then get a job in a café," I said. "Get a job in a libreria."

"I'm a gypsy," he repeated. "I don't have any papers!"

He now began smacking the butt of his hand hard against his forehead, his eyes squeezed shut even more tightly. I wondered if he was having a seizure.

Or if maybe he was a little crazy.

I wondered if he loved me enough to tell me what was going on.

And if I loved him enough to listen.

"Stop it," I said. I caressed his upper arms until he slowly stopped moving. "Tell me the truth."

"I-I'm a gypsy."

I pulled him down onto the bed beside me and wrapped an arm around him.

"Sandro."

And then it came out. Sandro was really Kevin Stovall of Orem, Utah. He'd been a Mormon missionary here in Italy and had known before the end of his first month that he never wanted to go back to America. He studied the language longer each day than the time allotted and had a good ear to begin with, so by the time his two-year assignment was nearing an end, he could convince most people he was from "up north." Napoletani had such a sloppy accent to begin with that anyone speaking crisply seemed upper crust.

"I couldn't go back to my family," he said, "once I knew I was gay and needed a man. They'd be so disappointed."

"What did you tell them?"

He shook his head. "I ran away in the middle of the night. I never told anyone anything."

"But Sandro—I mean, Kevin—they must be worried sick."

"Don't call me Kevin. My name is Sandro now."

"Sandro, you've *got* to call your parents."

He put his head in his hands. "What could I possibly say?"

"Even the truth is better than what they must be imagining."

"I'll think about it, Gaetano. Really, I will." He smiled. "You've already made my life better than it ever was before. Even getting slapped at work can't change that."

But I couldn't let the man I loved continue in that job. I understood now why Sandro didn't have any papers. He didn't want anyone to know he was American. Of course, even as an American, he wouldn't be able to work without a permit. But if he wanted to pass himself off as an Italian, that really did put him in the same position as the zingari. Unless…

I knew a guy at the newspaper who said he knew a guy in the Camorra. I arranged to meet the man and ask to have a birth certificate and ID made. I expected it would cost enough that I'd need to talk my father into a small loan, but the guy with the Camorra agreed I could pay simply by transporting something for him. He didn't say what it was and I didn't ask. A week later, someone showed up at my apartment with a camera, and a few days after that, Sandro had his papers.

"Jobs still aren't easy to find around here," I said, "but at least now you have a fighting chance."

"I'd take any job in the world as long as I could come home to you every evening."

"Now you're sounding like Romina Power."

"Or at least like her father."

Three more months passed. Sandro did call his family and tell them about us. Instead of being relieved to hear he was okay, they hung up the phone and made no effort to contact him again. Perhaps someday they'd change their minds.

My father was unhappy about my living arrangements, too, but said that as long as I didn't tell anyone at the newspaper, he wouldn't disown me. When my mother invited Sandro over for dinner, I knew we'd passed our biggest hurdle. Sandro entertained everyone with an a capella rendition of "Storie di Tutti i Giorni" that left even my father impressed.

"You know," he told me over the phone the following day, "your…friend…has a strong presence in front of people. He'd make a good tour guide. I know a fellow who runs a tour company in Pompeii—he did some advertising with the paper—and I think I can get him to talk to Sandro. If you want."

"We want."

I didn't tell Sandro until the appointment was confirmed. "Make sure he knows you can give tours in both English and Italian," I said. Sandro had to call in sick in order to meet with the owner of the tour company, which left Cerasuolo yelling and making threats, but Gennaro filled in for the day and eventually took over the position when Sandro got the new job.

We promised to help Gennaro find something better, too.

A month later, once we'd finally saved a little money, Sandro and I held a party at our place to celebrate a new beginning. Gennaro came with Vittorio, a guy he'd just met over the counter at the pizzeria, and Valeria came with Stefano, a guy she'd met over an aranciata a couple of weeks earlier, who was cuter than any of the rest of us. Sandro sang "L'italiano" quite convincingly but saved his last performance until after the others had left. "Tu Cosa Fai Stasera?" he asked.

And I answered by holding out my hand.

A Life of Horror

"No," Albert said into the phone, distracted by a poster of *When a Stranger Calls*. "I can't see you tonight."

"Why not?" Brad asked with a note of concern. "You okay? We had this planned."

"I'm not feeling good."

"What's wrong?"

"I don't feel well enough to talk about it, Brad. I gotta go."

"I hope you feel better, hon. I love you."

Albert didn't say anything. He just closed his eyes and hung up the phone.

Albert was tired of West Hollywood, tired of L.A., tired of his apartment, tired of his job, tired of Brad, tired of everything. He'd been living in this basement for over eighteen years. It was rent-controlled, and he simply couldn't find anything else for the price. Even with all his movies, though, he wasn't really crowded. He simply wanted something different. A change.

Albert leaned back on his black leather sofa and looked about him. A poster advertising Dario Argento's *Opera* was tacked to one wall. A narrow poster advertising a William Castle movie hung from another, at the top a life insurance form promising any moviegoer a thousand dollars if they died of fright while watching the film.

There wasn't much wall space available for posters, of course. Almost every inch of every wall in the entire apartment was filled with shelves, and those shelves were filled with DVDs and VHS tapes. OOP movies. Out of print. Thousands of them.

Albert had always liked movies, horror movies mostly, and he'd even earned a film degree at Loyola Marymount, hoping to get into the business. He'd worked on a handful of projects back in the 1980's, in the lowliest possible positions, until he realized it would take more years and far more energy than he possessed to ever force himself into a position of power where he could influence the way a film turned out.

He'd taken a couple of office jobs in the industry, had gone to the Cannes Film Festival once and to Tokyo another time. And he'd even been asked to take part in several film commentaries by a couple of directors he knew, credited as a "film historian." But as much as he liked movies, he decided he was simply going to have to forge his own path.

He ran into someone who was closing out their inventory of VHS tapes, getting rid of a bunch of movies about to go out of print. Albert bought them for almost nothing and decided to try selling them on Amazon. And to his surprise, people bought them. For $50 each, $85 sometimes, even $100.

From that moment on, Albert made his living scouring the internet for news on which tapes and DVDs were going out of print, looking for stores or individuals selling them cheap, and finally selling them in turn for whatever people were willing to shell out. He'd paid his way through life for almost seventeen years now feeding people's twisted desires to own, to collect, at any price.

Cannibal Apocalypse. The Butchers. The Deathmaster. A Polish Vampire in Burbank. The Psycho Lover. A Scream in the Street. Slumber Party Massacre III.

Albert wasn't sure why people were willing even to pay regular prices for some of this crap, much less top dollar. Only one in a hundred horror movies was worth seeing. He should know. He'd seen them all.

He walked to the kitchen, large enough to house three more shelving units on wheels, which he'd bought for a few dollars each from a Blockbuster going out of business. He started to eat a banana but then stared at it, half peeled.

He needed to see Brad.

He pulled out his cell phone and punched in Brad's number.

"Hey there!"

"Brad, let's go ahead and have dinner at Hugo's tonight after all."

"You're feeling better?"

"No, but I still need to see you."

"Great! I'll be there at 7:00."

Albert looked at his watch. It was not quite 4:00. His mail run was done for the day, always tedious because he had to stand in two different long lines, one to send packages and another to pick up mail. Maybe it was time to take Wilbur on a walk again. "Wanna go out?" he asked the gray-haired, shaggy mutt staring up at him from his toy mouse.

Wilbur wagged his tail furiously, and Albert hooked up the leash. They walked out of the apartment, up some stairs, then down some more, and out onto the street. West Hollywood was the kind of place where you had to lift weights for ten minutes before taking out your trash. Buff men walked by at almost any hour.

Albert was a bit short at 5'5" but slim and defined, with dark, straight hair, a goatee and a labret. For Wilbur's walks, Albert stayed away from the main street and wandered through the residential area, historic two-story homes and newer three-story apartment buildings. There was Susan, walking her Lab. And there were Jeff and Carl, walking their poodle.

Wilbur strained at the leash, hoping to visit his doggy friends, but Albert held him back. He was so tired of the same old mundane conversations he had every day with the other dog walkers in the neighborhood.

Susan waved and Albert nodded politely, yet he made no effort to head over toward her. Wilbur peed, and they made their way back to the apartment.

Back inside, Wilbur was still excited from his walk. He grabbed a chew stick and threw it in the air and chased it. Then he threw it another time and chased it again. Albert smiled. Wilbur could entertain himself like this for an hour.

But Albert couldn't. He felt he was staring at the four walls of a prison cell, trapped inside an iron maiden. He wanted to scream. He wanted out.

Blood Bath 2. Bollywood Horror Collection. Revenge of the Living Dead Girls. Phantasm.

Albert found himself absentmindedly rubbing his arm, and he finally looked down to see what had distracted him. He saw the scar his mother had left when she bit him once when he was thirteen.

His parents had divorced when Albert was twelve. All three of his siblings had immediately chosen to move in with their father. Albert hadn't liked his siblings and so stayed with his mother. But she threw Kleenex boxes at him, threw ink pens, threw forks at him. She bopped him on the head, slapped him, yelled at him, and bit him. She'd leave him alone for two or three days at a time while she headed out to the bars and went home with different guys.

Even at the time, Albert realized he shouldn't be left alone for so long, but since it was the only peace he ever got, he certainly wasn't going to complain about it.

Popcorn. Fright Night II. Sleepaway Camp. Let's Scare Jessica to Death. Clownhouse. Nightmares.

Albert watched Wilbur play for another moment. The dog was now messing up his throw rug, wrinkling it, trying to unwrinkle it, and then wrinkling it again. He looked at Albert and wagged his tail.

Albert shook his head. He couldn't do it. He picked up the phone and called again. "Hey, loverboy," Brad answered.

How could he possibly marry someone named Brad, Albert wondered. He'd be singing songs from *The Rocky Horror Picture Show* every time he introduced the man as his husband. "I'm going to have to cancel again," Albert said bluntly. "I'm sorry."

There was silence on the other end of the line for a moment. "Okay, honey. It's not the end of the world. We'll have dinner tomorrow night."

"Sorry."

Albert went to lie down, on his single bed in a little nook in the living room. The sole bedroom in the apartment was Albert's office, with his desk, his computer, more shelves, and his collection of *Famous Monsters of Filmland*, which he'd saved for almost forty years. He even had a *Vampirella* and *Creepy* collection, the only things he still kept from his childhood. The *Lost in Space* robot he'd bought as an adult. The *Alien* action figure, too.

Albert turned on the fan. The basement stayed cool most of the time, even when it was 88 degrees outside like today. And his electricity was included in the rent, so he could turn the air conditioner on any time he wanted without worry. He just didn't think it was very good for the planet to turn it on unless he really needed it.

Like he cared what happened to the planet. *He* was never going to have any kids.

He was never going to get married, either, despite Brad's proposal the night before. He was fifty-two years old, for goodness' sake. He'd never had a partner. A few boyfriends over the years, naturally, but none had lasted more than a few months. Mostly, he picked up guys in bars. The last few years, he barely bothered with that.

And then he'd met Brad six months ago. That had been at a local grocery. Brad was another fifty-year-old with a great body. A hairdresser in West Hollywood. Another flighty, self-indulgent jerk like everybody else in West Hollywood.

Only Brad wasn't a jerk.

Brad had been a Mormon missionary when he was just out of high school. He'd served in the Peace Corps after that. He'd been dumped by all his Mormon friends and family when he came out. Albert had heard that those people were supposed to value family more than anything else. Brad had explained that they were supposedly "sealed" for all eternity.

But even good families were worthless, it seemed. Yet Brad had made a life for himself, found a partner and been happy with him for over twenty years, until his partner died of pancreatic cancer a few years ago.

And now he wanted to replace the love of his life with Albert, who could never be that for anybody. It just proved how selfish humans were. Brad needed a body, and Albert was available.

That was love?

Albert looked at the DVDs on the wall beside his bed, reaching over to caress the plastic cases. *Demons II. Bleeders. Killer Inside Me. Horror Express. The Brood. Dangerous Seductress. Madman.*

Albert's oldest brother had died of a brain tumor when he was twenty-seven. Their father had died of a heart attack related to his diabetes when he was fifty-two. Fifty-two, sheesh. And Albert's remaining brother had died of melanoma just three years ago. The only ones left were his sister, living in Cancún, and his mother, still living in Boston.

When Albert visited every couple of years, his mother did nothing but sit in front of the TV all day. She'd have one TV on in one room on one channel, and another TV on in another room on another channel. It drove Albert crazy.

But she didn't yell anymore.

Of course, the lack of yelling didn't mean the presence of happiness. There was no such thing as happiness. Albert wanted to be happy. He wanted Brad to leave him alone. He wanted to be married to the man he loved. He wanted to watch a good movie and escape into another world. He wanted to die.

He grabbed the phone again. "Brad?" he asked when the line picked up.

"Are you okay, Albert?"

"I think we should break up."

There was silence on the other end of the line. Finally, Brad said slowly, "I love you, Albert."

"No! I don't want to hear that! I'm hanging up now! Good-bye!"

Albert slammed his cell onto the coffee table, mini-posters of *Sharktopus* and *The Boy Who Cried Werewolf* beneath the glass, and saw Wilbur looking back at him with his head cocked, his tail at half-staff, wagging uncertainly. Albert spread his arms, and Wilbur leaped into them. Wilbur licked Albert on the lips, and Albert buried his face in the dog's fur.

This was the first dog Albert had ever owned. He'd never wanted the responsibility, but his boyfriend John five years ago had adopted a puppy and then didn't take care of it. Albert had been furious, had taken the dog to his own apartment, and told John never to speak to him again.

And it *was* a lot of responsibility. He couldn't go on day-long DVD runs like before. He had to plan everything around Wilbur's three daily walks. He couldn't stay out all night. He couldn't take a weekend trip somewhere.

But he loved Wilbur.

Witchcraft 666. Don't Answer the Phone. Scanners. Zombie Chronicles. Ilsa. Slaughter Vomit Dolls.

Albert went to his office and checked his emails to catch up on the last bit of business for the day. He'd check again right before bed. He usually sold two to five movies a day, just enough to keep him solvent. He didn't need anybody else.

He remembered the time he was twelve, not long after the divorce. He'd come home from band practice and started feeling ill. Before long, his right side was killing him. He tried to tough it out, but the pain soon became excruciating. Albert tried calling his mother but couldn't track her down. No cell phones in those days. She wasn't at work, and she wasn't with the one boyfriend Albert was aware of.

Then he called his father and told him he needed to go to the hospital. His father had said he wanted to finish making dinner for the other kids and then he'd be over. His father never did show up, but his mother did, just in time to get him to the hospital minutes before the doctor said his appendix would have burst.

Albert walked to the kitchen and opened a bottle of mineral water.

Life sucked. Boo hoo.

He hated everyone.

Albert rarely took naps, but he felt so listless today that there was nothing else he wanted to do. He lay down on his bed, patted the mattress for Wilbur, and then cuddled with the dog. He listened to the whir of the fan and to Wilbur's heartbeat, and he slowly dozed off.

Later, he heard a noise. The clock on the wall said 7:00. He'd better get up if he wanted to get any sleep later. He threw his legs over the bed, and Wilbur jumped down and ran to the kitchen, whimpering in pleasure.

There was another knock. Albert rubbed his forehead and stumbled groggily to the door to look through the peephole.

No horror movie fan of any caliber would simply open up without checking.

It was Brad.

"What are you doing here?"

"We're eating at Hugo's. You like their breakfast food for dinner."

"I'm not going out with you at all. We broke up."

Brad came inside, ignoring the *Dawn of the Dead* poster near the kitchen door. He took Albert's hands, and Albert grew angry when he felt tears coming to his eyes. Why didn't Brad just go away? He was rude and insensitive to come over like this.

"Albert, I'm going to love you for the rest of your life, and it's going to be okay."

Albert shook his head, unable to say anything. He shook his head some more, and Brad pressed it gently against his shoulder.

They hugged for a long moment and then headed out the door. They went up some stairs and down some others, and then they were out on the street. They walked up to the main drag, turned the corner past the massage parlor, and, holding hands, walked up the street to the restaurant.

Elder Peterson's Penis

"Oh, Mom," Bonnie said breathlessly, "you should have seen it! Elder Peterson's penis was *this* big!"

"No!"

"Yes!"

Valerie sat on the bed in the next room, listening to the two talking in the bathroom and growing angry. How *could* this be happening again? Valerie hadn't been to church in two years and had only gone infrequently for five years before that because of the way the bishop had treated her when she'd confessed three times to having sex with Keith. But Bonnie and her mother, Sister Pecorino, were *excited* over the fact that Bonnie had had sex in the living room last night with one of the two Mormon missionaries who lived in their rented garage out back.

And Bonnie had just been to the temple to get her endowments not three months ago! It just made Valerie *furious*.

"All ready?" asked Bonnie, coming back into the bedroom. "You got your list of places to go?"

"I'm ready."

"Good." Then, turning on a big smile as artificial as her brows, Bonnie swirled around. "Don't I look cute in this?"

Valerie wanted to vomit. "Yes," she said. "You're beautiful. As always."

"Oh, well, I know I'm not *perfect*, but I guess I can get any guy I want."

"Come on," Valerie said, rising and grabbing her purse. "I want to get there before someone else gets the job."

They climbed into Bonnie's tiny car, and Bonnie looked longingly at the small garage apartment where the two missionaries lived. Elder Andrews had been there almost a year, and Elder Peterson for six months, but this morning Elder Peterson had completed his two-year mission and had left for home in Utah.

He'd promised to come back during Mardi Gras to pick Bonnie up, but as Valerie watched Bonnie's wistful gaze, she knew the guy would never be coming back. Guys never really cared about girls.

Bonnie drove over the Mississippi River Bridge, then across New Orleans and into Metairie, where she dropped Valerie off at an eye surgeon's office. "Okay," she said, "I've got shopping to do to keep my mind off Elder Peterson. You've got enough change to get home?" Before even waiting for an answer, Bonnie took off for Clearview Shopping Center.

Valerie stood on the street, watching her go. "Yes," she said to the exhaust fumes. "I have enough change for the three buses I'll need to get back. Thanks for asking."

She turned to look at the eye surgeon's office. Valerie had been a receptionist with a law firm for four years before Keith had talked her into going to nursing school. Now that she'd flunked out of Charity, she needed a new job until she could transfer to another school. But if she had to go back to being a receptionist, she at least wanted it to be related to medicine in some way. She walked confidently through the door and filed an application. She complimented the receptionist on her hair so maybe the woman would say something nice about Valerie when handing the application to her boss later.

The woman looked at her suspiciously, though, as if she were afraid Valerie would be too much competition, and Valerie wished she hadn't put her make up on so well that morning. You had to look good in the interview with the men, but you couldn't look too good when the women who were forwarding the applications to those men saw you.

After her first stop, Valerie started down her list of other offices, going next to a dental office, then to an optometrist office, another dental office, and to an orthodontist office. Did people in the suburbs all have bad teeth? Valerie walked or took buses the rest of the day until she'd applied at ten offices altogether and was too tired to try any more.

Since it was mid-January, it was already dark when Valerie walked back to Bonnie's house from the bus stop. Two of the streetlights were out and another flickered unhelpfully as she walked down the center of the street. She knew she was lucky Bonnie and her family had been willing to take her in when she'd been kicked out of the dorm just before Christmas. It was only for a few weeks, but it was more than Keith had been willing to do. Valerie wished Bonnie could help a little more with transportation, but Bonnie clearly didn't want to be bothered, so there was no point in asking.

Keith said she wasn't worth helping, anyway.

Valerie paused when she climbed to the porch, looking around back to where the elders lived. The window was dark. Peterson and Andrews had both originally served in Haiti until political problems forced them out, so they were here in the Baton Rouge mission as French-speaking missionaries. With Elder Peterson gone, Elder Andrews would need another French-speaking companion. Without one, he'd been sent to live for now with two English-speaking elders. Valerie wondered if she'd ever see him again. She might have to go back to church after all.

Trying to put him out of her mind, Valerie forced a smile and went into the house. "Don't I look cute in this?" Bonnie was asking her mother, modeling a new outfit she must have bought that day.

"No, sweetie," Sister Pecorino corrected gently, "you should say, 'Doesn't this outfit look cute on me?'"

Bonnie laughed. "Oh, mother." Then she saw Valerie and came bounding over.

"You look wonderful," Valerie said, wanting to preempt the question.

It was ten more minutes before Bonnie remembered why Valerie had been out all day and asked about the job hunt. Valerie was too tired to be perky, so she simply admitted she doubted she'd gotten any of the positions and that she'd have to try again tomorrow. "Well, you know I can't take you," Bonnie reminded her. "I have to meet with Elder Andrews for lunch."

Valerie was stunned. Andrews was *her* guy. She knew Bonnie didn't like that, but to actively steal him in front of her face seemed a bit much. "I thought you were engaged to Elder Peterson," she said.

"Peterson's gone," Sister Pecorino broke in. "Bonnie's got to cover all bases."

"But won't he write to Elder Peterson and tell him?" Valerie frowned.

"Not if I ask him not to." Bonnie fluttered her eyelashes and Valerie suddenly had to go defecate.

Sitting in the bathroom, she heard Bonnie and Sister Pecorino making plans for the upcoming lunch. Sister Pecorino would go along so the other elders wouldn't suspect anything, but it would be enough to keep Elder Andrews interested. "He's really been awfully good about it all," said Sister Pecorino. "What with you dumping him two weeks after proposing to him, just because Elder Peterson came along, after saying you'd wait for him."

"Oh, he understood." Bonnie shrugged. "It wasn't anything personal. And he got over it fast enough. Don't you remember when we snuck in to read his journal?" There was a pause, and then Valerie heard, "I thought I'd wear this. Don't you think I'd look cute in it?"

That night, Valerie lay on the couch at 10:00, ready for bed. Even Bonnie had gone off to her room, tired from getting too little sleep the night before. Valerie had heard the two fooling around until 3:00. Peterson usually didn't stay much past midnight. Of course, mission rules required him to be home in bed by 10:30, but he and Bonnie were hardly getting started by then.

Valerie remembered how fun the first week or so had been here. She felt like a teenager again rather than her true thirty-one years. Being with twenty-three-year-old Bonnie was like being at a slumber party. Of course, the house was usually in chaos, with Bonnie's parents sleeping in separate bedrooms, Bonnie in her room, and Bonnie's sister in another room with her illegitimate toddler son. When another sister came for Christmas with her husband and two kids, it had really been hectic, with so many lights and appliances running that once they'd blown a fuse, but it had also been nice to be with a family for Christmas.

Valerie had never felt terribly close to her own parents, and now that her mother had been dead ten years, and her father only yelled at her on the phone twice a month when she called, she didn't much feel like calling him even for

Christmas. She'd forced herself, though, only to regret it moments later when he began yelling at her again for not picking him up to do his grocery shopping.

"I told you," she shot back, mad at him in an instant. "The car's a wreck. No wheels. No battery. What do you expect, you stupid old man?" and she'd hung up on him. Didn't anything ever get through to the jerk? Couldn't he remember anything? He certainly remembered his twenty-one-year-old Hispanic girlfriend's name. Valerie told him Leticia was just using him, but he'd yelled at her that time, too, and then he was the one to hang up.

Valerie turned over on the sofa and saw the TV in the dim light. That had been the fun part of those first few days, when Andrews and Peterson would come over at 10:00 after everyone else had gone to bed. Andrews and Valerie would sit on the couch, and Peterson and Bonnie would snuggle in a large chair as all four of them watched rented movies.

At first, Bonnie had been very proper, saying, "No R-rated movies. I've been to the temple," as if the elders hadn't also gone to the temple. Valerie was the only one of the four who hadn't gone as an adult.

She'd gone to do baptisms for the dead with other teenagers in both the Washington DC and Atlanta temples, and the bus trips had always been fun, but ever since she was nineteen, she'd had trouble off and on with fornication and so could never get a temple recommend for the adult ceremonies. But then Bonnie, who'd had oral sex with one missionary, regular sex with another, and who'd then slept with two different guys on the riverboat she worked aboard briefly, had been able to get her endowments, the most sacred experience next to a temple marriage, only a month after confessing.

And not three months later, there she was in a chair with Elder Peterson, watching a PG-rated movie and kissing and petting. Even kissing a missionary was a sin. And after going to the temple, sins like sex which normally could get people disfellowshipped could now get them excommunicated.

At least, that's what Valerie had always been told. And there Elder Andrews and Valerie were, sitting on the couch, trying to ignore those sucking noises as they watched the movie.

Of course, one night, Peterson and Bonnie had fallen asleep on the floor in front of the TV, and Andrews had then slowly, inch by inch, made his way over to Valerie. He'd let his hand brush ever so slightly against her thigh, and she'd let one of her fingers touch one of his. A couple of minutes later, two of his fingers were touching hers, and finally, after about fifteen more minutes, they were holding hands, and he was resting his head in her lap. Then they'd kissed for half an hour. Valerie smiled as she remembered, pulling her blanket up more tightly to her neck.

The problem, naturally, had been when she'd told Bonnie about it the next day. "How could you do that?" Bonnie demanded. "You know it's a sin. You're corrupting the missionaries."

"Well, Bonnie, what are you doing?"

"That's different. It's not a sin if you're in love. You two were just lusting after each other. That's disgusting!"

And from then on, Andrews wasn't allowed to come over at night. Sister Pecorino would meet the two at the door and say, "You go on home, Elder Andrews. You know it's the right thing to do." And then she'd usher in Elder Peterson while waving goodnight to Andrews. As if it weren't one of the biggest mission rules that one companion never leave the other one alone! Valerie absolutely couldn't believe it.

She'd sit on the chair alone while Peterson and Bonnie made out during the movie. And now there were a couple of R-rated films as well. Not that those two ever saw any of the bad scenes. Only Valerie did, forced to choose either watching it on TV or in person. She couldn't even go to bed since they were making out on the couch where she slept. She just watched the movie and tried even harder the following morning to find an apartment.

She'd finally found a few in Metairie that looked livable. She had enough for a deposit, but she couldn't risk paying until she knew she had more income on the way. She desperately needed a job to get back her sanity. One day, she'd spent three hours getting to Kirschman's furniture store in Metairie for an interview, only to be told when she arrived that the interview was to be at the warehouse downtown. She spent two more hours getting there by bus, and by then the woman who was to have interviewed her had left for the day. So she spent another hour getting back to Bonnie's, still having accomplished nothing. It seemed most of her life passed the same way.

And now she couldn't even have Andrews. He was the only thing that had made flunking out of school bearable, had made Keith telling her she was a stupid moron bearable, had made Keith refusing to take her in or even help her move to Bonnie's bearable. She'd have to call and tell Keith tomorrow about what Bonnie was doing. Maybe she'd call it the Pecorino Penis Hunt to make him laugh and ask her over, but the last time she mentioned Bonnie, Keith joked that she sounded like the kind of girl he wanted to know.

"Biblically," he'd said with a repulsive snort.

With all these thoughts still racing about in her head, Valerie finally fell asleep.

"You did take your pill that day, didn't you?" Valerie heard Sister Pecorino asking in the morning. It was the first thing Valerie heard after waking, and she wasn't sure if it was part of a dream until she sat up and heard the rest.

"Oh, mother, of course I did," Bonnie answered. "You know I've been on them for two years."

"But you didn't forget that day?"

"Oh, mother."

She was on the pill when she went to the temple? How could the Church even function with people like this? Weren't the leaders supposed to be receiving inspiration direct from God? They never seemed to discern anything about Keith, of course, who'd been having sex with her for over six years and denying it in every worthiness interview.

And there was Eric, who'd gotten her pregnant and then dumped her, only to marry another girl in the temple not a month after Valerie's miscarriage. But everyone treated Valerie like a leper. She just couldn't understand it. If sex wasn't bad, why was everyone always torturing her, and if it was, why didn't anyone else ever get in trouble?

"Oh, it's different now," Bonnie had said after telling her about going to the temple. "It's not as if you have to tell the bishop *everything*."

"Of course you do," Valerie said. "That's the whole point of confessing."

"No, you don't!" Bonnie shouted, upset instantly. "You always contradict me. I'm telling you how to do it so you don't get in trouble. If you don't want to listen, that's your problem!" And she'd stormed off.

Valerie had wondered if maybe things had in fact changed, but then Bonnie hardly seemed the person to trust about Church doctrine. She didn't even know the Church had practiced polygamy for fifty years, and when Valerie told her, she'd called Peterson, crying and begging him to tell her it wasn't true. "He said it was only for a few years, to take care of the women whose husbands had been killed. And they didn't have sex. They just set them up in different households to take care of them."

"Bonnie, they were married. Brigham Young had sixty-seven kids. The Church doesn't even try to hide that."

"No! You think you know more than a missionary? You haven't even been to church in five years!"

So Valerie had let it drop. But surely, the Church didn't approve of single women being on the pill when they went to the temple. That must have been one of the unimportant things Bonnie hadn't bothered to tell her bishop.

Valerie didn't feel up to talking either to Bonnie or her mother this morning, so she left without breakfast to make her way back to Metairie to look again for a job. An attractive doctor worked in one office, but Valerie knew she looked too run down for him to hire her. She wished she'd thought to make better connections with the doctors and nurses back at school, so she could have asked for help in finding a position, but she hadn't thought she'd need that kind of help.

Around 2:00, she ate lunch at Popeye's, feeling fat as she ate a greasy biscuit, and then she applied at a few more places, even at a grocery store and a drug store. She had to get back on her own fast.

"Elder Andrews was so cute today," said Sister Pecorino around the dinner table that night. "He just had his hair cut. He looked like a little sailor."

Little was right, Valerie knew. The guy was eleven years younger than she was, too young really even for

Bonnie, but certainly too young for her. She knew she shouldn't care about him, and she knew she still wanted Keith, but she had to find a way to get Andrews back. No telling what Bonnie had told him about her today at lunch.

"Want to watch a movie?" Bonnie asked just after 10:00. "I rented this movie about a serial killer."

"I think I'll pass. I'm a little tired."

"You'd stay up if Andrews were here, wouldn't you?" Bonnie giggled.

"Why don't you just go over to his new place and fuck all three missionaries? You'd be sure to get *one* of them to like you."

"Oh! Oh!" Bonnie was too upset to say anything before stomping off to her room. Valerie wondered if she'd been out of line, but she'd meant it and so had no intention of apologizing. She pulled up her blanket and went to sleep.

Bonnie was rather cool to her the next day, but Sister Pecorino was nicer than usual, making sure Valerie had a good breakfast. After Valerie came back from job hunting, Sister Pecorino gave her ample portions of a nice dinner as well. But as she plopped a second helping of lasagna on her plate, the woman smiled and said, "It's not as if a few pounds now will make any difference." Valerie immediately stood up from the kitchen table, pretending not to hear Bonnie snickering.

"It was very good," Valerie said coldly. "I'm sure it's not the way you cooked that's making me ill." Then she ran to the bathroom and forced herself to throw up.

Bonnie strolled casually into the living room as Valerie prepared her bed on the couch later. "Elder Peterson got a letter today." Bonnie traced a line lightly across her bottom lip. "I forwarded it to his house in Utah. I didn't write a note or anything on the envelope. Just my initials."

"What did the letter say?"

"Oh, it was from a cousin. Nothing important."

Bonnie had already told her she opened any mail Peterson received that looked like it might have come from a girl. She resealed all the envelopes and passed them on to the missionary, but she still wanted to know what questions to ask.

"You get a letter from him yet?" Valerie asked casually, spitefully.

"You know he can't write me or his parents will get suspicious that there was something between us while he was on his mission. He's going to come for Mardi Gras and take me back."

"They won't get suspicious that he's taking you back after knowing you only one day?"

"We'll pretend we just started getting interested, and we'll date up there."

"You know he won't marry you. He already told you he wants to go to school."

"It doesn't matter!" Bonnie said, getting hot again. "If I don't marry him, I'll find another good Mormon guy up there and marry *him*. It's not like *you're* going to find anyone good down here."

"I'm not looking. I don't need a man." Which wasn't true, since the Church insisted she needed a temple marriage to get to the Celestial Kingdom, and though she wasn't even sure the Church was true, her MIA Maid teachers taught the principle so much it had somehow stuck.

"You don't need a man?" Bonnie laughed loudly enough to wake everyone else up. "That's why you're going after a child."

"Well, you're going after him, too."

"But I'm still young."

"Besides, we were just friends. That's what I told him in my letter. And then he said—"

"He wrote you?" Bonnie suddenly grew serious, then almost thoughtful. "I was sure my mother checked all the mail…"

Andrews hadn't written, of course. Valerie had called him after he didn't answer her letter, and he'd said pleadingly, "We can't have a future," as if Valerie had even wanted him to marry her. She knew perfectly well nothing would come of it. She simply wanted something to tell Keith to make him jealous. She wanted someone to care for her maybe just a little, for just a little while. But the phone connection had been too full of static for her to talk much to him that day.

"I don't tell you everything, you know," said Valerie.

Bonnie stalked off to her room, and Valerie prayed again for the first time in weeks. "Please let me find a job," she whispered. "Please."

The next morning, she left without breakfast and applied again at as many places as she could. But the hunt was getting depressing. Maybe she really was a stupid moron who would never succeed at anything. Keith was probably right. She'd meant to call him but had forgotten. Now she was too depressed. He'd yell at her, and she'd believe everything.

She found herself late in the afternoon in front of the eye surgeon's office, the place she most wanted to work, and she debated for several minutes over what to do. If they didn't want her, going in again wouldn't hurt. And if they were considering her, maybe she could pleasantly remind them again to review her application. So she smiled and walked through the door.

"Oh, Miss Gale," said a receptionist already working there. "I'm so glad you received our message."

"Message?"

"We called today to ask you to come by."

"Oh, of course." Valerie couldn't wait to get home to find out if they would tell her.

The woman asked if Valerie could start work Monday, and of course Valerie said she could. That meant tomorrow she could go out and buy the uniforms she'd need, and then she could relax over the weekend before starting work.

Or maybe Bonnie could help her move to her apartment. It wasn't much. Her TV and dining room set were at her father's. Bonnie's sister had "adopted" Valerie's bed months ago when Valerie had first moved to the dorm, and Bonnie had adopted her dresser for "safekeeping" until Valerie had a place of her own again.

Sister Pecorino had graciously offered to watch over the sofa, the very one Valerie slept on every night, but after six months here, the sofa was ruined, with chocolate handprints all over it. And since Valerie was only moving to an efficiency, she still couldn't take any of those things with her.

All Valerie really needed to move from Bonnie's place were her clothes, but there were several very nice dresses, easily two thousand dollars' worth of clothes altogether. She had to look good if she wanted to interest a man. She hoped she and Bonnie could patch things up so she could move. Even if Bonnie stayed mad for a little while, maybe once they were living apart, they could be friends again.

Valerie made a trip to one of the apartments she'd looked at before. It was still available, and she paid the deposit and a pro-rated rent for the rest of the month, and then she breathed a sigh of relief as she walked back to the bus stop with her very own house key in hand.

"You got a message," Sister Pecorino announced as soon as Valerie walked in the door. A part of her had been hoping really not to get it. Then she could wonder what else they hadn't told her. "Hope it's a job. The Church always teaches us the value of hard work."

"I start Monday," said Valerie. "I already talked to them."

"Well, congratulations." Sister Pecorino smiled and gave Valerie a hug, and it almost seemed genuine. It was only natural, Valerie realized, that she would get on Sister Pecorino's nerves after three weeks. Anybody would get on someone's nerves after that long in a little house like this. But Bonnie's mother had always liked her before. And Valerie herself had been a little bitchy sometimes, frustrated by all the tension of being unemployed. But maybe things would start working out better now.

Bonnie and Valerie watched a movie on the VCR, staying up till midnight and even giggling together again. Neither mentioned missionaries, and the evening went well.

The following morning, breakfast went well, too, and Bonnie even offered to drop Valerie off at a clothing store on the way to her part-time job. Valerie found the kind of uniform she needed, bought three with her credit card, and caught two buses to get home. She had a job. She had clothes for the job, and she had an apartment. The electricity wouldn't be turned on until Monday, and she'd have to wait for her first paycheck before she could get a phone, but everything was working out. Keith would absolutely hate it when she told him.

She wished she could talk to Elder Andrews, too, just so he wouldn't believe she felt the world revolved around her hopes about him. That would ease his mind and maybe help him still be friendly to her. But she didn't know his new number, and… well, wait, if he had to be transferred soon, he might end up in Metairie. Wouldn't that just kill Bonnie? Ooh, Valerie thought, smiling, I hope he does get transferred to Metairie.

At dinner, Bonnie showed off a new ring she'd bought, adding, "Elder Andrews liked it. I stopped by on the way home to show him."

Valerie refused to rise to the bait, only saying, "I hope he gets one like it for you one day."

But then Sister Pecorino interrupted. "She won't need it. She'll be in Utah and married way before he finishes his mission." She passed Bonnie some zucchini. "Which temple do you want to get married in, sweetie?"

"I guess whichever one's closest to whoever I marry," she said. "*I* don't care which temple. They're all the house of the Lord."

Valerie knew that last comment was directed at her, since she'd complained years ago that the Atlanta temple was too plain compared to the one in Washington DC. But she ignored it, finishing her dinner with just enough left on her plate to send a message and then excusing herself.

Still, they watched another video that night, and everyone was pleasant the next day, too. Bonnie didn't feel like driving across the river, so they didn't move any of Valerie's things, which was just as well, because Valerie still wasn't sure what she wanted to wear that evening. It was stake conference weekend, the time twice a year when all the congregations in the city came together for two two-hour sessions of talks.

Valerie decided she could attend because there'd be so many people no one would really notice her. And yet she'd still have a chance to see Elder Andrews.

She took a shower around 4:00 and started picking out an outfit. "What are you doing?" asked Bonnie.

"Getting ready for stake conference. Y'all are going, aren't you?"

"Mom! Valerie's going to conference!" Bonnie ran out of the room toward the kitchen. Soon both she and her mother were standing in the bedroom.

"What's this about conference?" Sister Pecorino demanded.

"Why, I'm going, that's all. Y'all have been trying to get me in church for weeks. So I'm going."

"No, you're going for the wrong reason. You're going to see Elder Andrews. That's not the reason to be going to church. You shouldn't go unless you have a testimony."

"Don't I have to go in order to get a testimony?" Valerie asked. She didn't much like talking to people while wearing only a slip, so she kept looking through her clothes for a nice dress. She still had several of the expensive ones she'd bought with her mother's inheritance, the ones she'd bought to impress Keith.

"You can't go," Bonnie spluttered. "It's not fair. I'll tell Elder Andrews you're after him."

"Tell him whatever you want. I don't care. I'm not going for him, so I don't care what he thinks." Valerie picked out a red and purple print and held it out. "Don't you think I'll look cute in this?" she asked.

"No!" said Bonnie, almost crying.

"You're going for the wrong reason," Sister Pecorino repeated. "You shouldn't go if you're going for the wrong reason."

Valerie turned and stared right at her. "So you're telling me not to go to church?"

There was silence for several seconds, and then Sister Pecorino turned and led Bonnie out of the room. Valerie finished dressing, putting on a nice pair of earrings, and dabbing a touch of perfume behind her ears, hoping to be subtle. Then she waited in the living room, watching TV, while Bonnie and her mother dressed.

They were pushing it, though, if they wanted to make it on time. She hoped they didn't decide to stay home. She could see them getting dressed, but one never knew.

Several more minutes passed, and suddenly Valerie heard a car sputter and then start. She jumped up and ran to the window. Bonnie and her mother were pulling out of the driveway. They'd gone out the back door and left her. She stared at the car as they drove off, her mouth hanging open.

They didn't return until well after the meeting was over. Valerie was already in bed on the sofa, pretending to read the scriptures. They said nothing to her, and she said nothing to them.

The next morning, she didn't bother getting dressed, staying even in her nightclothes until they'd left for conference. But then she did get dressed, in jeans and a shirt, and sat at the kitchen table trying to decide what to do. Since she hadn't challenged them this morning and had let Bonnie have her chance at Andrews, they might lighten up and talk to her again.

She called Keith. Maybe he'd come help her move. "I'm going with some friends to the casino in Biloxi," he said. "Why do you always provoke fights anyway? You get what you deserve." He said goodbye and hung up.

Valerie wanted to cry, but she was afraid Bonnie's sister would hear and report it to Bonnie and Sister Pecorino. Keith was so mean, and it wasn't true what he said. This wasn't her fault. How could anyone think it was?

They would come back from conference even more holier-than-thou, and with another story about Andrews. She should be gone before they came back. She looked through her purse but could only find fifteen dollars. Not enough for a cab to take all her clothes with her. She'd have to take the bus. She could pack her uniforms, toothbrush, and iron, all she absolutely needed, in her backpack. She could leave everything else and not even call. That would show them. Yes, that's what she'd do.

Valerie packed her bag and waited. If they came in the door either bitchy or refusing to talk, she'd just walk right out without a word.

She fixed her make-up so that the last they saw of her would be as a real rival, and she worked on that one problem area of her hair until it was perfect. She'd barely finished when she heard the car pull up.

"Hamburgers!" Bonnie announced as she came through the door. "Hope you're hungry!"

Valerie knew the Church taught not to buy anything on Sunday, but she managed not to say anything about it. In fact, she didn't say anything at all, too mad that they were talking to her again. It would have made a great story for Keith, telling him how she'd left with just the clothes on her back. That would have shown him her determination.

After lunch, Sister Pecorino said, "Well, hurry up, you two. Get everything in the car."

Valerie and Bonnie quickly packed, and though Valerie was willing to chat nicely for now, she kept trying to think of a real zinger to tell them after she got all her clothes in her apartment. She knew that wasn't nice, but she was always being too nice, and people were always walking all over her.

Only Bonnie was driving in the wrong direction, away from the bridge. She was going to Valerie's father's apartment, but for God's sake, why? There wasn't much else they could fit in the car.

Then Valerie realized what was happening. Bonnie wasn't taking her to Metairie but to Harvey, to dump her at her father's. Oh, God, that was worse than leaving everything at Bonnie's. Valerie thought furiously of something to say.

But as they pulled into the parking lot, Valerie saw a small U-Haul, and three elders standing beside it. One of them was Elder Andrews. Valerie's eyes grew big, but she remembered not to smile in front of Bonnie. Andrews shook her hand when she stepped out of the car, and Valerie managed not to yell at her father in front of everybody as they loaded her things. Soon they were in Metairie and unpacked.

"Missed you at church," Elder Andrews said as the elders got ready to leave. "Come visit us sometime on the Westbank."

Yeah, right, thought Valerie. "I wanted to come," she said with a shrug, "but I felt too nervous about moving. Thanks again for helping." She smiled as she shook his hand, but she was thinking, Shit! Why couldn't I tell him Bonnie held me prisoner at her house? Shit! Shit!

The elders left and then there was just Bonnie. "Thanks for helping," Valerie told her as well, wanting instead to spit on her. Now Bonnie would be able to show Andrews how helpful she was to poor Valerie, and that made her sick.

"Give us a call if you need anything else," Bonnie replied.

"No, that was plenty, but I guess I ought to get everything in order now." They hugged, and Bonnie left.

Valerie walked across the one-room apartment to the window and watched her friend drive off. Then she looked across the street at her new view. A Time Saver convenience store, a donut shop, and a lounge. One of those should certainly come in handy soon enough.

She started sorting through her things and had everything in its proper place in just over an hour. Looking at her watch, she saw it was 6:45 and decided to call Keith. She really couldn't wait to tell him about Elder Andrews coming to help her, and how good she'd looked. It might make him ask if he could come over.

She went downstairs and crossed the street, finding a phone between the lounge and the donut shop. The phone rang four times before the answering machine picked up. "Buenos dias," Keith said, using the Spanish he'd learned on his mission. "Leave a message, and if I feel like it, I'll get back to you."

"I'm in my new apartment," said Valerie. "And I'm all settled in. Feel free to drop by any time."

She gave the address and hung up, walked over to the Time Saver to buy some bread and milk, and then went back to her apartment. She lay on the floor where she'd be sleeping on a blanket later and spread her arms and legs to make a carpet angel. God, it felt good to be on her own again.

She ironed her uniform and two dresses, but then the iron grew cold. It was broken. Well, that figured. She knew she should be grateful the electricity was on at all today. She turned on the TV, but there was nothing to watch, and then she walked back to her window and looked another time at the Time Saver and lounge. She sat at her dining room table and reluctantly watched *Star Search*, finally turning it off in disgust.

Maybe she should write a letter to Elder Andrews. She'd have to mail it from New Orleans so Bonnie wouldn't get suspicious at the postmark, since Andrews still got his mail at the garage. Then if he ever got transferred to Metairie, he might drop by. Or would he feel pressured if she wrote? She had a legitimate reason to write a thank you note, though, so she decided to do it.

The note took forty-five minutes, what with composing it, revising it, and then copying it down again, and now it was 8:00. Still nothing good on TV. Sundays were always the worst. She picked up a romance novel she'd already read, but after fifteen pages, she put it aside. She walked over to the window and looked down.

"God," she said aloud, "Look at those sleazy guys coming out of the lounge." The girls were even worse. Real sluts. There was just one guy who looked kind of cute, but those others—God, who would ever go to a dump like that? Even when she and Keith had gone to a bar, it had been a nice one along the lake with a patio for dancing right out by the water.

The memory made her smile. Keith should be back soon from Biloxi. He bitched at her a lot, but she knew he wouldn't be able to resist seeing her again after almost a month. He'd be over before much longer. She hummed a few bars of "O How Lovely Was the Morning" and sat back down at the table. Picking up her book, she began to read, hardly able to wait for her life to really start anew, again.

Best Christian Example

I was the only boy in my high school's Christian Club. While afraid that being among an otherwise exclusively female group made me look gay, as the solitary Mormon in a Baptist high school, I had to do everything I could to prove that Mormons were not only Christians but also *good* Christians. Belonging to the Christian Club was one way to do that.

Another was by being an A student, even if I wasn't the Valedictorian. Linda, the sole Catholic in our class, was Valedictorian. As an "idol worshipper," she wasn't considered a real Christian either, but she didn't care.

"So at this week's Chapel service," said Mrs. Reynolds, the librarian who was also head of the Christian Club, "I think we need to do something special to encourage those who aren't saved to come forward and accept Christ as their Savior. Does anyone have any ideas?"

"I could sing a special song," Shawna offered. "I have a version of 'Yesterday' where I use the word 'Calvary' in its place."

"Any other ideas?" Mrs. Reynolds asked.

"We could talk about how accepting Jesus made our lives better," Kelly suggested.

Mrs. Reynolds put her finger on her chin. "I know," she said after a moment. "We'll call forward anyone who wants to accept Christ as their Savior, just like always, but this time all of you can come forward first. It will encourage the others who are wavering to come forward. Kind of like priming a pump."

"That's a terrific idea, Mrs. Reynolds," said Kelly.

Shawna frowned.

I was a little worried, too, thinking that coming forward might make it look like I hadn't been a Christian all along or make it appear I was converting to the Baptist faith. But that's what the club was doing, so I agreed.

Good Christians were followers, weren't they?

After our meeting during lunch, I went back to class. We only had thirty-three students in the senior class, so we were pretty much with the same kids all day, in English, in Algebra II, in History, in Physics, in P.E., in almost everything. I did take Typing as an elective, while most of the others took Study Period.

In Home Room this morning, we'd voted on Senior Superlatives. I'd won Most Courteous flat out, but there was still to be a run-off between me and Jose Lopez for Best Christian Example. Baptist despite his Latin name, Jose wasn't well-liked, always carrying his Bible and preaching to everyone. I'd come in second for Most

Popular, losing to Steve Berry, so that gave me an edge over Jose.

I really wanted to be Best Christian Example.

I'd placed third in New Orleans for Algebra I in ninth grade, had placed third in the entire state in English in tenth grade, then second in the state in eleventh grade. I'd really hoped to represent Living Truth Baptist High in English again as a senior, but Mrs. Sanford, the preacher's wife who was also the school administrator, didn't like me.

This year she'd made me compete in Typing. I'd come in third citywide for that but still irked not to compete in English. It was clear Mrs. Sanford was afraid to let Mormons shine. It made her prejudice against us look unfounded—if we were so good, could we really be that bad? I felt odd competing for Best Christian Example on her terms, but what choice did I have?

This morning after the runoff was announced, we were told to pray about it throughout the day and be ready to vote again the following morning.

In History two class periods later, Rebecca leaned over and whispered, "What year did World War I end?" We were all answering a sheet of questions, allowed to use both our notes and the textbook. It wasn't a test, just in-class homework.

"The same year as the flu pandemic," I whispered back.

"That didn't help."

"Have you tried the book's index?" I asked.

"Do you want me to vote for you tomorrow or not?" she said, laughing.

"Try the index," I repeated with a smile. She stuck out her tongue and turned to the back of her book.

After lunch, in Physics class, we had a test. Math was not my favorite subject, despite my success in Algebra I as a ninth grader. What my teacher didn't realize in selecting me to represent the school in the citywide contest was that I'd already had Algebra I in the eighth grade, back when I was attending public school. In fact, it had been an Honors class.

I'd performed poorly, ending up with a D. But taking the class again in ninth grade, at a more leisurely pace, I finally caught on.

Physics was different, though. It seemed inherently more difficult, but even if that weren't the case, our teacher was studying at the Baptist Seminary in Gentilly to become a pastor, and his heart was not in the subject. He would stand at the beginning of each class and say, "Read chapter such and such," and then we'd be on our own while he studied the Bible. I understood the importance of studying on my own to make up for any deficiencies a teacher might have, but my heart wasn't in Physics any more than the teacher's was.

"Okay, class," Mr. Wilkinson said, "before I hand out the tests, I want to offer you a bonus question. One of my colleagues at the Seminary stated that Christ would come back to the Earth at the Last Day, but my professor insisted Christ would only come to the clouds and call the good people up. My professor offered *my* class extra credit if anyone could come up with a scripture that said Christ would physically return to the Earth. Anyone know of anything? It's worth ten points on the exam."

Everyone looked at each other in bewilderment. But I'd just learned a verse in my own home study Seminary class last week that addressed this. I raised my hand.

"Yes, Brent?" asked Mr. Wilkinson.

"Job 19:25 says, 'For I know that my redeemer liveth, and that he shall stand at the latter day upon the earth.'"

Most of the other students stared at me with their mouths open. Mr. Wilkinson opened his Bible and read for a moment. "It *does* say that. I'll be…"

"Jiminy Cricket!" exclaimed Gary, a Seventh-day Adventist who played on the football team. He'd been praised in Chapel one day because he refused to perform on Saturday, even though the team then had to forfeit.

"Watch it!" said Kelly. "You know where they got the J.C. from!"

Mr. Wilkinson handed out the exams, and I suddenly felt significantly less intelligent than I had a moment earlier while quoting scripture. But I had to admit, the question came at a good time. That was sure to influence a few votes the following morning. I caught Jose's eye as the tests were being passed out, and his look was decidedly unchristian. I muddled my way through the exam, grateful for the bonus points.

"It's not very Christian to be a know-it-all," Howard said as we left class. He was Chinese and had become more withdrawn the past couple of years as he felt his difference more keenly. I wasn't sure what his religion was. We also had Nick, a student who was Greek Orthodox. I didn't know if he was considered Christian or not by the Baptists. He sort of flew under the radar.

Despite these attempts at diversity, the vast majority of students in school were not only Protestant but white Baptists. Blacks of any religion weren't admitted, to deter interracial dating.

As an exercise in unity, each year Mrs. Sanford announced that if we all attended services at the church attached to the school on a set Sunday two weeks before Easter, we'd get a whole week off. Otherwise, we'd only get two days. I never attended, going to my own ward instead.

This year, I got evil looks on the Monday Mrs. Sanford gleefully announced my name as the sole holdout while justifying not granting us the full week off. But really, even if I hadn't been anxious to be a valiant Mormon, I wouldn't have been interested in extortion. Still, I couldn't help but think now that my actions might have jeopardized my chances at winning Best Christian Example.

The rest of the day passed uneventfully. I didn't consciously try to court any votes for the runoff, but I was my normal friendly self. When Carl let the skins steal his basketball in Gym class, I told him it could have happened to anybody. When Amy was late getting out of Typing class, I ran out front and made sure her bus didn't leave without her. My own bus was always the last to leave, so it wasn't as if it were any great sacrifice on my part.

At dinner that night, Dad asked about my day. I didn't tell him about the bonus points in Physics class, but I did mention the tie for Best Christian Example.

"You know, son," he said, stabbing a scalloped potato with his fork, a meal my mother made once a week, "it isn't necessarily the best idea to fit in with Gentiles. We're supposed to be a peculiar people. They aren't *supposed* to like us."

Mom said nothing but nudged a platter of sliced beef toward me with a silent *tsk tsk* as if to assure me that of course everyone liked me. I slid a piece over to my plate with a smile back at her.

"But I just want them to acknowledge we're Christian," I said. "They keep saying we're not."

"Who cares what they say? They're ignorant."

"Don't you think it's good missionary work to get them to understand the truth?" I persisted. I'd be eighteen in just five more months and be serving full-time as a missionary for the following two years.

"They'll never really like you, no matter what they say."

"But I came in second for Most Popular."

"Of course you did, honey," Mom said.

"You didn't come in first, did you?" Dad pointed out. "It's because you're Mormon. And you won't come in first tomorrow. You may as well not get your hopes up. And like I say, it's not a good thing to be hoping for to begin with."

I went to my room after helping Mom clear the table and did my Seminary homework first, and then my schoolwork. Before I went to bed, I read a few chapters from Mark.

How could people think we weren't Christian? Did they not even know the name of our religion?

The following morning as Mrs. Eberhart took roll in Home Room, I wondered if it was sinful to be praying that Heavenly Father influence the runoff. We all stood to pledge allegiance to the U.S. flag, and after that, we pivoted and pledged allegiance to the Christian flag. I'd always felt awkward doing it, as that flag had nothing to do with Mormonism, but it had been clear from my first day at the school that not doing so would make me an outcast. So was I merely trying to fit in with the heathen? Was it like smoking just to be cool? Where did one draw the line?

I wanted to be Best Christian Example in my senior yearbook. Something everyone would see for years to come.

Mrs. Eberhart passed out the ballots and, after picking them all up, tallied the votes at the blackboard. I held my breath as she drew each line, scratching off four vertical lines with a diagonal one and moving to the next bunch. Yesterday there'd been a tie for first place, but that tie had only been 10 to 10 because thirteen of the other votes had gone to less popular candidates. But now all thirty-three would be tallied just for us two, and with an odd number, it couldn't end up in a tie again.

After a few moments, it was 16 to 16, and the final vote was about to be counted. I felt like I was in a sports movie. Please, Heavenly Father, help people see I'm a Christian.

"Jose Lopez is the Best Christian Example for the senior class!" Mrs. Eberhart announced, drawing the final line on the blackboard.

Everyone clapped, and a few people cheered. Rebecca leaned over and whispered, "The rest of us still think you're way cooler than Jose." I forced a smile back at her. I'd heard her use an ethnic slur against him a few months ago.

Classes were five minutes shorter today so we could squeeze Chapel in after lunch. And it was just as well we had the shorter periods because my attention span was suffering. All I could think about was the vote. Had it been rigged? I did get more votes today than yesterday, but I still couldn't help wondering. And did the majority really like Jose better or did they simply not want to vote for a

Mormon? Perhaps there was a hierarchy of biases. The ruling *felt* like discrimination, but who could tell for sure?

Or maybe the fact that the two candidates in the runoff were both "others" was a good sign, after all.

In the cafeteria, I ate with my friends, and they joked and laughed and told stories as usual, and I began to feel better.

But then Mr. Wilkinson came over to our table. "Hi, Brent," he said with a smile. "I just wanted to tell you I showed that scripture to my professor, and he said it meant that Christ's power and influence will be on the Earth at the last day, not that Jesus himself will be." He paused. "So you don't get the bonus points for your exam. Nice try, though." He clapped me on the back and walked off.

"What an a-hole," said Dennis. "Sheesh."

"Watch it!" said Kelly. "You know where that word comes from!"

I looked at her and thought, *I can't do this anymore.* "Where does it come from?" I asked, sipping my root beer. "Jesus? Or shit?"

Everyone at the table stopped talking and stared. Finally, Kelly swallowed and said, "That's not the way for a Christian to talk."

I nodded. "But I'm not a Christian," I said. "I'm a Mormon." Though, truth be told, my bishop wouldn't want me swearing, either.

"But…but…I thought…"

"I believe in a living prophet and scriptures written by American Indians."

There was silence for another moment. Then Kelly took a sip of her Coke, and Dennis took another bite of his sandwich. "Really?" asked Gary. "That's kind of cool. Maybe you should tell us more about that."

I smiled. "I will. But excuse me just a second first." I stood up and walked over two tables to where Mrs. Reynolds was eating with some of the other faculty. I told her I was resigning from the Christian Club and returned to my table.

Then, calmly eating my potato chips, I told my classmates about Joseph Smith's First Vision.

Temple Man

"Hey, Scoop," my boss said, "get over to Parleys Way in Sugar House right now."

"What's up?" I asked, ignoring Mr. Rutkin's insult. I was new at the *Salt Lake Herald*, eager to make my mark, and Rutkin couldn't help making fun of me. He was heavy and bald, like Lou Grant, only taller.

"Some guy just tossed a brick through a car window to rescue a dog." He slapped down a slip of paper with the address. "Go get the story."

"You're kidding me, right?"

Rutkin raised an eyebrow in reply. I grabbed my iPad and took off, grumbling to myself most of the way over to this older part of the city. It was the middle of summer, and we'd been having a heat wave, with temps almost to a hundred every day the past week. It would be cruel to leave a dog inside a car in this weather for even five minutes, but it hardly seemed like front page news. I wanted a real scoop.

When I reached the address on East Parleys Way, it was obvious at a glance what had happened. A dark blue Toyota Camry was parked on the street, with a police officer talking to an older woman on the sidewalk beside it. The rear window on the passenger side was bashed in.

I pulled to the curb just ahead of them and climbed out. Hanging back a few feet, I listened to the officer and the woman, typing what they said as quickly as I could. I wasn't sure how long they'd been talking, but the officer seemed to be finishing up.

"You're sure you've never seen this guy before?" the officer asked, a well-built man around forty, perhaps a few pounds overweight. "He must be from the neighborhood."

"I told you, I couldn't identify him even if he was my next-door neighbor. He had on a mask."

"All right, ma'am. Thanks for your help." The man closed his notebook and walked back to his cruiser. Normally, I'd have wanted to interview him as well, but I was afraid the woman would leave if I didn't approach her first, so I sacrificed the officer. I could always call the station later.

"Good afternoon, ma'am." I stepped in quickly. "I'm Mark Sanderson with the *Herald*. You mind if I ask a few questions?" I smiled the friendly smile that had won over my wife. "Could you tell me what happened here today?"

The woman sighed. She was probably sixty, short, with gray hair, wearing a simple green house dress not much more elegant than a muumuu. "I was walking home from the grocery," she began, and I now noticed her personal handcart filled with bags a few feet away, "when I heard muffled barking coming from this car." She pointed. "There was a little terrier inside. I tried to open the doors, but they were all locked. I stood on the sidewalk and called for help, and just sixty seconds later, this man showed up."

"And you didn't see where he came from?" I asked, agreeing mentally with the officer. "He must be a neighbor."

"I tell you, I didn't."

I nodded, not wanting to irritate her further. "Okay. And next?"

"Well, as I told the policeman, I was shocked to see his outfit. He was wearing a white, pleated robe, white slippers, and a white hat. And he had on this odd green apron in the shape of fig leaves. Plus, he had on a black mask like the Lone Ranger. I didn't know what to think, so I backed off."

Whoa, I thought. Some guy wearing Mormon temple clothes in public? That was a major no-no in the Church. This woman clearly wasn't LDS or she'd have recognized the outfit. Of course, the mask was a new addition. I didn't know what to make of that myself.

"The man came over to the car, saw the dog inside, and went up to that house right there…" She pointed again. "…and then grabbed a brick from the front porch. He came over, told me to go in the street and call the dog over to that side of the car, and then he bashed the window in. The man didn't even have to unlock the door. That dog just jumped out right into his arms, and the man walked off down the street with him."

"He stole the dog?"

"He saved that dog's life!" The woman wagged a finger at me. "The criminal here is the owner of that car. I want him arrested for endangering that poor creature!" She looked off in the direction of the officer's car. He'd driven away while we were talking.

I stepped behind the Camry and wrote down the license plate. We could look up the owner in the newsroom as well. I thanked the woman, typed in her name and contact info, and snapped a photo of the damaged car. Then I climbed back into my own vehicle and thought for a moment.

Within seconds, sweat began forming on my forehead. The dog's owner really had been a bastard. It was worth covering the story just as a reminder to the community. But I wanted something more. I turned on the engine and switched the air conditioner to high.

On my way back to the office, I thought and thought about how to approach Rutkin. It was the mask that intrigued me more than the temple clothes. That guy had been up to something.

Back at my desk, I typed and retyped. I called the police station and spoke briefly with the officer who'd responded. I found the name of the car owner. When I finished my story, I handed it to Rutkin. He read the headline and first paragraph, and his mouth fell open.

"'Temple Man, Salt Lake's Newest Superhero, Saves Dog's Life'? Are you crazy?"

"I'm telling you, we're going to see this guy again. KSL or KUTV or KSTU or, God forbid, *Main Street News*, is going to catch on eventually. We want to be first with the story, don't we?"

"*Main Street* would never print something like this."

"So we distinguish ourselves from them once more. Even if this guy never shows up again, we've got a fun piece."

"We'll get letters." Rutkin frowned.

"It's always good to be noticed, sir."

"I'll think about it."

The article appeared the next day, and that was that. I kept my ears alert for any more cases of a guy wearing temple clothes, but nothing showed up. So much for my intuition. Still, it had been an entertaining story while it lasted.

Then exactly a week later, it happened.

"Hey, Scoop," Rutkin said, slapping an address on my desk. "Seems some guy wearing temple clothes is on his cell phone at a local market over in Sandy calling for a tow truck to take away a car without a placard from a handicapped parking space. Go see what you can come up with."

I smiled and jumped out of my chair. Of course, the man was gone by the time I arrived, and I could see the tow truck heading off down the street with a Chevy Equinox trailing behind. Temple Man had just made an enemy, I thought. A small group of spectators was still milling about, so I approached and asked the entire group, "What happened?"

A teenage girl, maybe sixteen, with stringy blond hair, laughed. An older man around seventy, with a stern face and glowing white hair, pointed at a sign in the empty parking area.

"Some jerk was parked in the handicapped space. People don't realize we need those spaces ourselves. Not me personally, of course, but people like me. I was driving around, looking for parking, and I saw this guy in temple clothes and a mask calling on his cell phone, reading off the license plate. I thought, 'Good for him.'"

Well, *this* witness was a Mormon.

"Just how was the man dressed?" I asked. "You said he—"

"What the hell is going on?" said a thirty-something man coming out of the grocery with a cart full of food. "Where the fuck is my car?"

Hopefully not a Mormon.

The girl kept laughing. The older man said, "Got towed, you son of a bitch. You're not handicapped."

"Goddamn shit!" the man said. "I was only in there a few minutes. It's not my fault! Such a goddamn tiny parking lot!"

Two or three of the other onlookers started backing off.

"Stop laughing, you stupid bitch!"

The girl kept laughing but walked away. There was no more I was going to get here, but I drove back to the newsroom and called the towing company to get the car owner's name. Public humiliation sounded like a good idea. Then I tried to track down the mysterious caller, but it turned out the call had been placed on a burner. This guy planned to show up again.

I wrote my story.

Rutkin strode over to my desk, slapping it with his palm. "'Temple Man Tows Faker.' It's great work, Mark." Shelly, two cubicles over, stuck her head out and stared. Apparently, Temple Man was doing heroic work here in the newsroom, too, getting Rutkin to be more human. I smiled and called Cathy.

Over the next month, Temple Man made five more appearances. He showed up at a public park and stopped a bully from tormenting a kid. Two mothers reported on that, one of them catching a shot of the guy with her cell. That made page three. Another day, a man dressed in temple clothes and a mask handed out sandwiches and water bottles to the homeless. Page five. Late one evening, a guy dressed in temple clothes helped a young mother change a flat tire on the highway. Page six. Yet another incident involved someone identifying himself as Temple Man calling the police and reporting a drunk driver. Sure enough, the police found a drunk driver, and just like before, the call had been placed from a burner. Page seven.

Then one afternoon, Temple Man showed up at Trolley Square to give a man who'd had an apparent heart attack CPR until the paramedics arrived. That finally made the front page, complete with a photo by an onlooker. I wondered then how Temple Man always seemed to be at the right place at the right time. Was he inspired? Was he for real? Was it just a coincidence? Perhaps he kept his temple clothes in his car so he could jump into them at a moment's notice. The back seat of a car couldn't be any less comfortable as a changing room than a phone booth used to be.

Maybe he had a van.

Of course, I also realized we could have a copycat on our hands, someone who'd read the stories and was trying to emulate him. The paper published an Op-ed about the need for the common man to step up and do the right thing by his neighbors as Temple Man was doing. There was an Op-ed in *Main Street* bemoaning the sacrilegious nature of the "self-righteous, self-proclaimed superhero." Letters to the editor in both papers were published asking whether this was for real or if the guy was poking fun at the Mormon Church. One letter writer said simply, "Finally, a Mormon who *does* good rather than just going around *saying* all the time that he does good."

I wondered if maybe the man had been secretly called by his bishop or stake president to be a hero. Perhaps it was some kind of pilot program to replace the retired Home Teaching fiasco.

At least Temple Man wasn't picketing coffee shops or snatching cigarettes out of the mouths of smokers. Something a Mormon superhero might very well do. This guy seemed to be focusing on real problems, even if most of them weren't especially noteworthy.

People weren't going to care about towed cars forever.

Still, more readers began noticing my byline and Cathy could see the gleam in my eye. One evening over dinner, she was unequivocal. "You better not ever publish this guy's name and ruin what he's doing."

"It would be a great scoop," I said.

"You'd ruin the mystery," she replied. "He's more powerful as a mystery."

While my wife had a point, the desire to have a *real* scoop burned inside me. A few attention-grabbing articles would be generated through interviewing the guy and finding out what motivated him, and maybe some additional good could come from those revelations. Still, I'd read enough comic books as a kid to know that Cathy was probably right.

But it wasn't only my personal ethics being thrown into disarray by Temple Man. As a faithful Latter-day Saint, I attended the Jordan River temple once a month. When I started an endowment session several weeks after I began covering the story, I simply couldn't see the temple ceremony the same way. Here was a room full of men and women in their temple clothes. Part of me had always felt silly wearing the goofy little apron and the baker's hat tied to the robe to keep it from slipping off my shoulder.

In some ways, Temple Man was making the outfit "sexy," yet at the same time, he was clearly no Spiderman. There'd never be a movie about him. His latest two appearances had been to fill in a notorious pothole by himself and to hang an Olde Brooklyn Lantern from a post where a streetlight had burned out, apparently weeks earlier.

I looked about me in the endowment room as we performed one of the secret handshakes. Was one of these guys *him*? Or were we all congratulating ourselves on our faithfulness, while the real hero was out there rescuing a cat from a tree?

I shook my head at the mental image.

The following day at work, Rutkin came running over to my desk. "Get out to Millcreek. There's a fender bender. Apparently, Temple Man is on the scene trying to calm frayed nerves."

I drove on over, but not as quickly as I might have. A fender bender, I thought? Why wasn't Temple Man out there preventing murders and rapes? Why wasn't he foiling bank robberies and muggings? Was stopping at the scene of a minor accident the most we could expect out of a real-life hero? His escapades suddenly seemed less endearing and instead rather pathetic.

Was the guy just someone off his meds?

By the time I arrived, the police were talking to the drivers, and there was no sign of Temple Man. I interviewed the witnesses, got permission to use another cell phone picture, and soon had my story ready for the *Herald*. I went home early, wondering if I'd chosen the wrong profession.

I'd always liked ornithology.

"You didn't get fired, did you?" Cathy asked when I walked in the door at 3:00. We didn't have any children yet, but as good Mormons, we still felt it best she didn't work full time outside the home. Cathy worked fifteen hours a week as a real estate agent, which we figured was a good profession in case she ever did need to work after the kids came. Flexibility.

She'd also taken up designing stained glass windows to feel productive. And teaching ESL to immigrants downtown.

"I'm just not feeling well."

"You don't look so good, either. You better get to bed."

I heated a can of Campbell's chicken soup, ate a third of it, and climbed under the covers. I slept fitfully, dreaming about Arnold Schwarzenegger and Sylvester Stallone and even Halle Berry. I woke up at 2:00 in the morning, went to my computer, and thought about resigning. We could put off having kids a few more years while I went back to school and Cathy worked full-time. Maybe I could be a falconer.

Perhaps write something like *The Zookeeper's Wife*.

I'd read about people with big dreams, and when they finally fulfilled those dreams, they thought, "Is this all there is?" Writing about Temple Man may not have been my dream, but writing about something exciting was, and Temple Man had churned up a great deal of excitement. If not in the community at large, at least among a few news writers.

The national press hadn't picked it up yet, probably out of a sense of delicacy, afraid to be perceived as mocking religion, but every reporter in town—print, radio, and television—was talking about it.

Several reporters were buying squares to guess the date "it would all come out."

I listened to my police scanner when I could, always hoping for that "big moment," and half-heartedly turned it on now while reading my emails. I had three messages from folks claiming their neighbor was Temple Man. Four or five of those tips made it to my inbox every day. I'd given up checking them out.

One email today was from my cousin in Denver saying she was jealous to hear how well I was doing. Another was from Rutkin, saying he hoped I felt better because he was going to assign me to a drug case soon.

Just what I needed, to get shot by a drug dealer.

I'd never be a Woodward or a Bernstein, I thought. I'd certainly never be a Richard Engel.

The scanner soon crackled to life. A man was holding his wife hostage over in Magna. I breathed a sigh of relief. Something real for a change.

I jumped into my clothes and ran out the door. Since I didn't live all that close to the copper mine, I was surprised to discover the police still hadn't shown up.

The front door was open. I could see a man in his boxers and T-shirt holding a gun to a woman's head. But someone else was at the door, too, just off to the side as if afraid to block the message on the welcome mat.

"Love at Home."

Oh my god. It was him. Temple Man. He must own a police scanner, too. That could explain a few of the other incidents, I supposed, like the fender bender, but the guy was clearly small-time. This was something new.

All of a sudden, I felt like a journalist again.

I needed to get closer without provoking the armed man or putting myself in danger. I took a picture in case one of our photographers didn't arrive in time, but before I could do anything else, two police cars pulled up and four men filed out.

One of the officers, a tall African American, spotted me and held up his arm in warning. "You keep back." He stayed on his walkie talkie while his partner and two other officers slowly approached the house.

"I got a gun here!" the man at the door shouted, shoving it up against his wife's head. She squealed in terror, her flimsy nightgown offering little protection against the cool night. Temple Man stood by calmly. He seemed to be talking, but I couldn't hear him.

The officers stopped advancing, their guns ready. "It's okay," one of them shouted. "We're just here to talk."

"Get the fuck off my property!"

"Sir, we need you to put the gun down so we can talk. We don't want anyone to get hurt."

"Get out of here or I'll blow her brains out!"

The woman whimpered again.

"Hey, you!" shouted one of the officers, pointing toward Temple Man. "Back off!"

Temple Man said something to the husband which I couldn't hear, and to everyone's amazement, the man threw the woman to the ground and grabbed Temple Man instead.

The woman jumped up, one knee bleeding, and ran toward the officers. I was close enough to hear her. "That man asked Jerry to take him hostage instead of me! Said he was famous and Jerry would get what he wanted!"

I focused on the woman, looking up again when I heard the front door slam. Two of the officers ran to the entrance, standing just to the side as if debating what to do next. A moment later, there was a shot. The two police officers still near their cars ducked behind them, one officer dragging the woman with him. The officers nearest the house kicked in the front door.

When it was all said and done, the husband lay dead in the living room. There was no sign of Temple Man. No one knew if the husband had killed himself, if the two men had fought over the gun and it had discharged accidentally, or what.

The woman said that a guy wearing strange clothes had shown up shortly after the shouting started inside, long before any neighbors could have called 9-1-1. He'd tried to calm her husband down. She'd never seen the man before.

The officers didn't seem compelled to find him, even to take a witness statement, and I wondered if their personal religious beliefs influenced that decision. Was the guy perhaps a police officer himself? In any event, the deceased seemed the obvious criminal, so Temple Man's statement wasn't absolutely essential. I wrote my longest story yet for Rutkin and he loved it. Another front page.

Three weeks later, Rutkin came by my cubicle and slapped my desk. "What happened?" he demanded.

"What are you talking about?" I asked.

"Where is he?"

"Who?"

"You know damn well who. There's been no sign of Temple Man for almost a month!"

I shrugged. "Maybe seeing real danger scared him off. Made him realize he was taking too many chances."

"I don't want to hear that. That's *Main Street* talk." He pulled a stick pin out of my cubicle wall, making one of my notes fall to the desk. He stuck the pin back in without the note.

"Maybe he was just some college kid looking for adventure and now he's had his fill."

"Hmmph."

"Perhaps he was some terminally ill guy out to fulfill a fantasy."

"Mark…"

I shrugged again. "Maybe he was one of the Three Nephites."

Rutkin slapped my desk. "Write it up," he ordered.

"What?"

"All of it. Everything you just said. There's still a chance we can get a Pulitzer out of this."

I did write it up, editorializing a bit on how there might be a hero inside each of us, if we dared to put ourselves on the line. Saving a cat from a tree might not change the whole world, but it changed the world for that cat. Saving a dog meant the world to that dog. Saving a bullied kid meant the world to that bullied kid.

Even saving an old man with a heart condition so he could live another six months was something.

I probably overdid it. The piece was far too sappy to gain any critical recognition.

But it persuaded me. I began to see the potential for heroism everywhere again. In my wife, the neighbor on our left, my cousin in Denver. Even Mormon missionaries, I supposed. If some guy wearing ridiculous clothing could make a difference, anyone could.

People often talked about the banality of evil, but perhaps the truth was that heroism could be just as banal.

That night, for the first time, Cathy and I chose not to use a condom.

After she fell asleep, I took the mask I sometimes used on Date Night and stuffed it in my pocket. Then I pulled out the little suitcase in our closet with my temple clothes, put it in the trunk of my car, and went for a drive.

Woman on the Wharf

"Anziano, we need to find a Golden Contact tonight." Elder Allred sat on the edge of his cot and wagged his finger at me. Every time he did it, I thought of my mother. "We haven't taught a single lesson in two weeks. I can't take being called out at district meetings anymore."

"Feel free to be inspired," I returned.

"You're the senior companion, Anziano Mortensen," Allred said. "It's your responsibility." He pouted, and I reflected again on how effeminate he sometimes looked. I caught him looking at pretty girls often enough and didn't really think he was gay. I thought of my non-member friend Barry from college, who could effectively pass for straight, and I wondered if people like Elder Allred ever tried to pass for gay.

"You're just going to let me lead you down the path to hell without putting out any resistance?" I replied. "If a wife is an equal partner to her husband, surely you have to take some responsibility in our companionship."

Elder Allred frowned, paused a long moment, and repeated, "We need to find a Golden Contact tonight." The expression on his face at that moment would probably fail to attract either a man or a woman. But then, the look of smugness on my own probably wasn't especially attractive either.

Our lunch period was almost over, and we'd have to leave our apartment at 3:30. Ostia was a small town, so there weren't many areas we hadn't already tried out. Italians this close to Rome weren't particularly interested in Mormonism. But my companion was right. As missionaries of the One True Church, we had an obligation to bring as many souls as possible to the gospel. I'd been out fourteen months while Elder Allred had been out five. We'd been together here in Ostia just over five weeks. It was the spring of 1993, and I had no idea my life was about to change forever.

"Let's do some Spirit Tracting down by the waterfront," I suggested. This was a tactic missionaries sometimes used when their assigned tracting areas weren't producing many investigators. We'd take a break from our routine for one night, going instead where the Spirit led us, and try to find someone who'd been praying for the Lord to send us their way.

Elder Allred smiled. "Cool! The waterfront's always fun."

We put on our suit coats, grabbed our flip charts, and stood by the door with our heads bowed while I offered a companionship prayer. Then we headed out of the apartment and down the stairs to the street. A few people glanced our way as we walked along the sidewalk, but most had learned long ago not to make eye contact. When

I'd first arrived in Italy, I'd felt special. Our polyester suits and white shirts seemed to scream "American!" and I could tell everyone was jealous of us.

Sometimes, I felt like a spy, that fantasy nourished by the fact that our mission leader, President Holland, had worked for the FBI most of his adult life. But as time went on, I began to feel more and more like one of the Three Nephites, so ignored while preaching that I could remain unnoticed for two thousand years. Lately, I'd begun feeling like a simple salesman. One who wasn't making much on commission.

It hadn't helped that my previous companion, Elder Becker, had disappeared one night while I slept, made his way to the nearby Fiumicino airport, and flown home without a word to anyone. Now I could hardly stop thinking about Orem. And Janine.

But Janine would never marry me if I came home early from my mission. Only an RM for good Mormon girls. Ten months longer wasn't forever. I could make it.

"Buon giorno," I said to a man waiting at a bus stop. He looked at me nervously and turned away. "We're representatives of The Church of Jesus Christ of Latter-day Saints," I went on. "Ami i tuoi figli?" Do you love your children? We could use the "tu" with men.

The man glanced at me worriedly again, his eyes darting in every direction. I'd seen the expression a thousand times. He clearly wasn't going to answer without further prodding, so I continued. "We know a way you can be with your family forever. What's the best time we can meet to talk more about this?"

The man closed his eyes, steeled himself, and looked up the street for the bus, which was nowhere in sight. But he was no longer part of the conversation. I tapped Elder Allred on the shoulder and we continued along the sidewalk.

I'd had companions who criticized every failed approach, but Elder Allred knew the stats, the number of approaches one had to make even to get a lukewarm response. A block later, he nodded at a middle-aged woman with a tinge of gray and started talking. It was against mission rules for elders to approach women or for sister missionaries to approach men. I didn't stop my companion, though, since he was at least making an attempt.

The woman muttered, "Sono cattolica," shook her head, and kept walking.

We continued with the "24-hour work" for another couple of hours. Then I pointed to a corner bar, and Elder Allred and I went in and ordered some acqua minerale. It was a chance to sit for a few minutes. I wanted to ask my companion what he wanted to be when he finished college. I wanted to ask what his favorite movie was. If he liked jazz.

But we weren't supposed to talk about anything that didn't promote the work. From the way he fingered his missionary haircut in the mornings, I could assume he didn't like short hair, but he never actually said anything about it. I had mentioned Janine a couple of times, but I had no idea if Allred had a girlfriend back home himself. I didn't even know Elder Allred's first name.

"Come on, Elder," I said. "Time to start feeling the Spirit."

"You're supposed to always speak Italian," he said, wagging his finger.

I nodded and we continued on toward the waterfront, stopping when we reached Via dell'Idroscalo. Most of the buildings in the area looked to have been built in the 1930's, though I was no expert. Anything that recent was considered "new." When I'd been stationed in Napoli earlier in my mission, our building had been built sometime in the mid-1800's. Even that was considered relatively new.

The apartment I shared with Elder Allred, though, couldn't be more than fifteen or twenty years old. While we saw occasional new construction, there wasn't really much need for it. Bishop Cuccia from the Trionfale Ward had given a talk once about how the birth rate in Italy had been decreasing steadily for years, and the only way to maintain the population was to allow immigrants into the country. The most noticeable were all the Africans, though it seemed likely there had been at least some Italians with African ancestry for the past two thousand years.

Someone told me Alessandro de' Medici was black.

Bishop Cuccia thought a better solution than new immigration would be Italian women bearing more children again, the way Heavenly Father intended. If Catholics had given up on large families, it was time for Mormons to take over the task.

Elder Allred and I knocked on doors from just before six until a few minutes past eight. Not a single person let us in. It was always a risk to go Spirit Tracting, of course, since the lack of success proved beyond a shadow of a doubt one wasn't in tune with the Holy Ghost. The same thing had happened last time we tried it, and Elder Allred had asked sarcastically, "What spirit are you following?"

I'd replied, "Don't blame me. Maybe there's some sort of sexual sin in your past. Have you been masturbating lately?"

Elder Allred had shut up immediately. I noticed he was holding his tongue tonight, probably preemptively. I hated being a jerk, but I hated being constantly criticized even more. My father kept asking when I was going to be promoted to district leader and then zone leader. Anything less would be a stain on his honor. He'd given up on my becoming Assistant to the President, he wrote me every week, but he still held out hope for ZL.

Meanwhile, Janine was asking how much longer it would take before I baptized my twentieth convert. For some reason, that was the magical number for her. She continually hinted we might not be able to resume dating after I returned if I didn't reach it.

Since the average number of baptisms per missionary in the Rome mission was three, and I'd only baptized one so far, I understood I might need to start looking for a new girlfriend once I was home.

When I'd written something to Mom about the relationship feeling a bit transactional, she wrote back immediately that couples didn't always marry for love.

"What you want," she said, "is someone who will help you become a god."

President Holland and the AP's were constantly on everyone's case about not baptizing more as well. One elder who'd been out twenty-three months was even sent home early because he'd never baptized a single person, and the mission president thought he had a "bad attitude" and therefore didn't deserve to finish his mission honorably.

Even my friend Barry back at the U kept asking me, "When are you going to do something useful on your mission?" He thought I should be feeding the homeless every day.

"We're giving people the bread of life," I told him. "What could possibly be more important?" As time went on, though, I couldn't help but wonder if feeding a convert or two whatever amount of spiritual sustenance we could provide was in any way equal to feeding dozens or hundreds of the *disoccupati* and *senzatetto* we saw every day some real, actual food.

Perhaps I'd ask President Holland about it at our next zone conference.

"Elder Allred," I said, "let's just walk along the waterfront for a while and see what happens."

He nodded and we strolled the rest of the way to the water. There were docks and wharfs and boats and several laborers and seamen. None of the men looked approachable. I didn't want to be thrown into the ocean by some guy we might annoy. But there were a few women in the area, too. Most of them seemed lost, just standing around and looking about listlessly. Perhaps they were waiting for their boyfriends to return on one of the boats due in soon.

Elder Allred grabbed my arm. "Let's go talk to her," he said, pointing to a lone figure staring down into the water from a wharf. This woman was not middle-aged, probably only a few years older than we were, so it would definitely appear inappropriate to any judgmental eyes looking our way. But I was tired of doing approaches, and if Elder Allred was willing to try one, I wasn't going to stop him.

As we came closer, I could see the woman tense, but she put on a brave smile. I realized she was probably afraid of being mugged, even if we were wearing suits. Sister missionaries always had to be back in their apartments a full hour before the elders every evening. Italian macho could become a little threatening at night. Once when a former companion and I got caught out late in the Napoli ghetto, I'd felt rather threatened myself.

"Buona sera," Elder Allred said with a big smile. "Come sta?" We had to use the "lei" with women.

"You speak English?" the woman replied with a strong accent.

People often tried to practice their English with us. Especially little kids asking, "What taim eez eet?"

"Yes," Elder Allred told her. "We're missionaries with—"

"You can to help me?" she went on, her thick accent making it difficult to understand. Both hands were outstretched in front of her, palms up. This seemed an odd time and place to be begging, and she didn't really look poor, though perhaps a little tarty, now that I saw her up close.

"What's up?" I asked, feeling I'd better take over the conversation.

The woman put her hand on my arm, and I couldn't help but feel a tiny thrill at the touch. Shaking hands with other missionaries and church members didn't fill all my sensory needs. "My name Loredana Lupei," she struggled. "You can to say that?"

"Loredana Lupei," I repeated. She sighed to hear it.

"I take job as housekeeper," she continued, "but when I arrive Italy, Signor Santi take the passport. I am trap-ped working here all the nights. He does not to let me leave. You must to help me. Please."

"Working?" Elder Allred looked confused.

Thick as I often was, I finally realized what was going on. "Can you come home with us?" I asked. "Or do you bring men to your place?"

"Anziano!"

Perhaps he wasn't as slow as I thought.

"I—I must to stay here," she said. Her eyes flitted about nervously. It was the same trapped expression I saw every day when I stopped people on the street. Only the look of fear on this woman's face was far stronger. I noticed what appeared to be a bruise on her left forearm, almost hidden with make-up.

"Are you here every night, or do you work different areas?"

"This place where I am work."

Elder Allred looked from Loredana's face to mine and back to hers again in horror.

"We'll talk to our mission president," I said, "and we'll be back tomorrow night." I made sure to catch her eye. "Tomorrow night," I repeated.

I turned and grabbed my companion's arm, and we hurried all the way back to our apartment. It was almost nine when I sat on my bed next to the telephone.

"Hello?" President Holland asked when he picked up in the mission home.

I wasted no time explaining the situation with the Romanian woman and asked if he could get us help immediately with his government connections. Elder Allred sat on his bed watching me, his mouth hanging open. Mormon chivalry was welling up inside me. I was doing something useful for the first time on my mission, perhaps the first time in my life.

"Elder Mortensen," President Holland answered crisply, "you need to report to my office first thing in the morning, and we'll see about doing an emergency transfer and demoting you back to junior companion."

"I don't understand," I said. "This isn't about me. It's about Loredana."

"You're on a first-name basis with a *puttana*?"

Odd that he struggled in every meeting with the language and yet he knew that word.

"You are expressly forbidden to talk to strange women," the president continued in a cool tone. "This is a local police problem, not ours. How would it look if it were known that two Mormon missionaries were talking to a prostitute?" He breathed out heavily in disgust.

"But President—"

"We don't get involved in things like this," he went on. "Bad publicity hurts the work."

"But—"

"See me first thing in the morning," he repeated. "And you'd damn well better be fasting." There was a click as the mission president hung up the phone.

Did I mention I was thick?

Elder Allred and I sat on our beds looking at each other in silence. "He's not going to help?" he finally asked, pouting.

I again noticed how effeminate he looked, and an idea began to form. I explained what I was thinking, and while my companion looked horrified at first, he was soon helping me formulate our plan. We made our way back to the waterfront, but Loredana was nowhere in sight. I wasn't sure what her work hours were, but we decided to wait a little, and twenty minutes later, she walked back to her spot. I grabbed my companion's arm and we went out to meet her again. She smiled weakly at seeing us, nervous but hopeful.

"We talked to our mission president," I said.

"He will to help?"

I shook my head and the woman winced as if she'd been slapped.

"But *we* will," I went on quickly.

"You—you can do what?" Her eyes darted about.

"You're coming back with us to our apartment," I told her.

Her eyes narrowed immediately and she stepped backward.

"You're about the same size as Elder Allred here," I explained. "We'll cut your hair, you'll put on his suit, you'll use his passport, and we're flying to the States on the first available flight."

Loredana's mouth fell open. She needed some dental work.

"I should have just enough money on my emergency credit card to pay for our tickets."

"I do not understand."

"The mission president may not care about helping you find your passport, but he won't have any choice but to help Elder Allred get a new one." I suddenly remembered with a shudder that my cousin Zack had served a mission to Brazil, and his mission president had kept all the missionary passports in a safe at the mission home. I reached for Loredana's hand.

She still looked confused. "I do not understand," she said again.

"We don't have any time to waste," I said. "Let's go."

We hurried back along the dark streets, looking over our shoulders to make sure we weren't being followed. Back in the apartment, Elder Allred got out the scissors, laid a spare suit in the bathroom, and we ushered Loredana in to wash off her make-up. She either liked the warm water or felt especially dirty because we heard the water running for a long, long time. I finally knocked on the door.

"We need to get moving," I said.

Elder Allred gave me a kiss when Loredana and I left the apartment around midnight, and I never saw him again.

As it turned out, getting to America was the easy part. There was lots of misery and grief that followed. But Loredana finally got her passport, she eventually got a green card after we married several months later, and we moved to San Francisco shortly after I graduated from the University of Utah. I found a job straight off with REST, Real Escape from the Sex Trade, and began doing what I could to fight trafficking in America. The actual scope of the problem was far beyond anything I'd imagined.

I never set foot in a Mormon church again, and most of my family haven't spoken to me in years. But I don't regret my time as a Mormon missionary for one minute.

These days, I get my spiritual satisfaction in other ways. Loredana and I go down to the waterfront and feed the homeless on weekends. She's a bank branch manager during the day, a mother to our two girls at all times, and gives a public lecture on trafficking about once a month. We've gone back to Rome, visited her family in Bucharest, and toured a few other world capitals. But everywhere we go, as we look at the beauty of the local attractions, we're always aware of what's happening just two or three blocks away.

Once, in London, we were stopped by two Mormon missionaries in Soho. "What do you know about the Mormon Church?" one of them asked, smiling eagerly. It wasn't until that very moment, when I saw the dull look in his eyes behind the dazzling smile, that I realized my wife had helped me escape imprisonment as well.

I wondered whatever became of poor Elder Allred.

I squeezed Loredana's hand, nodded to our young teens beside us, and we walked on.

Life in the Dungeon

I saw the short, hunchbacked woman shuffling toward the booth and waved her over. She was elderly and would probably want to buy November's senior bus pass for $27. As she drew closer to the window, I could see that her left eye looked off severely to the side. I wondered if she could even see with it.

"How can I help you?" I asked cheerfully.

"There's shit in the elevator. A huge pile of it. I stepped right in it, and I couldn't get it off my shoe."

I looked at the floor behind her and could see she was tracking something repulsive along as she walked. "I'll report it to the Facilities guys immediately."

"You know why they did it, don't you?" the woman continued. "They're mad you got rid of the Ride Free Zone."

I was a Bus Pass Sales Rep for Seattle Transit. Three weeks earlier, the city had eliminated its policy of allowing free rides within the downtown area, a program which had lasted forty years. The city could no longer afford it. Some pointed out that making it harder to get around downtown would discourage both tourists and locals from shopping, and the city would lose even more revenue than it would gain by charging $2.25 per ride. Trying to enforce the change might even cost more than letting folks ride free. This was all yet to be determined, but already known was that many, many people were unhappy.

And now someone had protested in the Transit elevator at the Westlake station.

Transit only had two offices, our main one near Pioneer Square, and the one where I worked, in the tunnel at Westlake on the other end of the downtown area. Seattle had long ago created a transit tunnel underground going the length of downtown, from Westlake on the north, not far from the Space Needle, to the International District on the south in Chinatown. A dozen different bus lines, plus light rail, avoided street traffic by operating below the surface. Sometimes, I felt like a Morlock servicing the Eloi.

"I think you got the winner for the day," said Tim, one of my coworkers. There were three of us working the tiny booth about the size of a handicapped bathroom stall. I felt I was spending my days in an airplane cockpit. The only festive feature was a garland of orange skeletons draped along the top of the Plexiglass windows. Tim weighed about 300 pounds and took diabetes medication every day, usually in pill form but sometimes by injection. Every afternoon during break, he'd bring back Halloween candy and hand it to the rest of us, saying he at least wanted vicarious pleasure. The only proxy work I could do since I no longer held a temple recommend.

"You didn't see *my* customer?" asked Sharon, a hefty 240 pounds herself. She was divorced and always talking badly about her ex. "The woman had $200 on her card and was complaining about being overcharged twenty-five cents on a bus. I had to do a goddamn cash adjustment for twenty-five cents."

Cash adjustments were tedious, I had to admit, often taking fifteen minutes. I did five or six a day, usually for teenage Chinese girls who'd accidentally bought an adult card and put a youth pass on it, where it wouldn't work. The card was never registered, which meant I had to spend more time registering it, not easy because I had to get an address, another layer of difficulty given the limited English of most exchange students. Then I'd have to refund the card, issue a new card and register that one, and then transfer the funds over. Not the end of the world, but tiresome, especially since a whole gang of girls would usually arrive just a few minutes before closing.

"Yes, your customer was a pain in the butt," I told Sharon. She sometimes worked as a senior, our word for supervisor, and I didn't want to get on her bad side. She routinely read her mail, clipped coupons, read the newspaper, played on the internet, filled out forms so her sons could attend various activities, ate popcorn, and did all sorts of other inappropriate things at her window.

When customers would come to her station, she'd take a minute before looking up from whatever she was doing, and then she'd look back down and continue her personal activities, ignoring the customer. The customer would glance around in confusion, and I'd wave them over to my window. Even when Sharon did address the customer, it was usually with an antagonistic tone to her voice. I didn't personally see the advantage in being a creep, even if most of it was displaced anger at one's ex.

Thankfully, I didn't have an ex. I was still with my first love.

"I don't know why people need to be such jerks," Sharon said. "Must be a full moon."

"Only a week or so until Halloween," Tim said. "The nuts'll be crawling out of the woodwork before long." He turned toward us, his back to his window, and didn't see the young Hispanic woman walking up to him. "You and your partner celebrate Halloween, Graydon?"

I nodded and then pointed to his window. Tim turned and jumped in surprise when he saw the woman standing there. "Thanks," he said to me after he'd helped her. "She was hot."

Sharon ignored us and kept painting her nails.

"Oh, my mother will probably haunt me for saying that." Tim was fifty-seven and had lived with his mother until she died nine months ago. He'd never married but was always talking about the "young chicks" who came to his window, or the strip clubs he frequented on weekends. "Every time I lust after a girl, Mom sends a pregnant woman my way to keep me in line." He looked into the tunnel and pointed out a pregnant woman in a burqa coming up off an escalator. "See?"

"You know, there's therapy for that," I said.

"Oh, I don't mean she's really haunting me." Tim shook his head. "I'm not hearing voices or anything. What do Mormons believe about ghosts?"

"We believe they pretty much leave us alone," I said.

"Do you still believe in God, even after being excommunicated?"

I'd been ex'ed two years before, a week after my twenty-fifth birthday. My coworker had never gotten over it. He wasn't religious but thought excommunication was barbaric. "You've been in a relationship for a year," he'd told me at the time. "That's already longer than anything I've had. How can they say you're a monster?" He was still marveling that I'd been with Alex for three years now.

My parents were instead marveling that I'd chosen a Jewish partner. Growing up, I'd only known white people from the congregation I'd been a part of for so many years. Even now, my parents knew only one "ethnic" person to any extent, and Alex was every bit as white as I was.

An elderly man came up to my window. "What can I do for you?"

"I'd like a senior transit card."

"How old are you?"

He handed me an Indonesian ID card. "I'm sixty-four."

"Oh, then you'll need to come back when you turn sixty-five."

Right then, two more people came to my window one after another, the first shifting over from Sharon's window where he wasn't being helped. I loaded $30 onto one card for a Danish exchange student and put a $90 regular adult November pass on another for a Japanese woman. I liked these transactions. People usually paid with cash or credit, so it was a quick, easy task. A couple of times a day, customers paid with vouchers from some company or charity paying their fare, and those took a little longer to process, but even those were relatively simple transactions.

Most of what we did every day was easy. The only thing I didn't like was standing on my feet all day. Tim and Sharon sat in chairs, but I found that if I sat, I couldn't reach the window or the receipt printer or the calculator. I had to move around and reach for too many things during every transaction. Sometimes, it was easier to do the harder thing.

"So you still believe?" asked Tim. He wasn't going to let it drop.

I knew that Sharon's oldest son was studying theology at Gonzaga in Spokane and thinking of becoming a Catholic priest. Alex attended Torah study on Saturdays but rarely attended services. "Sure, I believe." I shrugged.

Even if the last thing I heard my stake president say was, "You're on your own now. Don't ask the Church for any help when you get in trouble."

I nodded at Hector, the janitor, as he walked by the booth. He nodded back.

"Oh, that's good," Tim replied.

"Why?"

"I'd hate to see religion hurt you."

I laughed. "It's already hurt me."

"Will you guys shut up?" Sharon kicked the counter. "I'm trying to read." She could barely hold on to her magazine with her fingers spread wide to let her nails dry.

I waved a man standing in front of her window over to mine. "Can I help you?" I asked.

The man thrust a transit card at me. "Money," he said in a thick Middle Eastern accent.

I put the card on the reader and saw that he had $2.25 left on his card. I told him the amount.

"Money," he said again.

"Did you want to put money on the card?" I asked.

"Huh?" He looked confused. "Money," he repeated.

"What about money?" I asked.

"Money," he said again with more conviction.

I held out my hand. He still looked confused but handed me a twenty-dollar bill.

"You want me to put twenty on the card?" I asked.

He pointed to the bill.

I loaded the money onto the card and gave him a receipt with his card. He nodded brusquely and headed off.

"Oh, I got another hot girl," Tim announced. An auburn-haired woman was approaching his station.

"You know, they can hear you over your microphone," Sharon pointed out. She put down her magazine and waved impatiently for a woman with a stroller to come to her window. "Can I help you?" she said in a strained voice.

We'd already taken our morning breaks, and soon Tim took the first lunch, at 11:15. He didn't return for an hour, and I left at 12:20. It could be dreary working underground all day. I felt safe from nuclear attack, but that was about the only positive aspect of working in the tunnel. I worried that an earthquake would trap me in the booth, and I'd spend my last two weeks dying in the rubble, unable to escape Tim and Sharon. On some days, even without a tunnel collapse, I felt buried alive in a tight coffin.

Alex usually made my lunch, a turkey sandwich or peanut butter and jelly. Today I had turkey with a slice of dill pickle, a surprise treat. I could have eaten in the tiny break room behind the counter, an area about the size of a small walk-in closet, but I needed to get away. On sunny days, I sat on a bench outside in front of the Westlake Shopping Center, but as it was raining today, I climbed to the third-floor food court and grabbed an empty table.

I still thought of religion more than I wanted to. Could I truly be a good person without it? Or was I really the horror the Church said I was? Dracula never saw himself as evil. The Mummy felt completely justified in the murders he committed. It was only an objective person looking on from the outside who could see the truth.

On my mission to Minnesota, my companions and I had a motto: You must apostatize to baptize. Sometimes, you simply had to break the rules to do the right thing.

Though I'd tried to leave Mormonism behind, I sent a yearly protest letter to Salt Lake, and of course I donated to the Human Rights Campaign, Lambda Legal, the ACLU, and the Southern Poverty Law Center. Still, I wasn't much of an activist. I'd been contacted by the organization "Mormons for Marriage Equality" about the Washington state campaign to legalize gay marriage, and I'd written some emails to my elected officials as well as a couple of letters to the editor to complain about the Church pushing its members to vote against equality.

I was grateful to see the handful of straight, supposedly faithful Mormons who were standing up for us, but frankly, I didn't much care if they liked me or not. Part of me cheered the gay Mormons who picketed in front of temples and held kiss-ins on Temple Square. Another part of me didn't give a shit. The Church often gloated, "You can't leave us alone," as if that somehow proved their divine status, but it was the Church who couldn't leave *us* alone.

So Romney scared me. I'd already turned in my mail-in vote for Obama, but the race was still neck and neck in battleground states across the country. The prospect of a

Mormon president who wanted to ban gay marriage and abortion and who was part of a party that wanted to dismantle Social Security and Medicare was terrifying. My family emailed me about how Romney was going to save the Constitution which was "hanging by a thread."

I worried that the relative acceptance gays had in society might be ripped away overnight. Alex had told me just last evening, "I wonder if this was how the Jews felt right before the election where Hitler took control." Romney was no Hitler, and Hitler hadn't won a majority of the votes, but persecution was persecution. Even if he didn't win, another awful Republican with Draconian ideas was sure to follow him.

I looked around the food court. Several Asian youths sat at the table next to me, eating noodles with chopsticks. A heavy white woman with mussed up dirty blond hair ate a pulled pork sandwich a few tables away. A businessman in a suit devoured a McChicken sandwich. A thin brunette munched on a salad and two black teenage girls sipped Smoothies. An Ethiopian woman in a purple head scarf ate rice and broccoli while she looked at her phone.

America might not be "exceptional," I thought, but it was a great place, where all these people could come together in peace.

So why did I always feel an impending sense of doom?

I looked out the window at the rain misting down and luxuriated in being able to sit for a full forty-five minutes, even on a hard chair.

Once I was back in the booth, Sharon took off without a word. My first customer was an elderly Russian woman who wanted to put $20 on her card. "Spaseba," I said when she'd finished.

She laughed and said, "Pajalsta." I could never remember which term meant thanks and which meant you're welcome. But the elderly Russian women who came to the booth always got a kick out of even my one Russian word.

I learned that Ukrainians who sounded like Russians to me were definitely *not* Russian.

A Vietnamese woman stopped by to purchase a book of ten $1.25 youth fare tickets. I was sure she was buying them for herself and trying to pass off to bus drivers that she was still a teenager.

"You and your partner doing anything for Halloween?" Tim asked during a brief lull. "Going to any haunted houses?"

"I doubt it. You?"

"My mother loved Halloween. When I was a month old, she put me in a basket, put a note on top that said, 'Please take care of me,' and left me on the neighbor's porch. She rang his doorbell and then hid in the bushes and watched him almost faint when he found me. Then she jumped out and said, 'Scared you on Halloween!'"

"Your mother sounds very special."

"Oh, she was, she was. She's still with me. Look! There's another pregnant woman." He pointed.

A Hispanic man came to my window then and plopped down his card. "Want month," he said.

"You want the November pass?" I asked.

"Month." He nodded.

He had a regular adult card, which meant he was eligible for the $81 pass, the $90 pass, the $99 pass, the $108 pass, and on up to $126. "Which one?"

"Month." He said it firmly and nodded authoritatively.

I looked up Details to see if he'd had a pass in preceding months. Then I could just get him whatever he'd bought before. I saw the screen and took a breath. He'd had both an $81 pass and a $90 pass. "You want the $81 pass?"

"Yes. Pass."

"Did you want the $90 pass?"

"Pass. Yes."

I held out my hand, hopeful the answer would come in whatever the man pushed through the slot in the window. But no, he handed me a $100 bill. I marked it with my counterfeit pen. "$90?" I asked.

He nodded. I put the pass on the card and handed him the card, his receipt, and $10. He looked confused and walked off.

"You're really good with the customers," Tim said. "I get so impatient."

"Can I help you?" I waved at a forty-year-old white woman with stringy hair who looked as if she couldn't decide whether or not to approach. She did.

The woman thrust her application for a Disability card through my window. "The FBI wants this," she said. "And Jesus wants it."

"I'm afraid we don't process these here," I said. "The Disabled cards are printed at our main branch in Pioneer Square." I slid the paper back to her. She pushed it right back at me again.

"You keep it. I'll lose it. The FBI wants it. Satan wants it, too." She shuffled away slowly like a zombie.

I took the form and went back to the senior's office. Mike was watching a football game on the internet. "Can we interoffice this to the main branch so the customer will have it when she shows up to get a card? She doesn't want to keep it. She's afraid she'll lose it."

Mike took the form, looked at it for a few seconds, and then put it on his desk where dozens of other miscellaneous papers lay. "They have no place to keep these. She'll need to bring another." He turned back to his game.

I walked to my window and put thirty dollars on a youth card for a petite blonde teenager.

"She was hot," Tim commented after the girl left.

"She was fifteen."

Soon Sharon was back at her window, sipping coffee. The only time she really helped was when she had to sell taxi scrip, since she was the only cashier allowed to sell it. Taxi scrip was a type of coupon that allowed the customer to buy a certain amount of taxi fare for half price, say $30 for $15 or $50 for $25. People needed a special yellow card to be eligible.

At the beginning and end of the month, our line out front might reach fifty people, but the rest of the time it was never more than four or five long, and sometimes there was no line at all. Right now, it was the longest it had been all day, with four people waiting their turn. A thirty-year-old bypassed the other four people and came around from the side directly to my window. "Uh, there's a line," I said, smiling and pointing.

"But the sign said to step to the side if you wanted to avoid the line."

There were two signs on either side of the line, which directed customers to the Regional Transit vending machines along the walls to buy cards, load cards, or buy light rail tickets. All of that could be done without us, yet a great many people came to us anyway. "If you read the sign more carefully," I said, still smiling, "you'll see that it isn't an invitation to cut in line." I pointed for her to go to the back of the group.

She turned around, bewildered, and wandered away.

"You were too nice," Sharon muttered. "That little bitch knew exactly what she was doing."

Some days, I wondered if being cast into Outer Darkness when I died would mean having to live like this for eternity. If the Church were right about gays, it would be worth being celibate for sixty years to avoid such a fate. The devil wasn't scary only at the end of October.

Stop it, Graydon, I told myself. You're over this. You're over it.

"Boy, that was some good-looking gal," said Tim, turning around in his chair to face Sharon and me. I didn't even know which woman he was referring to. Sharon ignored him and kept looking at pictures on her phone. It was Tim's turn to take his afternoon break and he put up a sign in front of his window. "Maybe I'll follow her for a while."

"Think of your mother," I said to ward off the stalking. Tim looked at the floor glumly and went to sit in the back room instead. I saw a young woman walk purposefully toward the booth and thought about letting Sharon take her. It was Satan's plan, though, to try to force people to be good rather than let them choose. I waved her over.

"My transit card broke," the woman said with some difficulty, thrusting the card at me. It was a green and white Disability card that allowed the rider to pay seventy-five cents per fare.

"I'm afraid we don't print those at this location," I said. "You'll need to go to the main branch near Pioneer Square."

"They told…me I could…come here," she said with a whine, instantly petulant. Her mouth twitched.

"I'm sorry about the misinformation, but we simply don't have a printer here that can print those."

"Well, what…am I going to…do?" She was raising her voice.

"You'll need to go down to the main branch."

"But I have…a seizure disorder. You…have to accommodate…me."

"Ma'am, our printer won't print those cards. There's nothing we can do at this location." I could put in a request to squeeze one of the machines into the senior's office, but there was nothing I could do to get her a card right now. I wasn't a sorcerer, after all.

"Oh, for God's sake," Sharon snapped. "Wait on someone else already!"

"I don't…think you…understand. I'm disabled."

"Yes," I said, "and the branch that handles Disability applications and prints Disability cards is our main branch near Pioneer Square. Our space is limited here."

"I can't go all…the way down there!" She was yelling now, drawing looks from the people in line behind her and from passersby walking toward the stairs leading down to the bus and train platform. "I have my…paperwork *here*!" She threw it at me. The papers hit the window and then fell on the floor outside the booth.

"Ma'am, you're welcome to yell and argue as long as you wish, but that's not going to change anything."

As soon as I said it, I realized this was the same message the Church sent when it ignored our protests. Some things were simply pointless. I glanced briefly at Sharon, my superior.

Was being second-class going to be my fate the rest of my life, both in and out of the Church? What if the election in a couple of weeks made Washington the 32nd state in a row to deny marriage equality? Even my own family lovingly demonized me.

The woman in front of me slapped the counter, and I turned back to her, irritated for allowing myself to be distracted. "You can get a friend or family member to help you get there if you're having difficulty on your own. We also have the Access van if you need it."

"Give me the…number of the main…office!"

I wrote down our Customer Service number.

"Not…that one! The direct…line!"

"We don't give out the direct line. You can call this number, and they'll transfer you."

"I WANT…THE DIRECT…NUMBER!"

"This is what I can give you." I slipped the paper through the little opening in my window, and she pushed it back.

"I need…the manager's…direct number!" she repeated. "I can't go all…the way to the…other branch!"

"Ma'am," I said quietly into my microphone. "Blind people go down there. People without legs go down there. You can handle it."

Was that encouraging, I wondered, or condescending?

Maybe I *was* a monster. Monsters, after all, were really just ordinary people who followed awful rules.

"Stop talking into…that damn microphone! You're…going to make me…seize!"

I turned off the microphone to indicate the conversation was over and said through the thick glass, "You need to step away from the window."

"What?" She leaned forward.

"You need to—"

"Huh?"

I turned the microphone back on. "You need to step away and let me wait on the other customers."

"Well, you…haven't helped *me*…yet!"

"I've told you where you need to go to accomplish what you want, and I've given you our customer service number. You need to step away."

"You can tell her where to go all right," Sharon muttered.

The woman continued to yell, and I turned my microphone back off so I wouldn't have to hear. Then I walked to the senior's office. "Mike, I need help out here. I have an irate customer who won't leave." I explained the situation, and he walked through the two locked doors separating our booth from the tunnel, like exiting a high-security prison. I waited until I saw him lead the woman off, and then I returned to my window.

"I almost felt sorry for you," Sharon said, leaning over.

Almost, I thought. My own instincts were to feel bad for anyone disabled and go out of my way to make their lives easier, but some disabled people used their disability like a weapon and tried to bully everyone in their path.

Squeaky wheels only got greased if there was grease to apply.

I'd come close to saying, "I understand you're unhappy and that this leads you to want to make everyone around you unhappy, but no matter how much you yell, I'm simply not going to be able to help you." But even if I said it calmly, it would sound mean.

It would *be* mean.

I remembered a customer at my window justifying her imperious behavior a couple of weeks ago, "Well-behaved women rarely make history."

I'd wanted to say then, "No one's going to write a history book about the woman who ranted about having to wait in line six minutes." But I kept a blank face and let her gloat.

Was I like that when I wrote to the Church?

I looked at the ring on my finger, which I wore despite the lack of a marriage certificate. Even with this crummy job that took up most of my waking life, I still had Alex to go home to.

I looked out and saw Mike turning away from the woman, watched her defeated expression as her right hand twitched. There was no way I could offer to take her to the other branch on Saturday, my day off, because both branches were closed then. I'd already had my lunch break today, so I couldn't use that time to help her down to Pioneer Square. Sharon sat next to me, playing with an ink pen which had a skull on top that lit up whenever she pressed down. She kept lighting it while an Indian man at her window talked.

"Happy Halloween," she said as he walked off.

The disabled woman stood motionless in the tunnel, staring at the floor.

Why did I even feel obligated to help this unpleasant customer? Because I knew it must be harder to *be* her than merely to deal with her? Because I wanted some Mormon somewhere to be nice to me?

I locked my computer and passed Mike on his way back through the metal doors. "Where are you going?" he asked. "Isn't Tim on break?"

"I'm going to escort that woman to the main branch," I said. "I'll be back in thirty minutes, forty minutes tops. You can dock my hours."

"Are you kidding me?"

"Hey, I'm all alone up here," Sharon shouted into the hallway where we were standing.

"Be back in a jiffy, Mike. Thanks." I smiled and nodded, not waiting for his reply, and headed out of the cage.

Kugel Exercises for Men

I love my husband, but good grief, can he be exasperating. He doesn't mean it most of the time. It's just that some neurons in his brain seem to get rerouted in the middle of a sentence. During the last presidential election, Arnie was always complaining about the electrical college, about how the use of superdenigrates wasn't fair, how none of it mattered anyway. Every politician was corrupt. Tracy, he asked me one time, did you hear about that outrageous ornaments deal in the Middle East?

For the first three years of our marriage, I made the foolish mistake of correcting Arnie whenever he made these kinds of mistakes. But it was like correcting a cat for meowing. Arnie was going to meow, whether I liked it or not. As long as he wasn't giving a talk at church in front of the whole congregation, I tried not to be embarrassed anymore.

And then the shooting happened at Jessica's school. Thank heavens, she wasn't one of the fourteen students and two teachers killed, but it did mean we had to start speaking in public on a regular basis. I prayed Arnie could hold it together for the length of a sound bite. But at our very first rally in support of a ban on assault weapons, the inevitable happened. A reporter stuck a microphone in front of Arnie and asked, "What is it you want politicians to know?"

I held my breath as I waited to hear what might come out of my husband's mouth. "It's all fine and good for senators to say kids should be learning CTR," he said, "but that isn't enough. Let's stop the bleeding before it starts."

I suppose it was a blessing the reporter never used that footage, didn't know about the Church slogan "Choose the Right" or the CTR rings Mormon youth wore.

At another rally a week later, Arnie was approached again. He had a natural, earnest look about him that made him excessively approachable. It was why I'd first asked him out, after all, all those years ago. "What do you hope to accomplish with these protests?" the reporter asked.

"Arming teachers isn't a solution," he replied. "There's an elephant of surprise involved. And it's in those first few seconds when half the deaths occur. We need to get rid of the deadliest weapons themselves so no one can surprise us with them."

I can't tell you how awful it is to watch a seasoned reporter laughing at you during a serious rally. A shattered ego is better than a shattered liver, obviously, but it's no laughing matter, either. And I worried my husband's neural defect would be weaponized against us.

"Arnie," I said that night after we returned home, "you need to get a priesthood blessing."

"For what?" he asked.

"To see if the Lord can cure you of all those malapropisms."

"Oh, Tracy, that again?"

"You saw how that miserable reporter used the footage he had of you? He's making people who want sensible gun regulations look like idiots."

"Aw, honey, it was a slip of the tongue. Nobody takes that seriously."

"Exactly my point."

"Dad," Jessica chimed in, "I've already gotten two dozen comments on Facebook about what you said."

"At least people are hearing me. Maybe it's a blessing I talk funny."

"It's not a blessing, dear."

Arnie sighed. "You want me to stop coming to the rallies with you?"

To my shame, I did. I didn't know what else I could reasonably expect, after all. I'd already determined there was no way to keep him from meowing. "Maybe we can practice," I said. "If you memorize two or three different statements and just stick to those if you get asked anything, it'll be okay."

Arnie shrugged. "I'll do whatever you want," he said.

We did exactly that, but at the next three events we attended, no one asked him anything. I saw the same mean-spirited reporter at a different rally and hoped he'd try to embarrass us again, but even he left us alone. Part of me felt miffed, but mostly, I was grateful to hear fourteen-year-old students who spoke more eloquently than any of us could hope to. We kept the pressure up, or at least the students did, and we tried to support them as best we could.

Both Jessica and I quizzed Arnie relentlessly on his canned responses.

Meanwhile, I kept thinking about those cats. Felines were nowhere near as easy to train as dogs, but spray bottles did work, and cats did adapt quickly to litter boxes. So I got back on Arnie's case whenever I caught him making a mistake. And there were plenty.

"Is it ever appropriate to use a split infinity?" he asked once after reading one of my prepared lines.

"Split infinitive," I corrected as gently as possible. Though Arnie's version might make a good title for a science fiction novel.

"Do you think it's safe," he asked another time, "to let Jessica stay at a hospice when she goes to those rallies so far away without us?"

"They're called hostels, dear." Though, considering the reason for the rallies, perhaps Arnie's nomenclature was more accurate.

"Politicians really ought to pay attention to us," he said another day. "It's in their best interest, after all. When people get disinfected, they're liable to do anything."

"That's disaffected," I corrected him, less gently now. I remembered why I'd given up years ago.

Then came the news of another shooting. "You heard what happened at the Veterinarians' Home?" Arnie asked the moment he walked through the door.

"They have a home for veterinarians?" I asked, genuinely confused.

"Veterans," he corrected himself.

If he knew the word, why didn't he just use it?

"There was a shooting," he said, getting me back on track and explaining what he'd heard on his way home from work.

"I want you to get a priesthood blessing," I told him again.

"Aw, Tracy, it's embarrassing. I feel like a grown man asking for help to stop bedwadding."

"Bedwetting?" I suggested.

Perhaps an actual spray bottle might be the answer.

He nodded.

"Bishop Barnes has never been anything but nice to us," I said. "Doesn't call you to teach any classes. He's a good man."

"Okay, okay. I guess it can't hurt to ask."

After services on Sunday, Arnie had the bishop and first councilor give him a blessing in the bishop's office. They let me attend. I'd hoped for a "you will be cured!" type of blessing, but instead it was the typical, "according to your faith."

It wasn't that Arnie and I didn't have faith. It was just that those types of blessings so rarely seemed to work. Admitting such a thing felt like we were demonstrating a lack of faith, though, so I thanked the bishop, squeezed Arnie's hand excitedly, and we headed home for lunch.

"I just love Italian paisley," Arnie said when I set the meal on the table.

"Parsley," I said automatically before biting my lip. I should have given the blessing more of a chance to work. Now I'd jinxed everything.

Arnie gently put his hand on mine. "It'll be okay, honey. It'll be okay."

I knew blind people stayed blind. I knew amputees never regrew a limb. I knew even the faithful died of cancer. But I simply didn't understand Heavenly Father. This was such a *stupid* affliction. And it was hurting Jessica. It wasn't fair.

We weren't so faithful, however, that we refrained from watching movies on Sunday. That evening, I slipped in a DVD of *The Faculty*, and we watched as a family. Clearly, we weren't so faithful as to abstain from R-rated movies, either. It was a cute film, as kids were always thinking their teachers were aliens. We needed a diversion after the tension of the past several weeks. Seeing Frodo in high school was fun.

"I just love Penelope Cruz," Arnie said as the movie ended. "She was so good in this, even if it was a small part."

"That was Salma Hayek," I said.

"No, it was Penelope Cruz," Arnie insisted. "You know, the woman who was in *Frida*."

Maybe we watched too many R-rated movies. "Salma Hayek was the actress in *Frida*," I said. Arnie's lack of a cure was almost certainly our fault.

"Really?"

"Really."

A similar discussion occurred a few days later over dinner. Jessica complained about something difficult in her Physics class and Arnie offered a bit of encouragement. "I think Stephen Dawkins is great."

It was our daughter who caught him this time. "Do you mean Richard Dawkins," she asked, "or Stephen Hawking?"

"The Black guy who demoted Plato."

"Gotcha."

Jessica stayed in the kitchen while I put things away. Arnie was on the sofa flipping through channels, and Jessica peered past me to make sure he couldn't hear our conversation.

"I don't know if I want Dad to come to the rally at the capital this weekend," she said softly. "I mean, I was used to the weird way he speaks after growing up with him, but seeing him in public now is...well, it's embarrassing." She closed her eyes. "Does that make me a bad person?"

"Honey, you wouldn't be normal if your parents didn't embarrass you." I made a point of not asking what embarrassed her about me.

"Will you ask Dad?"

I stood with a plate poised over the bottom dishwasher rack.

"What is it, Mom? You're not having a brain fart, too, are you?"

I set the plate gently in the rack and turned to Jessica. "What if we asked him to tape his mouth shut?" I suggested. "Maybe we could tell him it was part of the protest. We could have him hold a sign that says—oh, I don't know—something like, 'The dead have no voice but ours.'"

Jessica smiled, but her smile faded almost instantly. "Since that's actually true, Mom, we *need* to have Dad be able to speak."

I tapped the top rack of the dishwasher absentmindedly until the sound reminded me of gunshots. "I see your point." Jessica looked so unhappy that I pulled her close and gave her a hug. "We'll figure this out," I whispered.

It felt like the bishop's blessing had backfired. Arnie seemed to be using malapropisms in every other sentence these days. Perhaps I was hypersensitive again after years of ignoring it.

Sometimes, I wanted to bean him with a frying pan. Like when he talked about "repairian" therapy for gays. Or when he called his sister "ex-mammon." Surely, he knew the word "Mormon," didn't he? Or the time he talked about the "apocalyptic" books of the Bible that Catholics read which we didn't.

"Apocryphal," I corrected automatically.

Then, the day before the rally, when we were doing a bit of last-minute shopping to get snacks for the trip, we ended up with a Russian sales clerk at the grocery. I wanted to sink into the floor when Arnie decided to impress her with his language skills. "Placebo," he said with a smile. The woman just stared at him. I couldn't get him out of the store fast enough.

This just wasn't going to do. Not at all. With hundreds or even thousands of people at the rally, the chances that a reporter would even see Arnie, much less approach him, were slim, but these students seemed on the verge of achieving a meaningful change, and I couldn't bear to have my husband make that more difficult.

Arnie wanted to have sex that night, just in case one of us got hurt by counter protesters the following day, or even by the police. The truth was he rarely missed a chance to explain why we needed more sex, so I wasn't fooled. I gave in because, frankly, since he didn't talk during intercourse, our lovemaking made for some quality time.

"I've been doing more of those kugel exercises for men," he prefaced hopefully.

There was a time and a place *not* to correct someone.

The next morning as we prepared to head for the state capital, Jessica pulled me aside. "I'm afraid," she said. "I had a dream that Dad made the whole movement look stupid."

"He doesn't have that much power, honey," I assured her.

"I so want this to be a positive experience."

"We're all on the same team," I said. "That already makes it positive."

I could see Jessica was still unconvinced, and suddenly, I felt a direct flash of inspiration enter my brain. "Honey," I said, "why don't *you* give him a blessing before we go?"

"Huh?"

"And I'll assist."

"But we don't hold the priesthood."

"We have...we have...goodness," I said. "That's power enough."

Arnie didn't even hesitate when I suggested our daughter give him a blessing. She laid her hands on his head and made a decent stab at it. When you thought you'd never have to give one, you didn't really pay attention to all the particulars. But she concluded with, "if you're approached by a reporter, you'll speak more eloquently than you ever have before." I was a little worried by her wording since she wasn't setting the bar exceptionally high, but both she and Arnie seemed satisfied, and we headed off with smiles on our faces.

Jessica carried a sign that read, "When I said I'd rather die than go to Physics class, that was hyperbole, ass-ault-holes."

It wasn't *technically* profanity, so she wouldn't have to report to the bishop.

There were other signs that caught my attention as well, like one carried by a woman wearing a black dress. "It's too late for my family, but can't we save any others?"

Another sign read, "I don't want you to run into my school without a weapon to save me. I want you to run up to the NRA and do it."

The sign that really affected me, though, was one held by a delicate twelve-year-old Black girl with short braids. "I don't want to text my mom I love her from underneath my desk."

After the march but before the speakers began talking, reporters mingled with the crowd, and I was both excited and nervous when a young woman put a microphone in front of Arnie.

No one ever asked *me* anything.

"What do you think about politicians who say kids should be nicer to each other so the outcasts don't feel they need to shoot anyone?"

"If only those six-year-olds at Sandy Hook hadn't been such bitches," Arnie said, "maybe they wouldn't have all been shot in the head." He paused half a second and added, "I think a better approach would be not to let people who are deeply offended by little kids and country music fans and moviegoers have the opportunity to buy weapons of mass murder in the first place."

I almost shouted I was so happy for Arnie.

Jessica, Arnie, and I all clapped that night when we saw the clip on CNN. I didn't know if Jessica truly did have the power to heal, or if we had just lucked out, but it was a good day for our family. Arnie bought a bucket of Kentucky Fried Chicken for dinner, and we washed it down with ice cold Cokes. It felt a little odd to be having a good time when the occasion was so somber, but it felt important to be happy, too. What was the point of being alive if we couldn't enjoy life a little? "Man is, that he might have joy" and all that. I turned to the Weather Channel to take our eyes away from the news, asking everyone what they wanted to see next.

"Oh, let's watch *Mom*," Arnie suggested. "It's both serious and light-hearted, and I love their self-defecating humor."

Jessica and I started laughing, unable to stop, the first real laugh we'd had since the tragedy all those weeks ago. Arnie soon joined in, though he clearly didn't have the slightest clue why.

The Sunday After

It was the first Sunday of the New Year. Last week, the tsunami had killed almost a quarter of a million people. I still hadn't heard word from my niece who was vacationing in Thailand. I'd started my fast right at midnight on New Year's Eve, twelve hours earlier than usual, hoping the extra hours would help persuade Heavenly Father to show mercy on Tabitha.

What could mercy possibly mean, though, to a god who'd just killed so many people?

I hadn't gone to church in a few months and wasn't sure Heavenly Father was going to listen to my prayers in any event, no matter how long I fasted. But what else could I do? I was in touch with my sister Amber, who was literally waiting by her phone hour after hour, staring at the landline on the end table, her cell phone in her hand. Charles was on his own phone making calls to every agency he could think of, but my sister accepted no calls from friends or family, trying to keep her lines clear, sending out two emails a day to reaffirm she was sure Tabitha would be phoning any minute.

Amber had stopped going to church three years ago, so she wouldn't be at Fast and Testimony meeting with me today. Tabitha had flown to Thailand with a girlfriend from college, church the last thing on her mind.

Not *a* girlfriend. *Her* girlfriend.

Would Heavenly Father spare a lesbian?

I looked in the mirror and straightened my tie. No matter how many years I'd been tying the damn things, I still couldn't do it without a mirror in front of me. I hadn't had to wear one at work in years, but church services still required the accessory.

I saw the reflection of the freshly made bed in the glass, and my shoulders slumped. Six months had passed since the divorce became final. Erin had even insisted on a temple divorce to ensure I couldn't "recapture" her in the next life. She'd moved to another stake. The two kids were both finished college and married, living their own lives in other cities.

The house was so big.

I picked up my scriptures and headed out the door, obeying the speed limit on the ten-minute drive to church. Sunday was the only day I paid attention to the speedometer. The parking lot was almost full by the time I pulled in, but I found a space at the far end and started walking toward the front entrance. I nodded at Brother Higgins and his wife. He nodded politely but she looked at me with her lips set a little tight.

It's not as if I'd committed adultery or anything. I'd just told Erin I wasn't sure I believed anymore. I still loved her, despite our differences. And though I never gave her all the children she wanted, she'd never tried to get pregnant elsewhere. That had to say something about her character, about the strength of our relationship. But my no longer believing was simply more than she could bear.

I looked at the windows high up on the chapel wall. I had to make myself believe today. For Tabitha's sake.

"Good morning, Jake," I said to one of the other high priests as I entered the foyer.

"Welcome back," he said with a friendly smile. "It's good to see you starting the New Year off right." He grabbed my hand and squeezed hard.

I forced a smile back.

"Hi, Jake," said Brother Robertson, the Gospel Doctrine teacher, pushing past two other men to reach me. He clapped me on the back. "We've missed you."

"Have you missed my questions?"

Brother Robertson laughed heartily. "Well, we've *mostly* missed you."

I wasn't going to be a pain in the butt today. I needed whatever brownie points I could get. "I'm looking forward to your class after Fast and Testimony."

"It'll be a good one today, for sure."

I shook Bishop Franklin's hand next and then moved on into the chapel. For the past few years, I'd been sitting closer and closer to the back, but today I sat in the fourth row, right in the center, not in either of the two side sections. "I'm trying, Heavenly Father," I prayed. "I'm engaged. Please help Tabitha and her girlfriend. Please." I checked my phone to make sure it was on vibrate. There were no texts from Amber.

The Killian family sat in the row ahead of me: husband, wife, and five children. The Raleighs sat a few spaces away: husband, wife, and four children.

Erin and I only had the two. She'd always wanted at least six, had said so right from the start, but I'd insisted on condoms early on. Erin was justified in being miffed. Ten years into our marriage, I'd noticed a speck on one of the condom packages. In some back corner of my mind, I remembered I'd seen specks on several of the other packages before, and for some reason, I was finally curious enough to look at it under the light, realizing then to my horror it was a pin prick. Erin had inserted a pin through each of the condoms, hoping one strong swimmer would find its way to success. I never said anything but instead started wearing two condoms. It didn't do much for me sensually, but I didn't need more children to have a forever family.

Or maybe I did. My current family certainly hadn't lasted forever.

Was Tabitha still sealed to Amber and Charles, I wondered? No one had been excommunicated officially, of course. They'd just become "inactive."

Was Tabitha gone forever?

Please, Heavenly Father. I'll believe again. I will. Please help us.

The organist seemed to be playing music more somber than usual. But then, she played so slowly even on good days that any normally upbeat music often sounded dreary. Finally, though, the bishop stood up to start the meeting. "Welcome to all on this fine, beautiful morning. I hope everyone is starting their New Year on the right foot. Let's keep all our resolutions, to make it to church every single Sunday of the year, to read the scriptures every single day, to have Family Home Evening every Monday night, to pay our tithing regularly." He smiled beatifically out at the congregation. "We have a few announcements before we begin." The man proceeded to mention several lackluster events coming up and then named which opening hymn we'd be singing and who'd be offering the opening prayer.

Odd that he hadn't mentioned the tsunami or asked us to keep all those affected in our prayers. Amber had told me specifically that she'd called her Home Teachers. "I may need some Church connections to get a flight out for Tabitha," she explained to me. "Who knows? I'll sell my soul for Tabitha."

We sang "We Thank Thee O God for a Prophet" and then Sister Williams offered the opening prayer. She was a sweet old woman, one of the members everyone loved. Surely, she'd ask Heavenly Father for a special blessing. I bowed my head.

Nothing.

When she finished, I looked up quizzically and followed her off the stage with my eyes. How strange, I thought. Did no one watch the news? The tsunami had been on the air every night for the past week.

Well, I was here to do *my* part, I reminded myself. I was fasting. I was attending services. I was being a good boy. Heavenly Father, I prayed, please have mercy. I looked upward toward the vaulted ceiling.

I remembered Tabitha's last visit to my house, two weeks before her trip. I saw her more often than my own children, who Erin had long ago turned against me, well before the divorce. "You're better off, Uncle Jake," she said. "Even *I* was never attracted to Erin."

I'd smiled wistfully.

She punched me in the shoulder. "Oh, cheer up, Uncle Jake. If push comes to shove, I know a few women who swing both ways. I could set you up sometime." Then she smiled mischievously and added, "I know some hot guys, too. You'd never have to worry about pregnancy again."

She knew of my long-standing battle with Erin. Of course, that had been a moot point the last several years after menopause had entered the relationship. But Erin had never let me or anyone else in the family forget that I'd deprived her of all the spirit children for whom she was destined to provide bodies.

"Thanks, honey," I'd replied. "A bisexual woman will do just fine. I'm free this Saturday at 8:00. Ask her if she's willing to stay over. Maybe bring a friend?"

Erin had looked shocked for a moment until she realized I was joking. "It's been a while since you've joked, Uncle Jake. That's a good sign."

A good sign.

I looked at my watch as we began singing the sacrament hymn. There'd been no sign of Tabitha for a week. Was she lying unconscious in some dilapidated hospital? Maybe her legs were broken. Had she cracked some ribs? I'd seen footage of people with terrible gashes in their arms and legs, on their faces. Had she been disfigured?

Had she lost a limb, needed to undergo amputation to save her life? Perhaps she was fighting to stay with us every minute, wondering why we weren't there to help. Feeling abandoned.

Maybe she was clinging to life, using the last of her energy to mourn Colleen. Please, Heavenly Father, let Tabitha keep the will to live.

After several bored deacons passed the sacrament, the bishop opened the floor to anyone who wanted to bear their testimony. Even back in my believing days, this had always been the most excruciating meeting of the month. And that was saying something. Sister Richards was always the first to rise. She never walked to the podium, having suffered a stroke twenty years earlier and being paralyzed on her left side. She stood and started speaking, not waiting for the microphone which one of the deacons hurried to her pew.

"I just want to take this opportunity to say that I know the Church is true. I took too long while listening to the missionaries, straddling the fence, not wanting to leave my former church. And Heavenly Father was gracious and gave me a stroke to let me know he wanted me to hurry up. I was baptized as soon as I could stand again. And I've borne my testimony every single month since. I want to say again that I know the Church is true. Joseph Smith was a prophet of God. The Book of Mormon is the word of God. Anyone who doubts God's presence in our lives, just look at this walker." She slapped the metal frame. "I say this in the name of Jesus Christ. Amen." She plopped back down in her pew.

Sister Richards was followed by a blond six-year-old girl who walked to the podium and stood on a box to reach the microphone. "I know the Church is true," she whispered, looking out at her parents and covering her mouth to hide a giggle. "I know the Book of Mormon is true. I love my family. And I say this in the name of Jesus Christ. Amen." When she said it, it sounded like "cheese and rice."

Next came Brother Carlton. He also liked speaking regularly on Fast and Testimony day. I took a quick peek at my phone to make sure I hadn't missed any texts.

Nothing, dammit. Please, Heavenly Father, have pity. Pity.

"Brothers and Sisters," Brother Carlton began, "I had a profound experience this week I want to share with you. I was walking downtown and there were lots of panhandlers and bums. One woman came up to me, her hair filthy, dirt on her face. She held out her hand, and I said, 'I'll give you some money if you'll answer a question honestly.' She nodded, and I asked, 'What do you know about the Mormon Church? Would you like to know more?' I was sure I could help her more by giving her the gospel than by giving her money to buy liquor."

He shook his head. "And do you know what she said to me?" He paused and looked out at the congregation searchingly. "She said, 'I used to *be* Mormon, but I started drinking, and I ended up on the streets. Tell everyone to stay true.'"

Brother Carlton smiled broadly. It seemed unlikely that any homeless woman would have said those words, but who knew? Brother Carlton followed this with the standard testimony and then returned to his seat. I could see the congregants in front of me smiling and nodding to one another.

I knew most people thrived under a system of positive thinking, focusing always on the good in life. "Smile, even when you don't feel like it," my therapist had told me. "Fake it 'til you make it."

The folks here today looked genuinely happy.

It's me, God, I prayed, not you.

More testimonies followed, by a couple of teenagers trying to compete with each other for holiest teen, by a young mother holding her baby, by a couple of the older women, by another six-year-old whose mother whispered in her ear what to say.

The Spirit wasn't testifying to me.

Perhaps I was too far gone. But if that were the case, there was no reason for Heavenly Father to answer my prayers. Or Amber's. She was even further gone than I was. She was an atheist to my agnosticism.

I squeezed my eyes shut as tightly as I could, trying to will belief back into existence. "Choose the right…"

Someone said "Amen" and I realized I hadn't been paying attention. Damn.

Heavenly Father, don't the heathen deserve your pity, too? Tabitha still believes in you, even if she isn't Mormon. Forget about Amber and me. Just help *her*.

And Colleen.

Amber was in touch with Colleen's parents, too. But they hadn't had any contact from Colleen ever since they'd disowned her, so there wasn't much hope for news there.

The meeting dragged on, no longer than usual, but each minute feeling like fifteen. Finally, the bishop stood again and announced the closing hymn and closing prayer. We sang "Let Us Oft Speak Kind Words" and then Brother Bartlett offered the benediction.

As the other congregants started to stand and move off to Sunday School, I continued to sit, staring at the pulpit.

Not a single person had even mentioned the tsunami. No prayers had been offered for the injured or the families who lost loved ones. No one said a word about what was probably the largest natural disaster in recorded history.

Were we all living on the same planet?

I picked up my scriptures and followed everyone out of the chapel. Brother Robertson shook my hand as I reached the foyer again. Even though he needed to start teaching in a few minutes, he always made sure to greet everyone a second time. "We're still in the Relief Society room," he reminded me, as if I'd forgotten the location for the class in three short months.

I stared at him and then looked at all the other smiling people in the foyer.

"What is wrong with all of you?" I asked.

"Huh?" Brother Robertson tilted his head.

"Here," I said, handing him my Bible and triple combination. "Maybe you can find some use for these."

I walked out through the front doors and made my way back to the car. A few other people were ducking out early as well, skipping the rest of services so they could break their fast ahead of schedule. I sat down and turned on the car radio to hear the news. I checked my phone again for messages.

Then I put my head down on the steering wheel and cried.

Sneaking in the Carpenters

It was cold and our landlord only turned on the heat for half an hour in the morning and half an hour in the evening. So even though we were in Quartu, on the southernmost tip of Sardinia in the middle of the Mediterranean, we wore our overcoats most of the time we were in the apartment. A few days earlier, it had been so frigid that there was ice in the middle of the streets even at noon, with a wind so strong it dragged a bicycle along on its side. But since we were dedicated Mormon missionaries, the weather didn't keep us from working.

"Can I get in your cot with you?" my companion had asked at the height of the cold. "I can even bring my blanket over, so we'll have two." He was the senior companion, so I usually did whatever he suggested.

"Of course not," I said.

But I could hear Elder Stuart's teeth chattering from five feet away and finally relented. I had to admit, the warm body felt good. I suspected he was gay, but the only thing on his mind that night was the same thing on my mind, staying warm.

Today was Christmas Eve and the weather had warmed to something easily bearable, about 7 or 8 degrees

Celsius, maybe 9. It wasn't as if we had a TV or radio where we could check the temperature regularly. Raised in Salt Lake, I was certainly used to colder weather than we were experiencing today. I hardly needed a jacket at all, except that it was mandatory mission attire. I wasn't sure what 8 degrees Celsius equaled in Fahrenheit, but we were no longer covering ourselves with blankets while eating breakfast in our tiny apartment kitchen. I looked forward to the day in May when the mission president would announce we could go jacket-free while tracting, though our suit coats would remain essential for Sunday services.

We still had to go door to door this afternoon, trying to convert disinterested Catholics. But this evening there was a special program at the church in Cagliari. We'd be taking part in a skit involving a raw egg and some other food. I was chosen to carry the egg and worried it would break on the long bus ride into the city.

"Ready, Anziano Blake?" Elder Stuart asked, pulling on his suit jacket.

"Sí." I pulled mine on as well, setting the egg gingerly in my left jacket pocket.

"Too bad we can't wear something festive to the party."

"Like what?" I asked. "All we have are white shirts."

"I want to wear a bright red tie," he replied. "Or bright green. Or something."

I nodded. My family had mailed me a Christmas package which arrived three days ago and which I'd opened immediately. In it were three pairs of black socks, another cassette tape of the Mormon Tabernacle Choir, and three ties—one featuring a dinosaur, one featuring the NASA space shuttle, due to make its first flight this coming spring, and one that was bright purple with metallic stripes. None of the ties were acceptable for missionaries. I understood how Elder Stuart felt.

As we prepared to leave, my companion offered a prayer. He wore a blue polyester suit while I wore a brown one. Gray might have been acceptable, too, but I had yet to see one among the other elders. Then again, I'd only been out two months since leaving the Missionary Training Center in Provo. I was still learning every day.

Which meant I should probably be paying attention.

"Nel nome di Gesú Cristo. Amen." Elder Stuart looked up and smiled, and we headed out the door. I'd finally learned how to pray in Italian, thanks to my companion's help, and I'd finished memorizing all eight missionary lessons this past week. While I could speak haltingly in Italian myself, I rarely understood a single word any of the Italians said to me in return.

The bus stop was a block away, in front of the Upim department store. The district leader and his companion had already left for church twenty minutes earlier. I could hardly tell Elder Jones and Elder Smith apart. Same height, same build, same hair color, same hair style, same clothes. The only noticeable difference was that Elder Jones, the district leader, talked more. "No classical music!" he'd shout, walking through the apartment on Preparation Day as we did our chores. "No *Saturday's Warrior*! No *My Turn on Earth*! Only MoTab!" Even other church music outside of the Choir was banned. "We'll be so righteous we can call down the Holy Ghost to testify for us!"

I was glad we were taking separate buses.

It wasn't long before a 13 stopped and we climbed aboard. It was a mission rule never to sit on a bus, always offering our seats to other passengers to show how generous we were. There were about ten empty seats now but we remained standing, holding onto the bar over our heads. I kept my free hand wrapped around the egg, wanting to shield it from any inappropriate bumps or nudges. The last thing I wanted was a runny yolk in my pocket.

Elder Stuart was looking at a young Italian man sitting near us. "I want to grow a beard when I get off my mission," he said, motioning toward the man's short, dark beard.

"I thought you were going to BYU." Everyone knew that beards were prohibited on the Brigham Young campus.

"You can apply for a permit," Elder Stuart replied. "They're good for a year. Then you can reapply to have your case examined again."

I frowned.

"If you get the permit, you just wear a lanyard around your neck at all times to prove you have one, so you don't get stopped by campus security."

"Seems like a lot of bother," I said.

"I suppose it's a step forward for them. They didn't used to allow it at all. If you get your permit, you wear a white shirt and tie all the time to compensate for the beard."

"Aren't you tired of white shirts and ties?" I asked. "I've only been out four months and I'm sure tired of them."

He shrugged. "Yes, but I really want a beard." He motioned again toward the young man. "Don't you think it's attractive?"

I raised an eyebrow but didn't comment. No one ever said anything about Elder Stuart's possible homosexuality. It wasn't the kind of topic you could bring up in decent conversation. I myself happily liked girls and couldn't imagine life without them, hoping to get married to Jeanette as soon as I returned home. I wondered how long Elder Stuart would last after his mission before falling into sin. Maybe longer at BYU than elsewhere, of course. Besides, we also knew the Church practiced electroshock therapy for students who had a problem with this crime against nature.

I frowned again. I wasn't sure how we knew so much about things we never talked about. We just knew.

Soon we'd passed through Selargius and Quartucciu and then through the marshes, smelly even in winter, and finally reached the big city. We rode halfway through town before getting off the bus and starting our climb up the hill toward the church. My left hand was still wrapped carefully around the egg. I hated that as a greenie I was given all the unpleasant jobs. I supposed carrying a raw egg wasn't the worst thing in the world, but it was unpleasant enough that none of the other elders wanted to do it. A definite pecking order.

"We're still six referrals short for the week," I said as we walked along. "Do you think we should stop someone?"

"On Christmas Eve?" Elder Stuart asked. "I don't think so."

"But it's a work day," I pointed out.

"Be my guest."

How could he so brazenly flout the rules, I wondered? The mission president in Rome had told me in our interview two months earlier that I had to make sure to learn something important from every companion.

"Is *this* what I'm supposed to learn from my trainer?" I asked myself for the fiftieth time since being assigned to Elder Stuart. I frowned again and continued walking. I ended up not talking to any of the men we passed on the sidewalk.

Several minutes later, we came upon the tiny storefront that the local congregation rented for church. We went inside, where twenty members and several missionaries, including the Cagliari zone leaders, as well as Elder Jones and Elder Smith, were chatting and laughing.

I'd made it. All the way to the church without breaking the egg. I was so relieved I sighed heavily and plopped down in one of the metal folding chairs. There was a sickening crunch.

Oh, my heck. I'd sat right on my own coat pocket! What a complete idiot!

I stood up and looked at the thick, shiny liquid oozing through the fabric. I wanted to curse. "Flip!" I said in disgust. I took off my jacket.

Elder Jones was at my side in a second. "What do you think you're doing?" he demanded. "Put that jacket back on. You're in church. You need to set an example."

"But I just broke the egg in my pocket."

"Non me ne frega. Put that jacket back on."

I stared at him in disbelief, but it was clear he wasn't joking.

"Fa schifo," I protested.

"Put it on," he repeated. "And thanks for ruining our skit. Now we'll have to come up with something else."

Elder Stuart had been watching the exchange and now walked up beside me. "It's okay, Elder Jones," he said pleasantly. "We'll just go back to the apartment and change real quick and be right back."

"Anziani, you'll miss half the program."

"Well," Elder Stuart pointed out, "we'll set a bad example by staying and wearing filthy clothes."

Elder Jones paused a moment and then nodded. "Okay," he ordered, "sprigatevi."

I followed Elder Stuart out of the church, and we started back down the hill, my pocket a complete mess. "I could have kept the coat on," I said. After all, I was still wearing it now.

He laughed. "Are you kidding? I saw the look on your face. Why don't you trust yourself to make your own decisions?"

"He's our priesthood leader," I said.

"And you have a broken egg in your pocket."

Just *what* was I supposed to be learning from him?

"Elder, what say we go back to the apartment, put on some of those ties you got for Christmas, and go to a pizzeria and grab a slice of pizza?"

"Skip the Christmas program?"

"We'll never get back in time anyway."

I thought for a moment. It seemed so radical, so outrageous, so decadent. But I had to admit, it also felt good.

"Let's stop in here for a second." Elder Stuart pointed to a music store just across from the bus stop, busy making last minute holiday sales. Now he was really flouting the rules.

But I looked to see which names I recognized. Sometimes, we overheard the neighbor's radio, and there were two Italian songs I really liked.

"Tell you what, Elder," said Stuart. "If you give me your purple tie as a Christmas present, I'll buy you one of these tapes. Quale vuoi?"

I looked about, adrenaline pumping as I considered breaking away even a tiny bit from the life set out in such detail for me.

I was a slow learner, but I did learn.

"You can use your earphones on P-Day," Elder Stuart said casually. "No one will ever know." He leaned closer and whispered, "I listen to John Denver."

I nodded. I would do it. I'd be daring, too. I picked up a cassette of The Carpenters and handed it to my companion. He took it, grabbed another cassette featuring Zucchero, and patted me on the back as we headed to the cashier. "The pizza will be my treat as well, Elder." He kissed me on the cheek and handed the check-out girl a ten mila lire note. I smiled as I watched the transaction.

The temperature outside seemed to have warmed a degree and I pulled off my coat. Then we waited in the dimming light for the bus back home.

Ronnie and Clyde

"Hey, Clyde." My lover looked dreamily into my face after we made love. "You want to be Friar Tuck or Maid Marion?"

"I can't be Robin Hood?" I asked.

"No. I'm Robin Hood."

Ronald always liked to choose his role first. If we went out for Mardi Gras as a Victorian couple, I'd be the gentleman and he'd wear the hoop skirt. His brown hair came down to his shoulders, so he was really the better choice, and he practiced how to sit so that his bloomers wouldn't show. Sure, he had a moustache, but at least he didn't have a beard as I did.

Every time we'd go out together in costume, his was always larger or fancier than mine, one that would get the most attention. As dungeon master and slave, he was the slave because he got to wear more accessories. He was the sheep and I was the shepherd. He'd be the dragon's head and I'd be the tail. It didn't matter if he could be recognized. He just wanted to be seen. Even when we went as ourselves to a party or out shopping or whatever, he was the one who wore the T-shirts saying, "We aren't just good friends" or "Nobody knows I'm gay."

We'd met while walking in opposite directions on Royal Street in the French Quarter. Ronald wore a National Coming Out Day T-shirt and strode right up to me. "I have a family reunion this weekend and refuse to go alone. They're all Mormon. Will you go with me?"

"I'd love to." I was Mormon, too, had recognized him from one of the last Single Adult events I'd participated in. Ever since the reunion, I saw Ronald do whatever popped into his head, especially if it was showy or bizarre. And now a new idea had just popped in.

"So, Robin," I asked Ronald, "when do we start stealing from the rich?"

"Next Friday," he said. "I overheard two women while I was making groceries at Schwegmann's. One is leaving town next weekend. I followed her home."

"Not at all creepy, dear."

"There's a sign that says 'Beware of Dog,' but she didn't buy any dog food, and I didn't hear any dog when she opened the door."

"Just the same, you go in first."

"Don't you trust me?"

"Well, there was that time your brother came to town…"

"That's not fair. How was I supposed to know you couldn't tell us apart in the dark?"

"Maybe if you'd just remembered to tell me he was coming to visit—"

"Okay, okay, so you got a black eye. I'm sorry. But this is different. And you know how much we need that money."

I sighed and pulled Ronald closer against my chest. "All right," I said. "But I'm scared. I know people get away with this all the time, but this is *us*. I don't want to go to jail."

"Maybe they'll put us in the same cell together. Think of the fantasies we could act out."

We'd both lived sheltered lives, but we weren't *that* naïve.

The first burglary went well. The occupants were gone and had either taken their dog with them or didn't have one after all. We took the stereo, the VCR, the microwave, and a radio, leaving the TV. We certainly didn't want to be mean or anything. Just as we were leaving, though, Ronald gasped.

"What?" I whispered. "What's wrong?"

"Look!" He pointed to a glass cabinet filled with china and crystal.

"We can't sell that stuff, can we?" I asked doubtfully.

"Oh, I don't want to! I want to keep it!"

"Ronald! You know we're not doing this for us. I only agreed because we said all the money would go to charity."

"Yeah, you're right." Ronald looked a moment longer at the case. "I'm sorry." But still he looked.

"Come on. Let's get out while we can."

"We couldn't take just one piece of crystal?" he asked. "Kind of as a commission?"

We sold the appliances without any problem and immediately divided the money into three piles. We sent the first of it off to North Carolina to fight Jesse Helms, the second pile to the ACT UP group in New York, and the last of the money to Greenpeace. We sent it anonymously, of course, not wanting to take credit for money that wasn't ours, not wanting to get any of the organizations in trouble, and also not wanting yet to attract attention. My tips as a waiter at La Peniche weren't sufficient to justify large donations, and Louisiana was not the place to be if Ronald wanted to earn much as an elementary school teacher.

Besides, we were still saving up for Ronald to go to law school. He'd graduated with a 3.9 in English before getting his teaching certificate and had become more interested in law over the 3 ½ years we'd been together. Something about knowing that merely having sex with each other could put us in prison for five years kept him continually thinking about the law.

Louisiana was also the first state where the "gay panic" defense was used in a murder trial.

Our next three burglaries, every two weeks apart, were in different neighborhoods since we didn't want the police to start patrolling any one area too heavily. We again stuck to things we could sell easily, and we divided the money up three ways each time, sending the money to different organizations for each burglary.

The soup kitchen Uptown got some money, as did the Project Lazarus hospice, Amnesty International, the Salvation Army, the NO/AIDS Task Force, a national cancer research organization, a "foster parents" group helping children in Central America, the Helen Keller institute, and ACT UP/San Francisco. We also put aside eight dollars of our own money each week, but that didn't go very far toward our donations. I started to accept we *had* to steal if we were ever going to make a difference.

I remembered when I was seven, I'd wanted to do something special for my dad's birthday. I saved up for two whole months, picking up pennies and nickels I found on the street, watering the neighbors' flowers for a nickel, saving up my tooth fairy money, and anything else I could scrape up, and bought my daddy the best collection of bubble gum baseball cards available for $1.14. I knew my daddy watched baseball all the time. He'd not only like the cards, but he'd see how much I loved him since I wasn't just letting Mom write my name on her gift.

When I saw the cards in the trash the next day, I realized people lied when they said, "It's the thought that counts." I knew my daddy could never be satisfied with a $1.14 gift. It took real money to make people happy.

When I was twelve and started earning a little of that real money, I of course immediately began paying tithing. I was so proud at the end of the year to make an appointment with the bishop to discuss my tithing settlement. It amounted to $67.

I'd read the promises in the Bible to those who tithed, and I was shocked to hear the bishop tell me, "This is a really busy time of year for me, son. You shouldn't be wasting my time over this trifling amount." Even charitable institutions, even *God*, wasn't impressed with paltry figures.

I'd learned a little more about giving in the years since but had seen little to change my mind. A few select people could be satisfied easily, but to give anything worthwhile for most people truly did take money—money I never had. Just once I wanted to give something meaningful.

Hopefully, we wouldn't be caught for a while.

A week after our last burglary, I woke up in the middle of the night and found that Ronald wasn't in bed. I saw a light on in the kitchen and went to see if he was feeling okay. When I reached the door, I stopped and stared.

"What is that?" I demanded. Ronald was sitting at the table with his chin on his hands, leaning forward and staring at a crystal goblet.

"Isn't it pretty?" he asked.

"Where did you get that?" I snatched it up and looked closely at it.

"I slipped it in my jacket pocket at the last house." He looked at me pleadingly. "It was just too pretty."

I threw the goblet into the sink, where it crashed with a crackling roar in the 3:30 a.m. stillness.

"Why did you do that?" Ronald shouted.

"No stealing for us!" I said, trying to keep my voice low. "We won't steal for us!"

Ronald shut his mouth firmly and headed for the bathroom. I heard the lock click.

There was an "I'm sorry" card on my pillow the next evening, and Ronald set aside an extra ten dollars that week of his own money. The next two houses we burglarized let us contribute to research for autistic children, the Sierra Club, the National Gay and Lesbian Task Force, multiple sclerosis research, the Louisiana Gay Political Action Caucus, and Covenant House for teenage runaways. We both compiled a new list of possible organizations to donate to, and every day the list grew longer.

"We'll be breaking into houses for another year just to give to each group *once*," Ronald moaned.

"Should we stop spreading out the money and focus on helping a single group achieve something?" I asked.

"But which one?" he moaned. "Does a child in Sri Lanka deserve to eat, or does a blind woman in Morocco deserve to see? Does a child in Kentucky deserve to read, or do two consenting adults deserve to love each other?"

He huffed in frustration. "How do we make a decision like that?"

So we decided to keep splitting up the money. We almost decided to burglarize more homes, but though we were getting better and faster at it, we realized we were still very much amateurs, and we continued getting more and more nervous at every siren we heard, even when we didn't have any stolen goods in our possession.

I remembered another time I was a kid, and the son of a school board member used to steal my lunch money once a week. He said he was saving to buy a larger tank for his fish. One time, the creep was facing me with his hand outstretched. Looking over his shoulder, I could see the teacher approaching.

I stalled as long as possible, hoping the teacher would catch the bully in the act, but another kid called to her at the last second, and my money was in the guy's pocket. He realized then what I'd been up to and punched me in the stomach, but he never did get caught. His luck kept on throughout that long, miserable year.

Ronald and I had also been incredibly lucky, for a good while now. I knew it couldn't last much longer.

But it did for seven more houses and twenty-one more contributions. We doubted any of these groups would condone our methods, and I knew it wasn't fair to force our "targets" to make these donations. In a free country, didn't people have the right not to be nice? As Mormons, both Ronald and I, along with every other Mormon adult we knew, had committed in the temple to live the United Order.

But only in theory.

As a secular society, though, couldn't Americans come up with a basic, generic policy to work together for the common good? It would make life better even for the super-rich, who could then enjoy the great wealth they still retained while living in a country with less crime and misery.

Unfortunately, that probably wasn't going to happen anytime soon.

Over three years Ronald and I had contributed $1,100 of our own earnings to various groups and also donated countless hours to mailings, protests, letter writing, and a walkathon.

We tried to encourage others to get involved, but if they didn't, that was their right. They weren't *obligated* as people owning fifteen movie videos to help a twenty-three-year-old woman enter a drug rehabilitation program before she gave birth to another baby.

People were going to be robbed anyway, I told myself. At least we were using the money for good causes.

One evening, I found myself unable to concentrate while we watched a movie at the Pitt. We hadn't bought any popcorn, but a viewer during the previous showing had left a partially filled box on the seat that staff hadn't cleared away. I'd reached in to grab a few pieces before I realized what I was doing.

On the way home, Ronald tried to talk about the movie, but I didn't respond.

"You okay?" Ronald asked.

I couldn't answer.

"Clyde?"

"How can we justify going to see a movie if we're stealing other people's VCRs?"

"It was only a dollar movie."

"Still."

We were quiet the rest of the way home, but we stopped going to dollar movies and stopped going to the bars once a week as we'd been doing to meet friends. We raised our own donations by $5 a week, plus put a little more aside each week for law school. The sooner Ronald became a successful attorney, the sooner he'd have more legitimate money to donate.

Yes, we knew what people said about lawyers.

Two more burglaries and six charities later, even though we were only eating generic food and no treats, were watching TV in the dark, and were keeping the air conditioner off completely despite the increasingly warm days of late spring, I felt guiltier than ever about stealing. When another waiter at the restaurant told me his house had been burglarized, I felt so angry I almost yelled at a customer who took too long to make up his mind.

"Let's lay off for a while," I told Ronald that evening, intending to stop completely but afraid he wouldn't go for the idea without a little weaning first.

"We still have two whole pages of charities we haven't gotten to yet."

"They can wait."

"But what if someone dies of leukemia because we waited? What if—"

"They can wait. Let's lay off for a while."

But I wondered. What *if* we could help by giving just that last tiny amount needed to make a breakthrough somewhere?

If it were that close, I told myself, within a week other people would have made up for our small missing donation. And yet, it wasn't fair for me to put the burden on others and just wash my hands of it. I felt guilty no matter what I did.

I escaped my thoughts by reading two used paperbacks I indulgently bought at a garage sale for twenty-five cents each. I'd found a quarter on the sidewalk and felt I could splurge.

Three weeks passed without any burglaries. On one of the nights we'd normally have broken into someone's home, we felt so restless that we had to get out and take a walk through the Quarter, looking in the windows of antique shops on Royal Street.

"Look at that crystal," Ronald said, pointing.

"Nice." We looked at the set of glasses on a dark wooden table. "And look at that oil painting." I pointed.

"Ooh."

We walked to another shop. And then to another. And to yet another.

"$2000 for that little table." Ronald pointed.

"I see it."

"How can people pay that when others are starving?"

"They're preserving history," I said. "Isn't that important, too?"

"Yes, but look at that bed. $10,000. Think what we could do with $10,000."

"If I have to think of money another minute, I'll scream."

We walked home through the Quarter and into the Marigny, crossing the street once when we saw a suspicious looking guy, and then watched TV until we fell asleep.

Another month went by during which I tried not to think at all and was surprisingly successful. Before I knew it, our fourth anniversary was approaching, and I had something positive to occupy my mind.

What should I give Ronald for our anniversary? A piece of crystal? Maybe he'd like a contribution made in his name. An agreement to start up with the burglaries again.

What would he want, that I could live with as well?

Most of our friends had stopped seeing us over the past few months. Since we wouldn't allow ourselves luxuries like popcorn or movies or going out dancing, we became boring. Maybe we already were before but even small amounts of money had been able to mask it.

Perhaps we were only now boring because we couldn't talk about TV shows or what Ricky Graham did in his latest skit at The Parade. Maybe it was because we were no longer planning new Mardi Gras costumes as they were. Or maybe it was because we couldn't even talk about the weather anymore. All we could talk about was supporting causes.

We didn't have to worry about the cost of including friends in our anniversary celebration.

About a week before the big event, while I was working at the restaurant, a group of six guys from the Gay Men's Chorus came in after rehearsal for a late dinner. They laughed and joked and talked loudly, attracting the attention of the other patrons. When I set a dish down in front of a man dining by himself, he smiled up at me and motioned toward the table of six men.

"I love coming here on Tuesday nights," he said. "Those guys always look so happy. It makes me feel good."

I nodded briefly in response and returned to the kitchen, unable to get the comment out of my mind.

My shift ended too late for me to dare walking home, but recently I'd begun feeling so guilty for spending money on cab fare that I risked it anyway. Ronald was already in bed when I got in, of course, and as I crawled in beside him, I whispered, "It is you, isn't it, Ronnie? You're not your brother, are you?"

"No, but I'll give you a black eye anyway for waking me up."

"Oh, I'll make it worth your while." I started rubbing his thigh.

"It's too late. Can't we do this in the morning?"

But I knew what to do and kept him up for another hour. He finally rested in my arms with a contented sigh.

The next day, I bought an "I love you" card for Ronald and left it on his pillow.

"What's that for?" he asked. "You could have just told me. You didn't have to spend a dollar fifty."

I said nothing, and the next day, I left another card on his pillow. "What are you doing?" he asked. "I appreciate it, but you better not leave one each day up until our anniversary. I'd rather you put the money in our fund."

But I didn't. I left a different card every day, and though Ronald looked disgusted at first, he didn't complain any more, resigned rather than pleased. Trying to decide on a gift, I remembered the Christmas after my dad lost his job. He and Mom went to the Thrift Center to buy clothes for my brother and me.

Mom had a friend at church who worked for Hershey and got all the old chocolate, so we each received a stocking full of Halloween candy. I didn't bother any longer getting gifts for my dad, and I wrote a poem for my mom. It was not the "magical" Christmas in the midst of poverty that people claim is so wonderful and special, but it wasn't our worst.

Yet.

We'd taken a long walk in the cool air to look at Christmas lights, and Mom told us stories about Christmas when she was a kid. When we got home, we found that someone had been in the house while we were out. The TV was gone, along with my dad's rifle and my mom's costume jewelry. Mom sat down and cried while Dad drove off somewhere. My brother and I just looked at each other, and then I handed Mom one of my candy bars.

She looked at me, cried some more, then took the candy bar and headed for the kitchen. We spent the next hour breaking up expired candy and making chocolate chip cookies.

I couldn't figure out what to get Ronald, so I finally gave up trying to make it meaningful. On Monday evening, our anniversary, I suggested we stop in briefly at a couple of bars, just to say hi to people.

Ronald nodded his assent. "But only for a few minutes. If we spend any money, I'll start looking for our next house to hit."

We stayed out for half an hour. As I looked around at everybody drinking and laughing, I noticed how different the scene looked from the way I remembered it. These people had smiles on their faces, but many of them didn't really seem happy, and being here in the bar didn't appear to be making them any happier.

Maybe we'd made the right choice after all. We certainly weren't the happiest people in the world, but at least we had a sense of purpose. That had to count for something. For more than sitting at a bar drinking because you didn't want to be home.

"Come on, let's go," I said after a while, and Ronald agreed immediately.

We walked past another bar on our way home, and there was a group of several guys laughing as they came out, a few still holding drinks. A single, grim looking man went in.

"God, he seemed like he was in pain," Ronald said as we walked on.

Maybe he was, I thought. Maybe he really did need companionship this evening. Perhaps he even just needed sex, or simply to feel life in the people next to him, to remember that he was alive, too. Surely, there were other needs besides food and medicine. Didn't quality of life count for anything?

But then, wasn't being able to read, or having cataracts removed, exactly the kind of thing that brought quality of life to people, too?

"I bet these people could have just as much fun organizing a protest rally together, or working at the Task Force," Ronald said. "They'd still be able to meet people, and they'd be doing something useful, too."

"Is it wrong to relax?" I asked. "Maybe that's a legitimate need, too."

"How can we sit back and have a good time when people are suffering and dying all around us?"

I thought for a moment before answering. "Because maybe we'll die ourselves if we don't."

"What?" He stopped and stared at me.

"I want to help, and I'm going to help, but isn't the key word 'help'? It isn't 'solve.' Weren't we born to live, not to give up our lives? Is it so wrong just to want to live?"

"You're being selfish. It's natural to be selfish, but we've got to rise above that."

I remembered how many times the verse claiming that "the natural man is an enemy to God" had been used against us at church.

"How many people have we helped?"

"I don't know. Not enough."

"How many people have we hurt?"

Ronald's face grew hard and he started walking again. "We haven't hurt anyone."

"How do you know? Maybe someone we robbed was trying to fight cancer. Maybe we crushed her spirits and instead of going into remission, her cancer kept progressing. Maybe someone was just on the edge between doing something good or something bad, and we pushed him over to the bad. Maybe—"

"Maybe, maybe, maybe. Maybe we just took some money from people who needed to be giving to charity instead of enjoying life all by themselves and ignoring other people's pain. 'There must needs be opposition in all things.' Maybe they needed to feel a little pain of their own."

"Maybe so," I said. "But why is it wrong for others to inflict pain but okay for us?"

"Because we're helping more people than we hurt."

"So the end justifies the means?"

"Yes!"

"So in order to prevent the spread of AIDS, we should quarantine everyone who is HIV positive? That's a good end, isn't it? Think of the millions of lives we could save."

"That's different, and it isn't practical anyway."

"And our ability to cure every disease and feed every hungry person is?"

"If we want to live Celestial lives, we have to give more than Telestial donations."

"But aren't we just recreating Satan's plan? It was his idea to force people to be good, while Christ said they should have a choice."

Neither of us even believed in the Church anymore.

We walked the next several blocks in silence. Neither of us wanted to speak, even at home. Ronald went off to the bedroom and I opened the hall closet to get out his gift. I knew he wouldn't like it, that I'd made the wrong choice, and I wondered if this would be our last anniversary together.

Perhaps that was best. I did love him, and I admired his conviction, but I didn't think I could live like this any longer. I wasn't strong enough, or bold enough, or whatever it was that it took to do it.

But if I was being selfish, perhaps it was good to stay with Ronald so I could learn to sacrifice more. Even if what we were doing was a sin, perhaps allowing myself to be damned through helping others was still a worthwhile goal.

What was I supposed to do?

I sat at the kitchen table, staring at the wrapped box in front of me. Maybe I should put it back. Maybe—

The bedroom door opened and Ronald came out with a plain, unwrapped box in his hands. He set it on the table next to the other, but neither of us said a word. We must have sat there in silence ten minutes before he slowly pulled his gift over and halfheartedly ripped off the paper.

In the box were two crystal goblets. It had been a long time now since Ronald had asked for any luxuries. He looked at them carefully for a moment, slowly put them in the cabinet, and then went back to the bedroom.

I waited a few more minutes and then opened my package. Inside was a note signed and dated the day before which said, "I'll do anything you want me to do."

I looked toward the bedroom door. That note was still saying "the end justifies the means." He was just changing what "the end" was.

Perhaps therapy was what we needed to get over the past several months. I'd ask him tomorrow to go with me.

Ronald was already in bed, facing away from me. I turned off the light and slipped in beside him, but we didn't touch. I lay awake, unable to sleep, and a few minutes later, Ronald asked, "Should we pay them back? I still remember all the addresses, you know."

"Do you realize how much money that is?"

"Law school can wait another year or two."

"Do you think it'll be enough?"

There was a long moment of silence.

"No."

"Then…"

"I knew from the start it would come to this, Clyde. I've known you for a long time."

"Are you mad at me?"

"I love you."

"Maybe if we get more involved with Lazarus House or the soup kitchen or with Amnesty International, we won't have time to worry about burglarizing."

"I already signed us up."

I smiled in the darkness. "Go to sleep, Mother Theresa."

He turned over toward me. "Not for another hour yet. This is our anniversary." I felt his toes brush against mine.

"Hey, mister," I said, "thanks for four good years."

He said nothing but reached for me in the dark.

The Date

We stood looking at each other, in our creased suit pants and white shirts, our short hair and our business ties. Our black shoes shone brightly from their recent polishing. Elder Tanner grinned at me nervously and pulled my nametag off my shirt. I grinned back at him and pulled his off as well.

"Tonight we go out just as two men," he said. He took my hand. I could feel it trembling. He glanced at the front door. "Would you like to offer a prayer, Elder Smith?"

I nodded and bowed my head. "Dear Heavenly Father," I began, "please help us to have a good time tonight getting to know each other not as missionaries but as people. We ask this in the name of Jesus Christ. Amen."

It felt a little strange asking God for a blessing when we were about to break the rules.

It wasn't as if going to a restaurant was a sin, of course. It was just that it wasn't Preparation Day, and we were supposed to be out working on Saturday night. Also, Mormon missionaries weren't supposed to date for the entire two years they were on their mission.

Certainly not each other.

It was raining lightly, typical for springtime in Renton. I'd enjoyed my last district in north Seattle, but I had to admit, the suburbs down south felt more like home back in Toledo. Elder Tanner was from Logan. It was the only piece of personal information I knew about him. As missionaries, we weren't supposed to talk about our former "civilian" lives. We were supposed to focus on missionary work.

We climbed into the car, Elder Tanner behind the wheel. He was the senior and always drove. He'd been in the mission field thirteen months, me just six. He was nineteen now. I was still eighteen. We'd been together a full two months, and I loved him more every day.

He tended my foot for a week when I stepped on a nail. He traded chores with me that I didn't like, letting me get all the easy ones. He let me win at basketball at church on P-Day, the only thing that made the boring game bearable. He bought me a piece of cheesecake when an investigator turned on us last week and yelled at me.

Last night, he read me the Song of Solomon.

We drove from our apartment past Fred Meyer and Walmart and the Ford dealership and pulled into the parking lot at Buddy's Steakhouse. When we stopped the car, neither of us got out. Elder Tanner grabbed my hand and smiled. I smiled back. Both our hands were trembling now.

It was raining a little harder now, so we ran across the asphalt to the door of the restaurant. Inside was a tiny waiting room with an empty bench. A stuffed goose hung from the ceiling. A stuffed wolf looked out a window. From our vantage point, all we could see was the animal's behind. Elder Tanner pointed and giggled.

We walked through another door just as a huge man and slightly smaller woman came out. He wore a T-shirt that said, "Don't tread on me." She wore a white blouse with a drop of barbecue sauce on it. I fingered my white shirt and frowned.

In the main restaurant, we were greeted by three teenage girls. "How many?" asked one perky little thing. Her T-shirt read, "Preciate Ya!"

"Two," Elder Tanner said.

"The wait is about twenty minutes. This will light up and vibrate when your table is ready." She handed my companion what looked like a huge cell phone and then brushed us aside as another couple walked in.

Elder Tanner nodded to me, and we headed back out to the waiting area and sat on the bench. "I'm so happy to be here with you," he said.

"Elder, we eat together every night."

He punched me in the arm. "You know what I mean."

I put my hand on my stomach. "I have so many butterflies, I'm not sure I'll be able to eat at all."

"We're going to have a *great* meal."

Two teenage girls came in with two teenage boys. The door slammed behind them as they walked into the restaurant. "So, Elder Tanner," I said nervously, wanting to get to the real date stuff, "what's your first name?"

He threw up his hands helplessly. "I knew this moment had to come sooner or later." He took a breath. "It's Felix."

"Felix?"

"I'm afraid so. It means happy."

"Gay?" I suggested, smiling.

He looked quickly toward the door to make sure no one had come into the waiting area. "Happy," he repeated with a fake frown, a twinkle in his eyes. "And you?"

"Billy."

"Not William, or Will?"

"Billy is written on my birth certificate."

He put his finger on his chin, absentmindedly circling where a cleft would be if he had one like mine. "How do you feel about that?"

I shrugged. "I'll probably never be a CEO with a name like Billy, but that's okay."

Elder Tanner looked at me a moment. "It's odd, but I still want to call you Elder. That feels like your real name."

"I'm fine with putting that on our mailbox when we move to Capitol Hill after our missions." I grinned, and

Elder Tanner looked nervously toward the doors again. A group of maybe eight thirteen-year-old girls and a couple of adults passed through the room. Two old people in their sixties walked out of the restaurant, followed a moment later by another heavyset man in his thirties and his heavyset wife, with a boy about six.

"I'm sorry," he said. "I'm not used to this."

"Then maybe we should go on a date next Saturday, too."

Elder Tanner smiled. "We'll go on a date every Saturday for as long as we're still companions."

"How long do you think that'll be?"

"Don't know. Could be another week, or it could be four more months. As long as we keep our stats good, they'll leave us alone."

"Oh, I hope it's four more months. We'll have to work hard this week."

We chatted about our two investigators for a bit, and soon the device in Elder Tanner's hands lit up. He opened the door for me, and we went up to the perky girl again. She handed us off to another perky girl with repulsively tight pants, pointing out much too clearly that she did not have well-formed legs. Odd that she might think she looked sexy in such an outfit, even to straight guys.

A man in a suit looked sexy.

Well, *this* man did.

The girl in tight pants led us to a table in the middle of a vast room, handed us menus, and set some cutlery wrapped in cloth napkins in front of us. Country music played softly, but the roar of the other diners was almost deafening. I hoped I'd be able to hear Elder Tanner. But I supposed the roar also meant no one would overhear us.

"What would you like to drink?" the girl asked after we sat down.

"Water," said Elder Tanner.

"Water," I said.

"We have several great beers," she pressed. She pointed to a page on the menu.

"Water," Elder Tanner repeated.

The girl nodded and headed off.

I looked at the menu. The steaks were expensive, from $18 to $23. This meal would put a huge dent in our budget. Maybe our next date should be at McDonalds. I looked over at Elder Tanner. Still, I was glad our first was going to be memorable. I was torn between two options on the menu, a T-bone for $22 or Fish and Chips for $13. Elder Tanner was paying, so I wondered if I should go with the Fish and Chips.

I'd been on several dates with girls since turning sixteen a couple of years ago. In retrospect, those all felt like going to a dance with my sister. Tonight felt like the real thing.

I wondered if Heavenly Father was going to punish us, and how.

Elder Tanner closed his menu, and I closed mine. While we waited for the waitress to return, I noticed two older men at the table next to us, in their fifties. One of the men, with a goatee, smiled at me with a bemused expression.

I turned to look at the table beside the men. A couple in their thirties, both heavyset, were feeding a blond-haired boy about two, and a slightly older girl in a highchair. The girl looked listless. As I watched, the father pulled her out of the chair, and I could see a piece of plastic tubing hanging down from the girl's side.

Life wasn't fair.

Heavenly Father had put me in a church that condemned gays, but he'd also given me the love of my life.

Was that kind of him, or mean?

The perky girl with tight pants came back to our table. "Have you decided?" she asked, her pen ready.

"I'll have the sirloin," Elder Tanner said, "medium rare, with a Caesar salad and a baked potato."

"Did you want anchovies with your salad?"

"Definitely not."

She turned to me. "I'll have the sirloin, too, medium well, with baked beans and sweet potato fries."

The girl left and I looked at Elder Tanner. We'd done it. We'd ordered. We were officially on a date. I smiled at him and a moment later felt a hand on my knee under the table. I closed my eyes. Would we kiss later? I wanted him so badly, but we were still missionaries, after all.

"What do you want to be when you grow up?" Elder Tanner asked, squeezing my knee before removing his hand.

"An accountant," I replied. "I like numbers."

"Ugh, that sounds horrible." He laughed. "But my choice isn't much better. I want to be a UPS driver."

"Why is that bad?" I asked.

"It doesn't show any ambition."

"But you like to drive?"

He nodded. "I like being out and about. And lifting packages all day will keep me in shape."

"Then I don't see anything wrong with it."

"My father hates the idea. Says I'm a loser."

I saw the pain in his face and wanted to slap his father. I almost said, "Then we won't invite him to our wedding," but what I ended up saying was, "You could never be a loser."

Elder Tanner's eyes fell. "We're going to the Telestial Kingdom, aren't we?" He was hard to hear over the ruckus in the room. "Or to Outer Darkness."

"We're going to wait till we're married and living on Capitol Hill before we have sex," I replied. "Heavenly Father will just have to make allowances. You can only be as good as your situation permits. A diabetic can't fast."

Elder Tanner sighed and cracked open a roasted peanut from a little paper tray on our table. He ate the two peanuts inside and threw the shells onto the floor, where they joined hundreds of others. "I hope you're right."

"Elder Tanner, I love you. And that love doesn't feel evil. It's the best feeling I've ever had. Even better than the feeling I get when I bear my testimony. Loving you *can't* be wrong."

Elder Tanner looked at me and smiled, not a weary smile but a hopeful one. "I love you, too," he said.

"The Church'll come around."

"Do you really think so?"

"It *has* to. The Church is true. So it has to accept all truth. And the truth is that our loving each other is right."

I saw the man with the goatee at the next table motioning to the other man, who took a quick glance over his shoulder at us. Were they old gay letches ogling younger men, I wondered? Or did they recognize us because of our outfits?

Maybe they were interested in hearing the lessons. As much as I wanted more investigators so I could stay with Elder Tanner longer, I was irritated by their glances. Elder Tanner and I should have worn our P-Day clothes, even if it wasn't P-Day.

But we had an appointment at 8:00 with a member family and couldn't risk not being ready in time.

The father at the other table put a shoe on the little girl's foot. It had fallen to the floor. The girl seemed oblivious. The mother continued eating her fries. The little boy played with some kind of action figure.

Three servers shouted a fast-paced happy birthday song and brought what looked like a sundae to a table near us.

"Elder Smith, tell me something else about you that I don't know."

I thought for a moment. I wasn't terribly interesting, but like any young man, I supposed, I felt the need to impress my date. "I used to volunteer at the animal shelter," I said. "We killed most of the animals, but I wanted them to be as happy and comfortable as they could be in their last days."

"Now something else," he said. "I want to know more."

"I like reading Agatha Christie," I continued. "I like growing tomatoes. I like gargoyles. I hate sports, but I do want to train for a marathon one day."

Our server brought our meals and I picked up a fry while Elder Tanner stabbed a piece of Romaine from his salad. I watched him eat.

How could someone look so attractive when he was chewing?

"And you?" I asked, scooping a spoonful of beans.

Elder Tanner looked thoughtful. "I hate reading. I hate tomatoes. I hate gardening. But I love sports, especially football."

"Excellent!" I said. "That means we'll always have time to ourselves and won't get on each other's nerves by being together all the time."

Elder Tanner choked and began coughing. I patted him on the back while he swigged some water and wiped his eyes. "I'm with you all the time now," he said, "and love every minute of it."

Something about the way he said it made me feel hopeless, as if we were secretly spending money we'd found in a lost backpack on the sidewalk.

"I love grocery shopping with you," he went on. "I love cleaning the park every week when we do our community service. I love straightening up the apartment with you."

I wanted to massage his back, rub his chest, grab his penis through his pants. "I love spreading the Gospel with you," I said.

"Maybe we can be stake missionaries together after our missions."

The older man with the goatee was still looking at me every few minutes. What if he was a member and knew we had deliberately removed our nametags? We could get in trouble. We might be separated at the upcoming transfers next week. If we were still together next Saturday, maybe Elder Tanner and I should just have a special meal together alone in our apartment. That's what married couples in love did, wasn't it?

The little girl's shoe had fallen off again, and the father patiently returned it to her foot.

I began eating my steak. Elder Tanner and I talked about applying to attend the University of Washington after our missions. He'd find an apartment here while I was still serving and get everything ready for my arrival. We'd be living on student loans and part-time jobs the first few years. But we were used to being poor. We lived out of two suitcases now.

We chatted about high school. I'd been president of the math club. Elder Tanner hadn't had the right build or skills to play football, but he attended every game. He almost tried out for cheerleading, but he was afraid that would give him away.

We talked about our pets, about our brothers and sisters, about our parents. We talked about the music we liked, our favorite movies. I was beginning to see a completely new person than the one I thought I knew.

I liked this one, too.

Elder Tanner continued to put his hand on mine underneath the table every few minutes as we ate. The servers sang another happy birthday song to another couple. The family with the sick girl left, and a man with a cowboy hat and a woman wearing a tight T-shirt sat at their table.

I thought of Elder Tanner's crotch. Maybe Heavenly Father *should* separate us next week. Even if we couldn't have a temple marriage, I still wanted to be a virgin when we married.

How could this man look so attractive when he chewed?

I finished my steak, quite full, but still wanted dessert.

I wanted Elder Tanner.

Maybe this was all a hopeless dream. What if he forgot about me after transfers? What if he didn't move to Seattle after his mission as he said? What if tonight was all we had?

Would he still love me after we were excommunicated for each other?

I watched as the two middle-aged men got up from their table. They started to pass us on their way to the door. One of them, a little heavy, with a trim gray beard, leaned over when he reached our table. "Hi, Elders," he said before pointing to the other man with the goatee. "We served together in Madrid."

And then they were gone.

Elder Tanner and I looked at each other, my companion's mouth hanging open slightly.

He looked so attractive with his mouth open. I licked some salt off my lips.

Heavenly Father *approved.* It was a sign. We could grow old together. It really was possible. God had sent that other couple here tonight to show us. There really were miracles today like in olden days. The Church was true. I felt a burning in my chest and sent a prayer heavenward.

Elder Tanner took my hand on top of the table and smiled. I leaned over and kissed him.

I couldn't wait to go tracting with him in the morning.

Spirit Prison Blues

"Who died and made you boss?" Ian said testily.

"I did," Marcus replied. He looked at the picture on the wall featuring the Salt Lake temple. On the opposite wall was one of the San Diego temple.

"Well, I'm dead, too. So when do I get to start making rules around here?"

"As soon as we pass the parole board tribunal, I guess."

Ian sighed and stared gloomily at Marcus. "What's on the agenda today?"

Marcus looked over at Ian and wished again he had a different cellmate. They weren't technically in cells, of course. The doors were only locked in the evenings. But they weren't allowed to go anywhere without their assigned companion. Since they never needed to go to the bathroom, this meant they never even got a few minutes alone throughout the entire day. Marcus was with Ian and his negativity every second of what was apparently an intermediate eternity.

"We've got the library this morning," Marcus began.

"Ugh."

"And then film class."

"Oh my god."

"Then the museum."

"Of course."

"But tonight, instead of classes, there's a special concert."

Ian looked at him sharply. "Who is it this time? Not Florence Foster Jenkins again?"

She'd converted almost immediately after arriving and been given the chance to perform as a probationary reward until Judgment Day.

Marcus shrugged. "It's better than the Mormon Tabernacle Choir emeritus."

"Not by much."

"Would you rather the BYU a cappella choir again?"

Ian stared at the floor. "No," he said. "I guess not."

Marcus and Ian dressed. It seemed strange that in Spirit Prison, where they'd been sent along with other non-Mormon dead, they'd be allowed, even constrained, to sleep in the nude. Marcus was pretty sure it was only to emphasize the fact that they no longer had bodies. Marcus could see his dick, could touch it, but he couldn't feel it or get an erection.

It was rather depressing, but every evening just before lights out, they were told to take a good look in the mirror, and if they wanted their bodies back anytime soon, they'd better repent and hope someone did some proxy work in the temple for them so they could be resurrected sooner rather than later.

Marcus and Ian trudged down the hallway, buzzed out of the building, and walked across the campus to the library. Marcus remembered the shock he'd felt at being told he wasn't in heaven. He'd been an activist for ACORN most of his adult life, had helped to register poor Black and Hispanic voters, had worked to improve conditions for immigrant workers, had sought to increase the minimum wage, and had been a union organizer. He'd believed in God, attended a liberation theology church, and spent his life helping the poor and working class.

So why hadn't he gone to heaven?

"Actually, *no one* goes to heaven when they die," the warden had told him that first day. "It's just that good Mormons go to Paradise."

"And Paradise isn't heaven?" Marcus had asked in confusion.

The warden shook his head. "It's a resort where Mormons go until Judgment Day." He shrugged.

Bad Mormons, Marcus had learned since then, were sent to Spirit Prison with people like him.

"But I suppose Paradise is kind of like the semi-final round of the Miss America pageant. You already have to score pretty high to get there. It's only the exact order of the final reward that's still a mystery."

Marcus and Ian scanned their badges at the library entrance. Everywhere you went, you were monitored to evaluate how good you were. All the data were collected for analysis at the end of each week, and you met with an officer to discuss your progress. Marcus had to set short- and long-term goals so he'd be ready for the parole board when the time came. Marcus felt like he was in kindergarten, being told when he could and couldn't take a nap.

At least they still had sleep up here. It was the only respite he ever got. Apparently, even spirit bodies had spirit neurons that needed time to recuperate. They were allowed exactly eight hours a night. Then at the crack of dawn, they had to jump out of bed.

But there was no coffee, no matter how much he longed for it.

Marcus hadn't been able to determine exactly where they were, but it seemed to still be Earth, just another dimension. He could still see the moon at night, could still see Venus up in the sky. He'd overheard two guards say once that an inmate had snuck back to the other side for almost an entire day before being discovered and had to be severely punished as a result.

"Good morning, Marcus," said the librarian, a vapid woman named Camilla, smiling cheerily. "And Ian. What'll it be today?" She waved her arms toward the stacks. "We have Glenn Beck's latest book. And Spencer Kimball has just written a new one."

Marcus grimaced. He'd learned the names of all the Mormon leaders of the past century and a half and had read two dozen books by them since arriving three months ago. Camilla had explained that the only books available here were whatever might be found in LDS bookstores on Earth, tomes written by Mormons, new books by Isaiah or Elijah, or occasional "edgy" material like Jane Austen, *Lassie*, *Pollyanna*, or *Anne of Green Gables*.

Marcus typed *Northanger Abbey* into the computer, which didn't look all that different from an Apple, but he heard Camilla sniff pointedly, and he instead ended up with a slim volume called *Fatherhood* by Rex Pinegar, whoever he was. There were still more names to learn.

Marcus had never been a father as far as he knew. He hadn't wanted to bring children into a corrupt world, hadn't wanted to take time away from trying to improve the society he lived in. But he'd heard since his arrival how important it was to seem like a family man, so he thought he'd give the book a try.

As he started off toward the couches, Camilla called after him in a stage whisper, "Have the best of all possible days…and smile!"

Marcus closed his eyes for a moment but then did force a smile through gritted teeth. He didn't like being ordered to be in a good mood, but he knew there were cameras everywhere.

Posted in his and Ian's cell was a sign that proclaimed, "Attitude Counts!" He'd tried to remove it his first day, but it seemed adhered to the wall with some kind of superglue. A guard had passed by the cell later, pointed at the sign, and wagged his finger.

Marcus read for the next three hours. There was nothing else to do. He'd have to keep reading for two more as well. Once on the sofas, there was a strict rule against talking. You could only read and reflect on what you were learning.

The history was moderately interesting, but the theology was ludicrous. If Marcus hadn't wanted three children brought into a miserable world on Earth, he sure as hell didn't want to father six or seven billion spirit children who would all be forced onto another planet of similar misery.

Of course, chances were slim he'd ever have that opportunity. Only those who made it to the top degree of the Celestial Kingdom became gods. If a person never had the chance to accept the gospel in life, they could hear about it in Spirit Prison, accept, and then, based on how they'd acted in life in relation to which true principles they'd been exposed to, they could still qualify here.

But Marcus had turned Mormon missionaries away from his door twice. He'd campaigned for Al Gore and later Barack Obama, voting against Mitt Romney. He'd given money to support abortion rights and universal healthcare. He might be eligible for one of the lesser kingdoms eventually, but only if he repented.

And he was still in no mood to repent.

Repentance implied that you thought you'd done wrong, and Marcus wasn't sure he had, despite everything he'd been taught here.

Marcus looked over at Ian. His cellmate was reading a book about *The Importance of Obedience*. He looked absorbed.

Marcus couldn't wait till Saturday, when they had visiting hours. Then he'd be able to visit friends and relatives who'd died before him. The problem, of course, was that these visits were monitored, too. If you spent too much time with a rebellious prisoner, it was marked down in a book.

Marcus closed his eyes, thinking of Nancy. She'd been his girlfriend years ago, in college. While Marcus sometimes smoked pot, he'd never tried hard drugs. One evening, he came home from work to find Nancy overdosed on the bed. He'd always regretted not being able to tell her goodbye, so he'd looked her up once he arrived in prison.

Nancy wasn't in a regular cellblock. She was in a detox center. Naturally, of course, without a body to detox, she was permanently in a state of withdrawal. Marcus had been horrified to see her shaking and screaming, to realize she'd been doing this for twenty years already. When Marcus protested to the guard, demanding help, the woman had simply said, "Too bad. So sad. That's what she gets for sinning."

Marcus had tried to hit the guard, but without a body himself, he'd been unable to. Still, she wrote down the incident in her tablet, and his case manager had berated him at length during his next weekly appraisal.

He'd had to listen to an extra hour of Primary songs to atone.

Marcus continued to see Nancy first thing every Saturday morning, though he could only force himself to stay for a few minutes. The other inmates had told him that Nancy probably wouldn't be resurrected until *after* the Millennium, so she'd be like this at least another thousand years.

"It's not that anyone *wants* her to suffer," one grinning doofus explained. "It's just that there are natural consequences to certain actions. It's not as if God is *cruel*."

But Marcus began to wonder. The religion classes ran from 6:00 till 9:30 every evening, unless there was a concert, and the more doctrine he learned, the less impressed he became. A volunteer teacher from Paradise came to see him every night, trying to earn a few extra points post-life because he was apparently a borderline case between the highest degree of the Terrestrial and the lowest of the Celestial.

But this guy, Terrence, insisted that gays were damned no matter how real they thought their love was. He said there was a hierarchy in heaven, that while technically a woman could become a goddess, she was still subject to her god-husband. You could have only one ultimate ruler in any universe. You never heard an Old Testament prophet saying, "God's wife told him to tell me to tell you…" And no one could become a god at all, man or woman, without being married.

But Marcus had never married. He'd always thought it too stifling for both the husband and the wife. He was horrified to think he'd now have to accept an eternal marriage that would never end.

"The problem is," Terrence had explained, shaking his head sadly, "that you were never married in life. So it's not as if someone can just go to the temple to do proxy work for you. You'll have to meet someone here. And *if* you qualify in other respects, you can be resurrected in time to get married in the Millennium." He shook his head again. "But it won't look good on your record."

Marcus heard a tapping noise and turned to look at the librarian. Camilla had seen he was daydreaming and wanted him to get back to his studies. He nodded and looked at the pages once more, but not before watching her write something down in a notebook.

She wasn't wearing a ring.

Thankfully, there'd been no lessons on arranged marriages.

Camilla tapped again. Someone else nearby must be daydreaming, too.

Marcus quietly slipped his pen out of his pocket. The inmates had been given pens and notebooks so they could take notes about the books they read or films they saw. Marcus hadn't written much so far, but now he uncapped his pen. He glanced over at Camilla, who was talking to another inmate, and he opened his book to the middle. "Fuck fatherhood," he wrote in long, bold lines.

Finally, reading period was over, and there was a half-hour break near the duck pond before the afternoon film session began. "What'd you think?" asked Marcus, standing under a tree and really, really wishing he had a cigarette.

"I'm seriously missing my Stephen King," Ian muttered in a subdued voice.

"And I wish I could have my Faye Kellerman back." Marcus paused. "Do you suppose we could start a petition?"

He was half joking, but Ian gasped.

Marcus's eyes narrowed. "Who cares if we have a few points deducted?"

Ian shook his head. "This isn't like cramming for some college exam that determines your grade for the course. This is for *forever*. I'm not about to louse it up."

Marcus looked at Ian closely, evaluating how much he could say. "I think," he began, "that I may try to sneak out of the cellblock tonight."

"What?"

"Try to get back to the other side."

"Whatever for?"

Marcus shrugged. "I don't know. I still won't be able to drink a beer or kiss a woman, but…"

"But what?"

Marcus shrugged again. "I don't know," he repeated. "I don't even know that I'd try to materialize and warn people. What would I tell them? I don't want to become Mormon even now. There's no reason I should tell anyone back there to get baptized."

Ian tilted his head. "Don't you *want* to be on God's side? Haven't you *seen* how awful Lucifer is?"

Marcus nodded. One of the first films they'd seen was a documentary about Satan, how the evil spirits who'd followed him never obtained a body, so when apostates were sent to join them, everyone jumped into the bodies and fought over them. They were in continual spasms from the competing spirits, and there were physical fist fights between the bodies, as groups of spirits in one tried to subdue or rape the group of spirits in the other. It looked like hell.

Marcus smiled for a moment at the unintended pun but then frowned. What *did* he want out of eternity? To sit in a meadow and listen to Pearl Jam forever? You had to do *something*, but was godhood the best answer?

Even among Mormons, only a tiny elite achieved that. Most people, even Mormons, had to accept eternal limitation, not eternal progression. It somehow didn't seem fair. Judging the few years of life out of an eternity of existence was like asking a five-year-old who could barely concentrate to take a test that would determine the course of the next seventy years of her life.

"Well, *I* think we'd better get with the program," Ian said. "There are degrees of unhappiness. And being Mormon throughout eternity has got to be better than the alternative."

Marcus wasn't so sure, but he didn't say anything more. He listened as Ian told him what he'd learned that morning, and soon it was time to go to the theater. In the lobby, there were a few minutes to chat with other inmates, but too soon, they were ushered to their seats by inmates trying to get extra rations of the "good music," whatever that might be. Then the lights dimmed and the film started.

Today's first show was a summary of the Spanish conquest of the Incas. They weren't watching a re-creation, of course, but the actual events, the actual people. There was a voice-over, like Cecil B. DeMille in *The Greatest Show on Earth*, talking about how the Lamanites had fallen away and were ripe for destruction. The voice-over seemed to be in English, but the voices of the Incas were in a Native American dialect, and the Spanish soldiers spoke Spanish. Yet even though there were no subtitles, somehow Marcus understood every word of the movie.

The film was followed by a break during which everyone took a quiz. The questions were multiple choice, but they never asked much about the actual events themselves. One of the questions today, for example, was:

To what did the Incas owe their destruction?

    A. Personal Depravity
    B. An evil religion
    C. Social injustice
    D. A and B only
    E. B and C only
    F. All of the above

Marcus circled C, but when the tests were graded at the end of the session, he learned he'd been mistaken. The teacher drew a smiley face with a frown on his paper.

Next came a film about the early Christians as they fell away from the gospel and into apostasy. It seemed to be a major theme today. After a quiz on the Thessalonians, Marcus whispered to Ian, "I'm going for it tonight."

"No!"

"What's the worst they can do? Lock me up?"

There was one last, shorter film about the Reorganized Church of Jesus Christ of Latter-day Saints breaking away from the main group after Joseph Smith's assassination, and then finally film class was over. Marcus felt like a boy again in math class. "When am I ever going to need algebra?" he'd complained to the teacher.

Now he knew the answer to that question. If he was going to create worlds, he had to know every fact of biology, physics, chemistry, calculus, and every other science. And he supposed he needed all these lessons about human nature and about right and wrong, too.

All while being told he possessed only the slimmest chance of reaching a level where he could use any of it.

One thing, though, confused him more than the rest. In life, Marcus had often felt there wasn't just black and white; there were lots of shades of gray. How could God be *more* complex than humans and yet have a *simpler* world view? Why wasn't there *more* complexity in making decisions now?

There was a fifteen-minute break, during which Marcus tried to talk with a petite female inmate. Marcus's spirit body was the image of his physical body at the age of twenty-four, when he'd been in his prime. But the woman still looked at him askance and turned away. There wasn't much chance he'd ever find a wife at this rate, with so little time for socializing.

The concert would give him more opportunities, though. He could mingle all evening. Maybe he could even find someone else who wanted to break out of prison.

At 6:30, everyone from his cellblock filed into a large auditorium. There was a little fidgeting and talking, but the guards quieted people down. Marcus made a point of sitting near the end of a row so he could get up. He'd stand most of the evening, trying to talk to anyone who looked bored and thus open to dissent.

"Welcome, everyone," said a woman, beaming from the stage. "We trust you've had another productive day. But tonight, we want to reward you with a little concert from George Osmond." Marcus wondered if Ian was enjoying himself, but he couldn't find him in the crowd. At least the event was giving Marcus some relief from his companion's constant presence. No one was pleasant company twenty-four hours a day, every day. Marcus wondered again if he should even bother attempting marriage.

"George puts on a good show," the woman continued. "You'll be glad you died." She chuckled. "And next week…we have a special performance by the King family."

Marcus looked at his neighbor, mystified.

"It'll be a real treat! So, everyone, be happy! And remember, you're a child of God!"

The lights dimmed, a spotlight shone on stage, and George Osmond walked out with a big smile. His first song was a cover of one of the covers his sons had sung, "He Ain't Heavy, He's My Brother." Marcus slipped out of his seat and started looking for anyone fidgeting.

And there *was* someone. Another guy, an Asian, kept looking at his naked wrist as if hoping to check the time.

He was at the end of a row, too, and Marcus motioned to him. The guy nodded and stood up. He couldn't know what this was about, but that clearly didn't matter. Any excuse was a good one.

"You want to get out of here?" whispered Marcus.

"You mean skip the concert?"

"No, I mean, get *out* of here."

The man's eyes widened. Then he nodded. "I don't care what your plan is. I'm in."

Just then, four guards came up to Marcus and his new friend. They had spirit handcuffs and slapped them on the two men.

"What's going on?" Marcus asked. "Can't two guys hang together at a concert?"

"Ian told us everything," one of the guards informed him. "He turned 'soul's evidence.' Admitted his own grumblings but gets points for turning you in."

"You're in big trouble now, mister," said one of the other guards.

"What about this guy?" asked Marcus. "*He* hasn't done anything."

"He's talking to *you*, isn't he?"

Marcus squinted. The guard looked like a twenty-something Joseph McCarthy. Marcus was led off in one direction by two of the guards while the other man was led away by the others. Marcus ended up in a small room behind a table, in a chair under a bright light that did not hurt his eyes. He looked off to the side.

"Oh my god," he said. "You have a one-way mirror!"

"Don't take the name of the Lord in vain."

"Fuck you."

One of the guards slapped the table in front of Marcus. "That's enough! We can throw you into Outer Darkness any time we want. Do you want to go to hell?"

Marcus looked at the two guards, and then glanced over at whoever might be watching through the mirror. "If there are degrees of heaven, there are degrees of hell, too. And this is certainly one of them."

The head guard gasped.

"You have a very rebellious spirit," the other guard said coolly, but Marcus thought he detected an almost admiring tone.

Marcus shrugged. "I don't like to see injustice," he said simply.

"Injustice!" the first guard exclaimed. "We're giving you chance after chance after chance to repent!"

"You're giving me chance after chance after chance to become a Stepford saint. I want to choose my own path, not be forced to choose the path you want me to take. What kind of freedom is that?"

"It's the only freedom there is," snapped the head guard. "You can take it or leave it."

Marcus thought for a moment.

"Well? What's it going to be?"

"I think your God is a bully," Marcus said calmly, eliciting horrified expressions from both guards. "And I think your Lucifer is a punk. I don't want to follow *either* of them."

"Those are your choices, buddy."

Marcus shook his head. "Why does this have to be a two-party system? I want an alternative. Or maybe four or five alternatives."

There were more gasps.

"There's an eternity ahead of us," said Marcus. "And unlimited space. And that's only in this one dimension. There's certainly room for another team or two."

The head guard slapped the table again, but the other guard, while still angry, began to look confused.

Marcus looked down at his cuffed hands, and suddenly, he experienced what could only be described as a revelation. Pure knowledge entered his soul. He stood up and held his hands out in front of him.

"What are you doing?" the main guard asked nervously.

Marcus stared at his handcuffs a long moment, and then they unlocked and fell to the floor.

"Oh my god," whispered the second guard, taking the name of the Lord in vain himself.

"What did you do?" the head guard demanded, a little frightened now.

"You only have power over me if I concede that power," Marcus said. "I just realized that all this time, I've been complaining, but I've *let* you control me." He paused. "And that's not going to happen anymore."

"What—what are you going to do?" The guard fingered his collar.

Marcus thought for a moment. He had a lifetime of political activism and union organizing behind him. Perhaps he'd organize the inmates into a prison uprising. He rubbed his chin.

Maybe after that, he'd go from universe to universe, creating spirit unions and pushing third party candidates. It was enough to keep him busy for a while.

A few million years perhaps.

Marcus didn't answer but simply walked out of the room. The second guard ran after him, keeping his distance but looking almost hopeful. Marcus smiled and headed back for the cellblock. He walked up to the first cell and knocked on the door politely.

"Yes?" said a meek voice from inside.

"May I have permission to enter?" Marcus asked.

The door swung slowly, and a man whose mouth hung open stood staring at him.

"Do you want to go to heaven or hell?" Marcus demanded bluntly.

"H-heaven," the man stammered. Now Marcus could see the fellow's cellmate in the background, peering forward timidly. They'd clearly been in prison a long while.

"Yes," said Marcus, "but that's a close-ended question. How about we ask an open-ended one now?"

The man looked confused.

"*What* do you want out of eternity?"

The man looked at Marcus, at the guard, and even back at his cellmate before looking at Marcus again. "Is this a trick?"

"Nope." He smiled at the guard, who nodded his support. "We're making our *own* heaven." He offered his hand and the man took it cautiously. "Mind if we come in and talk for a bit?"

The two cellmates looked at each other for a moment, communicating silently, and then opened the door wide, motioning him to enter. Marcus smiled and walked inside.

The Removal of Debra

"Gary, could you type up this bid for the job I'm hoping to get? Your mom's not feeling well."

"Sure, Dad."

I followed him to his office, the former dining room which now had a desk, two file cabinets, an adding machine, and a wall lined with trophies from tractor pulls. Dad was Texas State Champion in his category. I'd only gone to one of the pulls he competed in, though Mom went to almost all of them. Since her favorite song was Petula Clark's "Downtown," I wasn't sure what she thought of the rural crowds. The one pull I'd gone to was in Mississippi, just two hours north of our home in New Orleans, but it so bored me I could never force myself to attend again. I felt bad not to be more supportive, so I was glad to be of some help now.

"Here's the proposal," Dad said, handing me several papers. "You're the college student. Fix any problems you find."

"I don't know anything about building houses," I reminded him. "If there's something wrong, I won't know. I'll just type it like I see it."

Dad wrinkled his nose briefly. "Your mom never has any trouble with it, so I guess it'll be all right."

I took the proposal upstairs to my computer and started typing. It was mostly a long list of materials or jobs and the corresponding price for each. "Molding" was one of the items. I wasn't sure if it should be "moulding," so despite what I'd told my dad about not making corrections, I verified. Then there was an entry for "wainscoating," and I wasn't even sure what that was, so I looked up the term. And finally I saw an entry for "the removal of debra," and that one stumped me completely.

My mom's name was Debra. Obviously, there wasn't a fee for getting her off the property. But was there some other person stalking the workers who had to be removed from the site by a security guard? An arsonist had once burned two houses my dad was building. Perhaps it was a technical term I didn't understand. My dad only had a high school education, but he was certainly intelligent enough to use some technology. He'd had faxes and cell phones and email for years.

I was just about to go downstairs and ask him about the entry when a light went off in my head, and I laughed at myself for being so slow. It was obviously supposed to be "the removal of debris."

I finished typing up the bid and handed it to my father. We got along well enough despite having little in common. He liked baseball and hunting. I liked books and movies. He liked raising cows on land he inherited in Mississippi. I liked playing Scrabble with friends. So it felt good to have at least this one brief moment working together on a common project.

If he ever realized I was gay, of course, God only knew how he'd react. I'd hoped my missionary work would change me, but now I realized being gay was permanent and I was doomed to Outer Darkness. Yet I still hoped as a Sunday school teacher and stake missionary to help save some other souls, even if my own was damned. I wanted my parents to make it to the Celestial Kingdom, not be a stumbling block to them. If I could do some little thing for Dad today to help, even just for his business, then I felt happy.

"Thanks, Gary," Dad said as I handed him the papers. "I'll take a quick look at this, and then we're going to take your mom to the doctor."

"Is she feeling worse? I'll go in and check on her."

"She wants to be alone."

"You're sure you don't want me to take her? I have a test tomorrow, but I can study in the waiting room while she's with the doctor."

"No, I'll take care of it."

Though I was twenty-one, I was only a sophomore at the University of New Orleans, behind most other students because I'd served two years as a Mormon missionary in Romania. I still lived at home, and Dad paid my tuition. I had a part-time job delivering pizza on Friday and Saturday nights, but I felt useless much of the time, a leech living off my parents. I did the family's laundry every few days, but it was really the only chore I did around the house.

Dad didn't like the way I mowed the lawn and insisted on doing it himself. He didn't want me cleaning out the gutters.

And I'd overheard him once telling Mom he didn't like me helping in the kitchen.

That didn't leave much.

I went back to my room and studied my notes on *Hamlet*. I was reviewing one of the soliloquies when I heard the car pulling out of the driveway. Mom had been kind of sullen the past few weeks and clearly didn't feel well. She was the type who got grumpy when ill, so I'd mostly been staying out of her way.

She had a cliché personality when she had her monthly periods. She'd be fine one day and a monster the next. I'd never told her, "I guess it's that time of month" because I knew if I said it during "that time," she'd probably knock my head off. The rest of the month, she was as sweet as could be. The last few weeks, though, she'd been grumpy most of the time. Once, she'd even kicked our Chihuahua for getting in her way, and she loved that dog.

I'd finished reviewing both *Hamlet* and *Coriolanus* when I heard the car pulling back into the driveway. I went downstairs. The kitchen door opened and Dad came in. "Where's Mom?"

Dad looked tired. "They admitted her to the hospital. She's lost a lot of blood."

"She's hurt? I thought she was sick."

Dad gave me a weary look. "She's been bleeding for a month. I came back to see if you wanted to go to the hospital and keep her company while I do some work in the office. She still doesn't *want* company, but I think it's best."

"Sure, Dad. Which hospital?"

"Lakeside Women's Hospital."

"I'll go right now."

"You better eat a sandwich first. I won't be able to get back for a few hours."

I quickly shoved down a turkey sandwich and drove over to the hospital near my old high school. Soon I was in Mom's room. She was glaring at the bag of blood attached by a tube to her arm.

"How're you feeling?"

"Like crap," she said angrily. "I'm watching that blood go into my arm drop by drop, and I lose it as fast as it comes in. They're going to do a hysterectomy tomorrow morning."

Wow. This was serious. "What's wrong?"

"I've had fibroid tumors for years and apparently now they're causing this bleeding."

"At least you won't have periods anymore. That'll be good."

My mom shot me a dirty look. "I've had periods since I was ten. I'm forty-three. I'll be glad to get rid of this fucking junk."

I was shocked at her language. I'd once heard Dad say "damn" and another time Mom say "shit" and been surprised even at that. Mom must really be feeling awful.

She didn't *sound* glad.

We didn't talk much for the next few hours. Finally, around 9:30, I thought I'd better head back home to get some sleep before my morning classes. But Mom looked so miserable I didn't want to leave. I wondered where Dad was. I'd thought he was coming back to see her for a little while.

At 9:45, Dad walked into the room. "You can go on now, Gary. I'll stay the night."

I nodded and gave Mom a kiss on the forehead. She looked too exhausted to be annoyed. I was surprised my dad was staying the whole night. He was not an overly demonstrative man, and this seemed much more intimate an action than I'd have expected. I hoped my mom wasn't in any real danger.

It was difficult to concentrate during my exam the next day, knowing Mom was in surgery, but I thought I did well. Mom always liked to hear about my grades and I didn't want to let her down. After classes were over, I headed back to the hospital.

Dad was still there, though it was after 3:00. Surely, he hadn't been in the room since the previous evening. "How're you feeling?" I asked Mom.

"Like crap."

"I'm going to the job to get some work done. You'll want to fix a sandwich for yourself when you get home, Gary."

"Sure, Dad."

"See you tomorrow, Debra."

After Dad left, I sat beside Mom's bed. She had bruises covering half her arm. I wanted to hold her hand, but she had an IV in it.

"They did a goddamn bone marrow test this afternoon. Hurt like hell. I don't know what the fuck that was all about." She sighed and shook her head. "I'm sorry I'm cursing. I know I shouldn't make things any harder on you. I just don't feel good."

"It's okay, Mom. You've got more important things to worry about."

"But I should be stronger." She looked at her hands and suddenly got a disgusted look on her face.

We didn't talk much over the next few hours. The TV played, and Mom watched it intently, the look on her face now angry. I'd brought my Western Civilization notebook and studied a bit.

Around 8:00, the doctor came by and made Mom stand up beside the bed and walk a few steps. Mom swore but did it.

"We'll have you walking down the hall tomorrow," the doctor said, smiling despite my mom's scowl. "And you'll be home tomorrow night."

Mom was indeed home by the next evening. She still didn't feel well and went straight to bed. I left her alone but thought about her while delivering pizza in the rain later.

She loved Canadian bacon.

The next day after church, I went to sit on Mom's bed beside her. "All those bruises look painful," I said, hoping to convey my concern. Then I added impishly, "Maybe we should try some acupuncture to relieve the pain."

She smiled for the first time in days. "I think acupuncture is what caused all the bruises in the first place."

We chatted for an hour, and then she got a call from the Relief Society president, so I left her alone. She'd be back to normal soon. I checked on her just once more a couple of hours later, and since it was Sunday, I asked if she wanted me to bring her scriptures to her. She nodded absently, but when I handed her the Book of Mormon, she looked at the cover for a long moment and then put the book aside.

I didn't study for school on the Sabbath. Instead, I emailed some friends in Bucharest and my aunt Robin in Jackson. Then I read some of *Faith Precedes the Miracle* and a little of *Life After Life*, about near-death experiences.

Mom came down for breakfast the next morning and Dad cooked for her. I ate a bowl of cereal and headed off to school. Mom was back in bed resting when I returned in the late afternoon. Dad fixed Mom some soup, and I had a sandwich.

Then I headed over to the stake president's house. Their oldest daughter was hosting the Single Adult Family Home Evening. We had a brief lesson on charity and then played Truth or Dare. For one of my truths, I had to reveal my first crush, which was easy enough—it was my first-grade teacher, Miss Kavanaugh. At least they didn't ask for my second crush, which would have been Mr. Edwards, in second grade. Or my third, which would have been Coach Marks in 8th grade. Or my fourth, which would have been my classmate Jim in 9th grade. Or my fifth…

As much as I had to hide, I still always chose Truth in Truth or Dare. I was too wimpy to ever do a Dare.

The stake president, who'd left the Single Adults alone during the evening, walked up to me at the end of the meeting. "Your dad just called. He took your mom back to the hospital. She has a high fever. She's in East Jefferson."

"I'll stop by on my way home."

He put his hand on my shoulder. "If you were *my* son, you'd be working your way through college. I don't approve of your father paying your tuition. I'd teach you some responsibility. Make a man out of you."

My first impulse was to say, "Thank God you're not my dad." But I knew my father and President Brooks were friends, so I just smiled. I couldn't help but notice he didn't have any problem paying his daughter's way through college.

On my way to the hospital, though, I thought about what the man had said. *Would* it make me a better person to move out on my own, get a full-time job, and go to school part-time? If I was a bad person now, surely that was for being gay, not for making A's on someone else's dime.

I was two years behind most of my classmates as it was, but maybe that wasn't as important as being self-sufficient. Taking out student loans and being $50,000 in debt by the time I finished school would be a hard way to start my adult life, but hard wasn't necessarily bad.

Still, so what if I was a lazy bum for living at home while going to school? I was destined for hell anyway. Why bother with improving my character? I was taking five classes a semester. I didn't date or go out or waste the money Dad gave me at the beginning of each semester. I might be wicked, but I was still a good kid.

Yet a kid nevertheless. Even after a two-year mission. Even after going through the temple. Even after a year and a half of college.

When I got to the hospital, I headed up to my mom's room. I wondered if the fact she was in a larger hospital now meant the infection that had caused her fever was serious. I offered up a quick prayer, put a smile on my face, and went into my mom's room. My dad sat next to the bed.

"I want to talk to Gary alone for a minute," Mom said curtly. Dad nodded and left the room.

I took my dad's place in the chair and held Mom's hand.

"I am super pissed off," she said. "Do you know when they admitted me, the nurse looked at my chart and said, 'Oh, you're the leukemia patient.' So that's how I found out I have leukemia."

"You have leukemia?"

"Your dad wasn't going to tell me. He thinks I'm too fragile. But I can tell you this—if I'd known what I had, I'd have stayed at home and blown my brains out. But now I'm trapped here, on chemotherapy I don't want, and I can't get out. My whole life, people have been telling me what to do. Even now, I don't have any say over my own life. I am *really* pissed."

My mind was going a mile a minute. Mostly, I was thinking maybe my dad was right not to tell her, if it kept her from committing suicide. The Church said taking your own life was a terrible sin. There was no sense going to hell when you were so close to finishing your test.

But surely she wasn't about to "finish." She wasn't going to die. The chemotherapy was going to work. There were huge strides forward in cancer treatment all the time. And this was my mom. My mom couldn't possibly die. Those things only happened to other people.

Mom grasped my hand. "They won't give me a prognosis. But I got them to tell me the name of the leukemia. It's acute myelogenous leukemia. I want you to go to the library and find out how long I've got."

I nodded dumbly.

She squeezed my hand harder. "I want you to know," she said, looking at me intently, "I've always loved you. I've always been proud of you. I couldn't have had a better son."

"There's no need to talk like that, Mom. You're not going anywhere."

"We'll see. You come back and tell me my prognosis tomorrow."

"Okay."

"And for God's sake, don't let the Relief Society president come. I can't stand that bitch. I don't feel up to pretending I like her at a time like this. And I'm not going to apologize for it, either."

"I'll call and tell her you're not well enough for visitors."

"Hell, you can tell her the truth for all I care. I'm sick of pretending." She laughed a little bitterly. "Maybe I'm sick *from* pretending."

I nodded, knowing I'd find something more diplomatic to say. I'd been voted Most Courteous in high school. With so many defects in my character, being nice was one of the few things I had going for me.

Though I supposed there was no pressing reason to be nice if I was going to hell anyway.

"Call your Aunt Robin and ask her to come down. I want to see her before I die."

"You're not going to die."

"I want to see her. And call Grandma, too."

"I'll call them tonight."

Grandma drove a couple of hours from Brookhaven the next morning, and Robin left her two teens and husband in Jackson and came down early in the afternoon, before I was back again after school.

"What's the verdict?" Mom demanded as soon as I walked into the room. Three pairs of eyes stared intensely at me.

"If the chemotherapy doesn't work," I began uncomfortably, "you have about three months."

Mom deflated like a punctured balloon and I felt like a murderer. I didn't have the heart to go on, to say that even with successful chemotherapy, which was rare, remission usually only lasted a single year. All our worlds were being turned upside down.

Mom didn't say anything more the rest of the afternoon, other than muttering "shit" a couple of times. Robin and Grandma tried to carry on a cheerful conversation, but Mom took no part in it, and I didn't, either. Around 9:30, Dad came to stay with Mom for the night, and the three of us went back to the house.

"The chemotherapy will get rid of the bad cells," Robin said as we came inside. "It's all going to work out fine. Tomorrow morning before you go to school, you and your dad need to give your mom a blessing. You still carry your consecrated oil with you, don't you?"

"Yes."

"Then everything's going to be all right."

Grandma looked unconvinced but smiled weakly.

I knew God would never honor a blessing made by a homosexual, even if I was still a virgin. I wasn't a virgin in my thoughts and God would hate me for that. He'd certainly never save my mom on my account. Maybe I could get the bishop to do the blessing with Dad.

I went upstairs and called Bishop Tillotson, asking him to stop by the hospital in the morning before work. When he agreed, I sighed in relief.

The hospital was on my way to school, so I dropped Robin and Grandma off in the morning. Dad looked beat but said he and the bishop had given Mom the blessing. I looked at Mom while he told me, unnerved by the glare she was directing toward him.

I was finished with classes by 3:00 and went back to the hospital. A nurse came into the room to draw blood, but Mom's arms were already covered with bruises. A little later, I noticed that the tubing had become disconnected to the IV in her hand. I pushed the call button, and about five minutes later a nurse responded by intercom.

I explained what had occurred, and the nurse angrily told me that this couldn't happen. I insisted she come look, and the nurse arrived several minutes later. When she saw the tubing, she didn't say anything. She reattached the hose and left, still angry. For some reason, I felt guilty.

The next few days passed in much the same manner. Robin and Grandma did the mornings. I came in mid-afternoon, took them home, and went back until late evening. Dad came around 10:00 and stayed the night.

Mom didn't talk much, so on my shifts, I mostly studied or told Mom stories of my mission experiences in Romania. I'd had a favorite companion, Nicolae Petrescu, who'd just written me a long email, so I told her what he was up to these days. She didn't look overly interested, but we had to talk about something. I didn't tell her that Nicolae had said he missed me. "Mi-e dor de tine!" he'd said.

I smiled, remembering his voice.

I asked if Mom wanted me to bring her something to read. She had probably two thousand books at the house and particularly loved mysteries, though I'd found a few classics as well as a few books about sex on her shelves. She had a locked cabinet in her tiny study, and she'd never let anyone see what was inside. She'd collected first editions for a while, and I figured she kept a few rare books in there. Perhaps if I brought her something special from home, she'd feel better.

"My reading days are over," she said. "Take whatever books you want and get rid of the rest. And don't clutter up your house with all that junk like I did. Use the library."

"But you love your books, Mom. There's no sin in enjoying something."

She stared at the ceiling. "I wish I had actually done something with my life." I put my hand lightly on her arm, afraid of hurting her. "I wasted all that time being a good little girl. God, I wish I'd posed for *Playboy* or something when I was young. Or gone to college. Or written something. Or backpacked across Europe. Or gotten arrested. I wish I'd done *something* interesting."

"You got married in the temple and raised a family." I felt stupid saying it, knowing that forced her to say she was glad she'd had me.

"Having a kid shouldn't mean you never get to do anything else with your life."

"No," I agreed. "You're right."

Unfortunately, our talks tapered off quickly. By the next day, Mom started losing her sense of what was going on around her. Once, after a nurse left, Mom asked in a bewildered tone, "Who was that?"

"The nurse."

"Should we help her?"

"She doesn't need any help."

"Why not? Did we already help her?"

I nodded. "Yes, we helped her." I thought that should end the discussion, but Mom looked confused.

"What did we do?"

I didn't know what to say at this point. "You gave her some blood." Mom looked at me like I was crazy.

The next few days were worse. One morning, I stopped in to see her briefly while dropping Robin and Grandma off, and two nurses were lifting Mom in a huge sling so they could weigh her, since she couldn't stand to get on a scale. They had to push her over to one side to slide the fabric under her, and then push her over to the other side to pull it the rest of the way across. It was clear they were hurting her, and I wondered how knowing if she'd lost or gained a pound could possibly be so important.

After the nurses finally left, Mom turned to me and said encouragingly, "Gary, you can get your snakes now."

I smiled and thanked her.

Another time, in the afternoon, I watched as a nurse poked Mom's almost entirely blue arm to draw yet more blood. After the nurse left, Mom turned to me with a look of disgust. "Why did we join this club?"

That evening, Dad came a half hour early to relieve me. "Gary, I had to revise my proposal for the job. Would you mind retyping it before bed tonight?"

"Sure, Dad. But you didn't have to get here early for that. I can stay up a little later."

"It's okay, son."

I'd taken a couple more exams at school and was still making A's. I had to prove to God I could take the stress and still perform.

I thought about what my mom had said. We'd joined the "club" of Earth life so we could pass the tests God gave us and become gods. It was a miserable club sometimes, but if we could do well even at the worst of times, it would all pay off in the end.

I wondered, though, what it might be like to enroll in a class just for the sake of learning. What would it be like to enjoy life for the sake of living rather than trying to create a celestial resumé?

I retyped Dad's proposal and read a few more pages of my Book of Mormon in Romanian before going to bed.

The next afternoon when I walked into Mom's room after dropping Robin and Grandma off at the house, two nurses met me at the door. "We have to draw so much blood, and we're running out of veins, so we decided to put this tube inside her arm, and now we can always just stick a needle into the tube."

I was irritated they hadn't thought of that right at the beginning. Did they not know in advance they'd be using up all her veins? I almost said something, but then I thought I'd better be polite.

I sat off to the side and watched as the nurses cut and dug into Mom's arm. She grunted and cried, and I squirmed in my chair. But if they could manage this, it would lessen the suffering later.

The nurses kept working and shoving and muttering, and Mom kept crying and moaning. It went on and on and on. After fifteen horrendous minutes, I couldn't take it anymore and left the room.

But the nurses didn't come out for still another fifteen minutes. Half an hour of sheer, literal torture. But at least it was done. I felt ashamed for leaving Mom alone during all of that but relieved it was over.

"The tube is in?" I asked.

"No, we didn't get it," one of the nurses said. "Her veins are too damaged." She shrugged and walked off, unconcerned, and I had to fight not to hit her.

The next day was even worse. When I arrived to pick up Robin and Grandma, Mom was sleeping, but a nurse came in to draw more blood, and Mom woke up moaning from the pain. She'd always had veins that were hard to find anyway, and now the nurses had to dig and dig.

While the nurse was digging in her leg, Mom began looking around wildly, her eyes searching desperately and blindly for help. She threw her arms up to the ceiling and wailed, "I want my mama!"

Grandma sobbed loudly and rushed over to her but Mom seemed not to recognize her, crying as the nurse continued to work on her. Grandma cried, and Robin cried, and I thought life could never get any worse than this.

But it did. The next morning, Dad reported that he'd been up all night, that Mom was now bleeding from her bowels, and he'd had to empty the bedpan every twenty minutes. Mom's platelets were gone and she wasn't reacting well to the platelet transfusions.

He stayed a little longer so Robin and Grandma could do platelet pheresis, in the hopes Mom wouldn't reject familial platelets, and I went right after school to have my platelets taken out, too. It took about ninety minutes, a nurse taking blood out of one arm, spinning it in a centrifuge, scooping out the layer of platelets, and putting the rest of the blood back in the other arm, repeating the process over and over.

I didn't get to Mom's room until 5:00. I called Dad to tell him not to come till he'd taken a long nap, that I could do more than just five hours for my shift, since I knew I always had the shortest shift of anyone in the family to begin with.

Dad came at 11:00, though, and after emptying the bedpan every twenty or thirty minutes, even those six hours seemed an eternity. But Dad's shift was even longer, and he was trying to maintain a business as well. I wondered if I should drop out of school and carry more of the burden. But there was only a month left to the semester. It seemed like such a waste to just chuck two and a half months of work. And maybe managing all of it together really would help God to bless me.

If my dad could handle his heavy load, surely I could handle this little one. Maybe the blessing God bestowed would be an improvement in Mom's health rather than an improvement in my soul. Or an improvement in my mom's soul instead, a reconversion to the gospel. This illness seemed like the ultimate "trial of her faith." I'd started fasting every other day, asking God to help her however He could.

I hardly had any interaction with anyone at all these days, studying non-stop between classes, driving my car delivering pizza on weekends, and spending just a few minutes with my family during shift changes. Mom slept or moaned or talked crazy while I was with her. I wasn't sure she could even regain her testimony if she was no longer lucid.

The Relief Society president insisted on coming over one evening despite what I'd told her, but Mom didn't seem to notice. A couple of other ward members came by on other days, but really, Mom had never made many friends over the years, so no one besides us seemed to really care that she was sick.

It struck me that completely devoting yourself to your family must be a limiting, lonely life, no matter how righteous. Perhaps Mom wasn't losing her testimony now so much as repenting.

One day, though, without warning, Mom looked at me and seemed to be her old self again. It was like a miracle, and I smiled to see the recognition in her eyes. "You're getting better," I said.

"It would have been so much better still if I'd just shot myself."

I was surprised to realize she might have been right, but instead I smiled even more broadly. "The chemotherapy's working, and you're going to be fine." Then I had a horrible thought—what if in fact the chemotherapy *did* work, and she went into remission, and then a year from now had to die all over again? I hoped my gasp wasn't audible. And I suddenly hoped the treatments failed. Dying once was bad enough.

"Don't waste your life like I did," Mom said. "Time isn't something to be tossed away." She stared at her arm.

"It's like…blood dripping out of a cut non-stop. When you can't ever get a transfusion."

Mom had once told me she wanted to be Grace Metalious, but when I looked up the writer and saw that she'd been an alcoholic, I'd been appalled.

"You didn't waste your life, Mom. You read me stories. You made peanut butter fudge for Christmas. You went to the Smoky Mountains with Dad every year."

"I'm forty-three, and I only had ten good years out of all that."

"You went to the temple. You taught Relief Society. Didn't you enjoy any of it?" How could she not have liked feeling the Spirit?

Mom sighed. "So much time wasted doing what I was supposed to do."

"Well, if we're supposed to do it…"

"My only hope is to be myself the little time I have left." Her eyes narrowed as she looked straight ahead.

"We have all eternity, Mom. Even if you die, it's not the end."

She looked at me sadly. "You need to find yourself a nice young man," she said softly. "Maybe this guy Nicolae you like so much."

"What?"

"If there really *is* something beyond all this, what we get will depend on how well we used what we were given. Following the rules isn't the most important thing in the world. Live while you're alive." She closed her eyes for a moment. "God, the things I wanted to do. The things I meant to do." She looked at the IV pole sadly. "The things I'll never do."

She seemed exhausted and closed her eyes again. I realized I was tightly clutching the sheet on the bed, my mind reeling from the discovery that Mom had known I was gay all along.

But living in the Church was the only real way to have happiness in the next world. She was wrong to be upset that she'd been good all her life.

Yet however many "near death" experiences were out there, I'd certainly never talked to anyone this close to the other side. I wondered what else to ask while she was still reasonably coherent, but suddenly her eyes rolled up and she began shaking. The whole bed started rocking. I didn't bother with the call button but ran to the door and shouted for help.

The convulsions were over in a few minutes, but when the doctor came later, he said she'd had a stroke. It was too early to tell if there would be permanent damage or not.

The doctor left, and after I emptied the bedpan again, wiped Mom's legs, and tried to shove some clean pads underneath her, I sat with my head in my hands. Was Mom being punished for her heresy? Or was this a blessing, to knock her out so she wouldn't feel so much pain?

I hesitated before calling Dad, and he arrived by 9:00. I stayed a while longer but neither of us said anything.

I had an Italian test the next day. I'd picked Italian to fulfill my language requirement since it was the closest thing offered to Romanian. My heart wasn't in it today, but I forced myself to concentrate. I was sure I'd made an A.

To my surprise, Mom was awake when I got back. There seemed to be no lasting effects from the stroke. Another miracle. Maybe God really was going to bless her. I rushed back after dropping Robin and Grandma off at the house.

"I'm afraid I've been too protective," Mom said sadly as I held her hand. "God is getting rid of me so you can grow up."

"If I'm immature, that's my problem," I said. "God doesn't impose the death penalty for a thing like that."

She shook her head in a melancholy way and smiled weakly. Then I emptied her bedpan again.

Mom talked about growing up in the country, finding arrowheads in the pasture behind her house, the big day when the gravel road out front was finally paved, and the day her parents met two Mormon missionaries in town. I realized we'd never talked as adults before, and I suddenly wanted desperately for her to survive so I could finally get to know her as a person.

"You know, Gary," she said, "the Church will try to get rid of you." She patted my hand, her IV tube glistening in the light. "But that's okay. I worried about it for a while." She stopped and her face grew harder. "But you don't need to carry all that baggage around with you the rest of your life. Guilt and fear are useless emotions." She paused and then added uncertainly, "Do you think Nicolae might really like you? You know, the way you like him?"

I felt my face flush. It was just too strange to be talking like this. How could Mom be so calm? "I—I don't know," I said. "I hope so." I was going to be struck down with leukemia, too, for saying it.

She nodded. "Then you'll get a job this summer and save up some money to go see him. Or you'll invite him here to stay with you a few weeks to find out."

I nodded, my ears and cheeks still burning.

"These things don't happen on their own. You have to *make* them happen."

I looked down at the floor, too embarrassed to look my mom in the face. She put her hand on my arm. "I suppose everyone looks for meaning at a shitty time like this. But if I can just teach you not to throw away…"

Mom paused and managed a brief smile. "God, it feels good to finally say the things I've been thinking for so many years." She laughed a little. "Maybe you can never truly be the person you want to be completely. You'll always worry about how others are going to be affected. But Gary, don't worry about it as much as I did."

We talked about other things then, important and unimportant, just enjoying each other's company. She *was* more fun like this, more interesting, more real. I felt mystified and guilty that I could even consider the word "fun" in such circumstances. I always believed Mom and I had been close, but the definition of "close" had changed in the past few days.

As much as I loved Nicolae, how often had we ever talked about anything that mattered to us outside of religion? Was I up to spending the next twenty years writing him about how things were going in the ward and hoping the work was going well over in Romania? Never telling him anything deeper?

Mom whispered where she kept her dildo and told me to find it before my dad did. I didn't even know what she was talking about until she explained it. Two weeks ago, I would have been mortified, but now I just nodded and assured her I'd take care of it. I turned the nurse away once when she came to draw blood. The woman was angry, but she left when I pointed to the door.

Then Mom and I talked about how I'd need to help Dad by taking over the cooking and cleaning, how I'd give Mom's clothes to some of the poorer members of the congregation, how I was to keep no more than a hundred of Mom's books and donate the rest to the public library. I was to be sure to visit Grandma often. Robin was to have the one painting Mom had made, of their childhood home in Mississippi. I was to be nice to whatever woman Dad eventually chose to marry.

Mom was calm but firm about everything. I felt selfish, spending all this special time alone with her while everyone else was away. But maybe she'd talked to them this way, too. I hoped so.

I emptied the bedpan a few more times. Mom always moaned when I turned her over, and around 8:30, when I pushed her back into place after another bedpan moment, she had a glazed look on her face. "Why is it raining in here?" she asked in alarm. "Get rid of those rats!"

It happened so suddenly I didn't know what to do. In a matter of seconds, her eyes rolled up, her jaw clenched tight, and she started shaking again. There was nothing to be done, so I didn't feel a sense of urgency. I calmly pressed the call button and told the nurse what was happening.

The seizure was over in a couple of minutes, but by the time the doctor arrived an hour later, things seemed grim. "You can see by the way she's holding her hand she's had a severe stroke. I expect she's paralyzed on her left side. It's impossible to tell right now how much of her brain function is left, but it doesn't look good. The other tests show her kidneys are shutting down, too, and it looks like she may be developing diabetes."

Dad was due in a few minutes, but I didn't want him to hear this from the staff, so I called and told him what had happened. When I saw him looking down at Mom a few minutes later, I could see he'd finally given up. I knew he wouldn't like it, but I went over and hugged him anyway. He was unresponsive at first but eventually hugged me back. Then he released me. "You go get some sleep, son."

The next morning, Dad didn't leave when I brought Robin and Grandma. I thought maybe I should skip school for just one day, since Mom might die at any moment, but I had a geology test, and I didn't want to bother the professor by rescheduling.

I arrived at the hospital a few minutes after 3:00. Dad, Robin, and Grandma were in the hall outside Mom's door. They all looked exhausted.

Dad walked up and grabbed my arm. "Your mom died five minutes ago."

I felt a wave of guilt. I wasn't there when my mother died. Had I let a stupid class be more important? But then I told myself, "If God had wanted me to be there, He could have kept her alive five extra minutes."

Had *she* somehow timed this to spare me?

Was all of life just chance? *And* choice?

"I want to see her."

I went in the room and looked at Mom's motionless body, just an empty shell now. Then I looked up at the ceiling, and into the corners. Was she up there right now looking down at me?

Robin, Grandma, and I went back to the house while Dad stayed at the hospital to make arrangements. As soon as we closed the door behind us, our Chihuahua started pawing frantically at the carpet in front of the door, trying to get out. She knew Mom wasn't coming back.

I picked her up and held her, and she squealed pitifully for fifteen minutes. When Dad got home later, I had dinner ready for everyone.

After dinner and a little subdued conversation, I went to my room and chucked out my copy of *The Miracle of Forgiveness* with its hateful chapter on homosexuality. I looked online for gay support groups in New Orleans and found a chapter of PFLAG that met once a month, with a meeting to be held just next week. And then I emailed Nicolae, telling him about the last few weeks, and asking if he was up for a visit in August.

Splitting with the Sister Missionaries

Tanny peeked through the curtain to look at the two sister missionaries getting out of their car. They didn't seem happy to be there. She could hear them talking to each other. "Do we have to bring her along? She's so fat."

"She's weak. She needs us."

Tanny let the curtain fall back into place. The sister missionaries had only asked her to go on splits with them out of pity, not because they wanted her. She'd show them. When they went to teach someone, she'd bear her testimony and bring down the Holy Ghost upon everyone. Then they'd see.

The chimes rang and Tanny went over to open the door. "Hi, Sister Archer," she said sweetly. "Hi, Sister Blackburn."

"Good morning, Tanny. It's good to see you." Sister Archer smiled beautifully. She was so pretty. Flawless skin. She looked like a saint. Tanny giggled. She *was* one.

"Did you need to come in, or shall we start working right away?"

Sister Archer laughed melodically. "Are you sure you want to work all morning? It must be nice to be retired and not *have* to work."

"I'm not really retired," Tanny reminded her. "I'm disabled. It's not exactly the same thing. I'm only fifty-one." The sisters must both be around twenty, Tanny thought. To them, fifty-one probably sounded ancient.

"You're not *really* sick," said Sister Blackburn. "No one who lives the gospel is ever truly mentally ill." The bishop had told her the same thing. So had the Relief Society president. To her face. With real voices.

"Schizophrenia is a genuine disease," Tanny replied flatly. She remembered losing her friends over the years one by one after all her accusations. She remembered how her non-member family no longer talked to her. She remembered all the times she'd been called in by HR on various jobs and fired.

Sister Archer laughed sweetly. "Well, you seem perfectly fine to me. Let's get going."

Tanny wasn't going to argue about it. Life these past three years since she'd finally been diagnosed and prescribed meds had changed dramatically for the better. Instead of hearing voices constantly, she could cope most days. She still heard them, of course, but not as frequently as before. She could still have worked part-time if she wanted to, almost certainly able to keep a job now that her auditory hallucinations were mostly under control. She just didn't see the point when Disability paid enough for this tiny apartment and food to eat, even if sometimes it was only a can of tuna. She had a DVD player and checked movies out of the library since she couldn't afford cable. But books were free at the library, too. Being poor was infinitely better than being ill. She was content most of the time.

Except when she was unhappy.

"Who else is working with us this morning?" Tanny asked. "Veronica?" Veronica was another older single woman in the Relief Society.

"No. That fell through," Sister Archer said. "It's just us."

"But I thought the whole point of going on splits was to double the workload. I go out with one of you and someone else goes out with the other."

"It's just us," Sister Archer repeated.

The two sister missionaries stole glances at one another and Tanny knew exactly what they were thinking. It was almost as if she could hear them. They were both afraid to be alone with her.

"We're going to see Sister Bounds," said Sister Archer. "She's feeling ill and needs someone to lift her spirits."

"She has a real illness," Sister Blackburn pointed out.

"Are we wearing masks?" asked Tanny. It was all fine and good to knock on someone's door and hand them a pie and then run off, but to deliberately spend time with the sick? Who would do such a thing on purpose?

"We're missionaries," said Sister Archer, not really answering Tanny's question. "We help those in need."

They were driving along the road, stopping at stoplights, passing stores. Tanny luxuriated in the feel of the air conditioning, of the freedom and comfort. She always had to ride the bus when going somewhere by herself. It must be wonderful to be a missionary, she thought. She leaned against the back seat to enjoy the ride, but she could see the two sisters in the front talking softly to each other.

"If she acts all weird in public, we're going to have to dump her on the side of the road," Sister Blackburn whispered.

"We can always call the elders to take her home."

"Elders can't be alone with women."

"Who would ever be tempted by *her*?"

Tanny looked out the window at some children playing on a playground.

Soon they were pulling up in front of a beautiful, two-story brick home in a lovely neighborhood. The lawn was immaculately manicured, with blooming camellias along the front of the house. They all climbed out of the car and walked up to the magnificent front door, made of dark, rich wood and beveled glass. Sister Archer knocked. A few moments later, the door opened and Sister Bounds stood there, looking awful without her make-up. "Who invited her?" she whispered to the sister missionaries.

The three of them went inside and asked Sister Bounds what she wanted for dinner, and then Tanny and the missionaries got to work in the kitchen preparing the meal. Tanny couldn't even imagine what it must be like to have such a large kitchen, with so much food in the refrigerator and pantry. The family even had their Year's Supply, while Tanny would have starved to death two weeks into the Apocalypse. She saw Sister Bounds eyeing her suspiciously, as if Tanny were going to sneak a ham into her blouse.

"What's your favorite meal, Tanny?" Sister Archer asked as they cooked.

"I like Salisbury steak," she replied.

"Huh?"

"Frozen dinners. They're my favorite thing. So easy."

"I see."

There was a lull in the conversation after that, but a while later, Sister Archer tried again. "Have you read any good books lately?"

"Cordelia Kingsbridge is my favorite author," said Tanny. Once she found a writer she liked, she went through every book they ever wrote.

"What does she write about?" asked Sister Archer.

"Murder and mayhem."

There was another long lull after that.

Tanny didn't really mind the silences. Sometimes, silence was better than sound. Sounds haunted her. Even with the meds. It was just nice to be spending time with someone. She didn't really have friends at church, hadn't since her Young Adult days. Even the Visiting Teachers never came by. The missionaries, though, they made an effort.

It was probably because they had nothing better to do, she realized. It was either stop by Tanny's apartment or go looking for converts. With those choices, even Tanny looked good.

They continued with the meal.

Finally, they were done, and Sister Blackburn went to tell Sister Bounds they were leaving. Then the three of them climbed back into the car. Tanny listened as they pulled away from the curb. "She said never to bring her back to her house," Sister Blackburn whispered.

"We're almost through. Hang in there a little longer." Then, looking brightly into the rearview mirror, Sister Archer smiled and spoke up more loudly. "Is there anywhere you'd like us to take you before we head back to your place?"

"No. Back home is fine." She wanted to go to the grocery and buy all the heavy items so she wouldn't have to carry them on the bus. She wanted to go to the park and look at all the flowers. She wanted to go to a museum, but who could afford that?

She really wanted to go to another group therapy session. That sometimes almost felt like Single Adult Family Home Evening at church all those years ago.

They drove along in silence, but Tanny could still see the sisters looking at each other anxiously.

If only they held the priesthood, she thought. She could ask them to cast out the evil spirit inside her. She felt as if she were two people, a normal, happy woman, and an ugly, unpleasant freak everyone hated. How could that all just be brain chemistry? Couldn't Heavenly Father get rid of the ugly part of her no one liked? Why couldn't she be healed? What was the point of priesthood if it couldn't *do* anything?

She remembered reporting back to her doctor a few weeks after first going on medication. "It's a miracle!" she'd exclaimed.

"No," her doctor had replied. "It's science."

But it was a miracle she'd found the science, Tanny thought, though she kept that idea to herself. Then she'd seen the doctor turn to a nurse and whisper, "She's still delusional." And all her doubts and insecurities came flooding back.

If Heavenly Father couldn't cure her himself, why couldn't he at least let the doctors do it?

"I see my psychiatrist on Tuesday," Tanny announced. There was no response. "Every couple of months I need to go in and have my meds adjusted. Seems they're never quite right. I still hear the voices."

The two sisters looked at each other in the front seat.

Tanny laughed. "You'd die if you knew what words they were putting in your mouths." She chuckled again. "But I know enough now to realize what I hear isn't real." She paused. "Still, it's terrible to hear it. I'm never really quite sure what's real and what isn't. You could say something awful right to my face and then deny it and I'd never know the difference." She laughed again.

Sister Archer pulled into a Dairy Queen. "Why are we stopping here?" Sister Blackburn asked.

"Tanny, how would you like a great big strawberry shake?" Sister Archer asked, twisting her head to look into the back seat. "Or a banana split?"

"Oh, I'm already so fat."

"If you hear mean voices all the time, don't let yours be another of those voices. Tell yourself something nice." She smiled. "Let's go get some ice cream."

Tanny suddenly felt more alone than she'd ever felt. It was like being trapped in a cave-in, just barely able to hear sounds on the other side of the rocks and knowing your rescuers would never reach you in time.

They stepped out of the car and walked into the restaurant. It was so cool and fresh and clean inside. They stood in line and looked up at the menu on the wall. Such a luxury to eat out, thought Tanny. Should she be wasting the missionaries' money? They needed that money to serve the Lord.

Sister Archer leaned over and whispered into Tanny's ear. "Get a large," she said. Then she turned to Sister Blackburn and laughed. "A large shake for a large girl!"

They picked up their order and sat at a table to enjoy their ice cream.

Partying with St. Roch

I could see that Dennis had a drinking problem. It wasn't as bad as Glenn's had been, of course. I'd dated Glenn for almost a year before he died of cirrhosis, holed up in his apartment with empty beer cans around his bed. He'd frequently point to my flat stomach after we had sex and say, "You may have a six-pack, but *I've* got a whole keg," and then he'd pat his extended abdomen. I'd thought it was just a beer belly, but some of that enlargement was due to his damaged liver. After that experience, I vowed never to date another drinker.

Then I met Dennis at the Unitarian church in Uptown New Orleans on Nashville. We were both excommunicated Mormons, and we hit it off singing about a God who loved all people equally. We dated for five months and then moved in together, about one month before Dennis's T-cells dropped to 50 and he was diagnosed with full-blown AIDS.

It was late 1989, and we were looking forward to New Year's, hoping for a repeat of the Gay Nineties, at least in name, working together for gay rights with several organizations, not the least of which was ACT UP, carrying signs and shouting slogans in front of City Hall as we demanded more access to medicines. Shortly after we moved in together on St. Roch, just off of Chartres in the Marigny, Dennis developed an addiction to Coke.

That was Coke with a capital C.

He began having me purchase every three-liter bottle of the off brand the local Schwegmann's grocery stocked when I went to do our weekly shopping. I'd pile twelve of the monstrous bottles into my cart and plod my way to the checkout. Every single week, people would smile and say, "Having a party?"

"Nothing but fun at my house," I'd reply, smiling back.

"Kirk, you only bought eight bottles today," Dennis complained this afternoon. "I'll never make it through the week."

"I'll stop at the store again tomorrow."

"I need this. I get so little pleasure out of life."

"I'll stop at the store again tomorrow."

The sodas were not diet. I was afraid that at any moment, Dennis would have diabetes to add to his problems, but something about the HIV or his particular metabolism seemed to defy the sugar overload. He remained thin as a rail despite a full daily allotment of calories just from the cola alone. His other favorite treat was chocolate, which was a debatable violation of the Word of Wisdom. And perhaps because the caffeine kept him from fully hydrating despite the vast amounts of liquid he consumed, he also drank a great deal of black tea.

"Do you think I'm a hedonist, Kirk?" Dennis asked. "Do you think I should be obeying all the commandments now that I'm about to die?"

"Shut up and fuck me," I said, forcing a smile.

I was still negative, and Dennis always used a condom when we had sex. The irony was that he was basically a top. He'd only bottomed maybe three or four times ever, but he'd done it just once without a condom, and now he was paying the price. Every day, priests and pastors across the country were still proclaiming that AIDS was God's punishment for our abominable sins, thereby infecting everyone with their hatred.

It was impossible not to wonder if they were right. Every evening as I kissed the man I loved goodnight, I'd look into his face and wonder if God really despised us this much. One of the last things I heard my stake president say after he told me I was excommunicated was, "If Heavenly Father still loves you, He'll give you AIDS to help you repent. It's so much kinder than letting you live in your sins for a lifetime, thinking you're not sinning. I'll pray that God gives you AIDS, for your own good." He smiled and held out his hand warmly, as if he'd just said something comforting.

My hand stayed by my side and his finally dropped as well, a look of confusion on his face. I turned and walked out of his office, and I never went to an LDS church again.

Mormonism had always been my rock before, "the one and only true church." Four years passed, in fact, before I ever entered any other church at all. A friend invited me to a meeting at the MCC in the Bywater, in an ancient red brick building along the levee. I didn't like the congregation, so a few months later, I tried a Dignity meeting with some gay Catholics. I didn't care for that, either. I attended a Reform synagogue Uptown on St. Charles and liked that well enough, but I was afraid to stop praying "in the name of Jesus Christ," even though I wasn't sure I even believed in Jesus Christ anymore. I realized I was being superstitious, not religious. I attended a Methodist meeting on North Rampart in the Quarter and then an Episcopalian service Uptown and a Hare Krishna meeting on Esplanade.

At last I stumbled upon the Unitarian meeting. I'd been just about to give up my quest when I listened to a blonde woman with dreadlocks give a sermon on the importance of protecting the environment, and I decided to come back a second time. I'd been attending ever since.

"Really?" Dennis looked doubtful, almost mournful. "You're still attracted to me?"

"I want you, mister."

I grabbed my crotch, and Dennis's eyes lit up. He hurried over to the dresser and pulled out the two nametags I'd had made. He slipped one on his shirt pocket that said, "Elder Top—The Church of Jesus Christ of Latter-Gay Saints" and handed over a similar one for "Elder Bottom."

Dennis leaned forward to kiss me, rubbing against me and smiling as our two missionary nametags clicked against each other. Then, despite the costume, he took off his shirt and knelt in front of me, unzipping my pants as I rubbed his head, trying not to be distracted by the large black Kaposi's lesions on his shoulders and back. He didn't fuck me as I'd suggested but just sucked me off. I watched as his head moved back and forth, wanting to memorize every sexual encounter with him so I could replay them after he was gone. With a final thrust, I came. Dennis swallowed with a smile and stood up.

"Your turn?" I asked, pointing to his zipper.

He shook his head. "All I want is more Coke. I know it's a pain, but can you go to another store?"

I nodded and went to grab my cart again. We didn't have a car, and the Schwegmann's on Claiborne was the only store truly within walking distance, about nine blocks from the apartment. The next closest was a grocery on Franklin. I walked the five blocks to the bus stop, waited for almost twenty minutes, and then boarded the 57. A few minutes later, I was at the store.

There were no three-liter bottles here of the off brand that Dennis preferred, but there were several two-liter bottles of regular Coke. I'd tried making this substitution for Dennis before with negative results. He wanted what he wanted, and nothing else would do. It could be annoying, but how could I deny him what few indulgences he had left in life?

If what the Church taught were true, there'd be no Coke in heaven. I'd never even dared try a sip until I went to my first gay bar.

I wondered if it were true that the Church owned lots of stock in Coca-Cola.

I pushed my cart along the pavement until I arrived at the bus stop. Where could I try next? There was a Rouse's up closer to the lake. Since I was already taking the bus, I supposed it didn't matter how many blocks I had to go once I was sitting down. The bus jerked to a halt in front of me fifteen minutes later, and I dragged my cart on board. I was the only white person in the vehicle. Whites in general were afraid to ride the buses in New Orleans, afraid they'd be murdered by all the black people who filled the seats.

While I did get a few cold stares once in a while, obviously most other passengers ignored me completely. Once, I'd run into my Sunday school teacher Theautrey on the Elysian Fields bus. I'd said hi and shaken his hand. At the Unitarian church the next Sunday, he admitted he'd felt two conflicting emotions: one, surprise that a white person would acknowledge him in public, and two, embarrassment in front of other blacks that *he* was friends with a white person himself.

As a Mormon, I'd learned that blacks had been cursed with a dark skin for their lack of dedication to God in the Pre-existence. While I'd grown up watching *Diff'rent Strokes* and *The Jeffersons* and didn't feel I harbored much prejudice, whenever I saw a news report of another black murderer or listened to the uneducated speech of blacks around me, I'd doubt just a little my belief that all people were equal. Norman Lear could help, but he couldn't undo so many years of damage.

Maybe it *wasn't* oppression and lack of opportunity that hurt this community. What if they really were inferior spirits? Even while listening to Theautrey teach and feeling impressed with his knowledge, I'd doubt. Maybe he had some white blood, I'd think. Maybe that was why he was so smart.

I'd hate myself for thinking these things and then get mad at Mormons all over again for filling my head with nonsense. Gays weren't bad. Blacks weren't inferior. What kind of religion went around spreading such hateful teachings in the first place?

It was like shingles erupting across your body decades after you'd recovered from chicken pox.

I climbed out of the bus across from Rouse's and headed for the store. I went straight for the soda aisle, ready to be finished with this interminable chore and get back home to relax. I worked all week at the public library under a tyrannical manager and then came home to a sick partner. Saturday was my day to have fun, and I had to take my fun when I could get it. I tried to make these outings an escape from the confines of my apartment, but all I really wanted to do was listen to Roxette while putting together a thousand-piece jigsaw puzzle of Notre Dame or the Taj Mahal.

No three-liter bottles.

Why did Dennis have to drink so much? Was it his way of thumbing his nose at God?

I looked over the soda section a second time to make sure I wasn't missing anything. There was a section for three-liter bottles, all right, but there weren't any stocked. Was there an epidemic of cola addiction out there?

"Excuse me," I said, stopping a young black man with a nametag. "Could you check in back to see if you have any more of the three-liter bottles?"

The man looked at me, looked at the empty shelf, looked at me again with his lip curled ever so slightly, and headed off without a word. I waited fifteen minutes and then decided to try one last store, a new one that had opened next to the projects near Canal. This would be the last stop on my pilgrimage, regardless of the outcome.

I arrived thirty-five minutes later and pushed my cart quickly to the soda aisle. There was a lone three-liter bottle. An elderly woman looked as if she was contemplating it. I debated snatching the bottle before she had a chance to reach for it, but I bit my lip and waited until she slowly moved on down the aisle. I put the bottle in my cart, added one more item from a few aisles away, and headed for the checkout.

Dennis was not going to be pleased.

Was I a bad partner for giving up before I'd accomplished what Dennis asked of me? The man was dying, after all. He'd be gone in only a few months. Couldn't I sacrifice just a little more? Perhaps this proved what everyone said about fleeting gay relationships.

It was what I felt every Sunday, too, that my new religion was only a lackluster replacement for the real thing, no matter how much I told myself I preferred these services to the Sacrament and Priesthood meetings of before.

I dragged my cart off the bus twenty minutes later and pushed the metal cage ahead of me slowly, careful going over the cracked and uneven sidewalks of the Marigny. I passed the funeral home and the corner where a jogger had been mugged and killed. I walked past a gay Bed and Breakfast and finally made it to St. Roch.

The patron saint of the plague.

I unlocked the door underneath the balcony and headed up the stairs. "Kirk! I was afraid something had happened to you!"

"I could only find one more bottle."

Dennis stared at the bottle in disappointment but then managed a smile. "Maybe there will be more later in the week. I just want you to spend the rest of the day with me. We have so little time left together. Tell me more of your mission stories from Germany. You know I like that."

Dennis sat down on the sofa eagerly, and I poured him a glass of cola. Then I opened another purchase, my first bottle of red wine, and poured myself a drink, too. I brought both glasses over to the coffee table and set them down. Dennis picked up his and looked at mine for a long moment without saying anything. Then I picked up mine and took a sip. Not bad.

"Tell me again about that time you decked your zone leader," Dennis said, leaning back and smiling.

"Well, naturally, it was an accident," I began. I sat back on the sofa, too, and Dennis swung his legs up so that his feet were resting in my lap. I sipped my wine with one hand and rubbed his feet with the other, looking over at the man I loved and wondering how I was going to fit the whole of eternity into the next few months. "It all started the day my zone leader told me in front of everyone that I didn't measure up to his expectations…"

I continued with my story, distracted by a new lesion on Dennis's leg. I began embellishing, just to add some variety, and Dennis grinned as I went on.

These are the good old days, I realized. One day soon, I'd look back and miss these times. I tried to memorize every detail of the room, the torn vinyl sofa we'd bought at Goodwill, the coffee table I'd carried two blocks from a garage sale, a mediocre piece of art Dennis had painted. When I finished my story, Dennis asked for another, this one about the middle-aged German who'd fucked me one day when I'd broken the mission rules and took a long walk on my own.

We both smiled as I began telling the story. When I finished, I poured Dennis another glass of cola, and I sipped a bit more of my wine. Then I had Dennis tell me one of his own favorite mission stories, back when he thought it was a healthy thing to spread the teachings of the Church. We smiled and laughed and drank, happy for a few brief moments on the torn sofa.

In the back of my mind, I wondered where I'd packed my Book of Mormon, and if maybe I should read for a while after Dennis fell asleep.

An Eternity of Mirrors

I put my hand on Elder Cooper's arm. "Ecco," I said. "Those guys again." I nodded toward two olive-skinned Italians in their mid-twenties near the Fontana dei Quattro Fiumi.

"They aren't interested, Elder Shaw," my companion replied.

"I'm not going to do an approach," I assured him. "Just going to say hi."

I walked up to the two men with a smile and waved. One of them grabbed the other's arm and reached for his suitcase, pulling it in front of him like a shield.

Mormon missionaries weren't *that* scary, were we?

Fire suddenly exploded around the gurgling water. There was the sound of roaring wind mixed with screams and breaking glass, a brief moment of pain, and then blackness.

***

The alarm went off at 6:30 and I stumbled out of bed toward my desk. I knew better than to leave the clock within arm's length of my mattress. In the dark, I heard a groan from my companion's bed on the other side of the room. Since he didn't have to turn off the clock himself, he always managed to stay under the covers an extra fifteen minutes. Against the rules, but that was his problem, not mine. It was late spring of 1981, and the mission president had just changed the time we were to wake up from 6:00 to 6:30, a glorious miracle, but we'd somehow adapted overnight, and what had once seemed absolute luxury now felt way too torturous again.

I pulled up the serranda to let some light from the balcony into the room, and another groan drifted over from Elder Cooper's bed. I thought of teasing him some more, but I needed to pee and hurried down the hall. When I opened the bathroom door, I saw I was already too late. One of the zone leaders was in the shower, humming "Give, Said the Little Stream," and the other, Elder Walker, was standing at the toilet. "The Lord blesses those who take the initiative to wake up early," he said.

"You're special, all right," I agreed. "You prove it every day."

Elder Walker's face hardened, and for a moment, I was afraid he'd aim his stream at me. I left and walked a few feet down the hall toward the kitchen, where I poured myself a bowl of Corn Flakes and sprinkled some Coliseum sugar over it. I snipped the corner off a triangle container of milk and poured.

I heard a snort as Elder Walker joined me in the kitchen. A second later, he knocked my arm so that I spilled some of the milk.

"Sorry," he said coldly.

"It's okay," I replied casually. "It's your mess, so you can clean it up."

Elder Walker's eyes narrowed, and he slapped the table, making droplets of milk jump into the air. "You're getting more rebellious every day, Anziano Shaw. If you don't shape up, I'll have to report you to the mission president."

"I have four months left," I said. "If the Church wants to send me home because I'm making you wipe up the milk you spilled, I can live with that." In fact, I almost welcomed it. One door after another after another had been shut in my face these past several months, day after day after day. A mission was supposed to be the best two years of my life, but it certainly wasn't that.

Of course, I'd learned a lot about myself out here, which could potentially be positive, but not all of what I'd discovered was good. I also learned a great deal about the world, having taught people from seven different countries so far. It was eye-opening to realize there was more than one way to do things. More importantly, I'd managed to learn a tiny bit about the complexity of human behavior, just the very tiniest particle, of course, yet far more than I'd known before. I didn't regret coming to Italy, even if I wasn't sure I'd miss my mission after it was over.

I might miss Elder Cooper, though. But there was always the possibility we'd end up at college together someday.

Elder Walker slapped the table again and headed off to his bedroom. I started eating, and a moment later, Elder Cooper staggered into the kitchen. "I need coffee," he moaned. I laughed and offered him my box of cereal. He grabbed a bowl and began pouring with his eyes closed. I put my hand on his back when he was about to spill over onto the table.

"Buddy," I said, "hang in there. We'll get a Coke when we leave the apartment later."

Elder Cooper opened his eyes and smiled. "I like it when you call me buddy."

I clapped him on the shoulder. "I gotta get in the shower before Walker jumps the line and uses up all the hot water." I walked back down the hall to grab my towel, but while I was undressing in the bathroom a moment later, Elder Walker burst in, already naked, and pushed me aside. He pulled the shower curtain in front of him, giving me a wide but cold grin as he did so. I waited a moment and then flushed, smiling when I heard a loud grunt from the tub.

"Stronzo," I heard him mutter.

"Not yet," I replied, "but I'm not feeling very well, so prepare yourself for some noxious odors." I didn't actually sit down, but I put my hand in my armpit and made a few offensive noises. Then I flushed again.

Soon it was Quiet Hour and I sat at my desk reading the Book of Mormon. "And it came to pass," I read. "And it came to pass." "And it came to pass." The same thing over and over and over. It seemed odd that Nephites, so concerned about limited space on the gold plates that they used reformed Egyptian instead of their own language, would keep wasting that precious space using the same useless phrase again and again.

One of the mysteries of the universe, I supposed.

"Almost time for Devotional," I said after the hour was up. "What plans should we make today?" I always let my junior companion make his suggestions first. It saved me the trouble of figuring something out and it let him gain confidence. I usually went with whatever he suggested unless I really felt the need to override.

Cooper, who'd been out ten months, had enough time under his belt to be made senior, but the mission president told him during every interview that he wasn't impressed with Cooper's attitude. At least, that was my companion's version. Despite being a bit of a slacker, Cooper and I had gotten along the past two months after his transfer to Rome Four. I probably only had one more companion left before I returned to California. But while Cooper could be trying at times, he was also probably my favorite companion. Not my best companion, to be clear, my favorite.

"Anziano," Elder Cooper said slowly, "io so certamente che you don't want to hear this, but I'm veramente not in the mood to do 24-hour work sta mattina." He often protested the rule that we only speak Italian by making whatever Italian he did use irritating.

"Truamente?" I asked.

"Sí. Can we just hang out at il parco this morning?"

"The one on Via Nomentana?"

He nodded.

I considered for a moment. "How about you relax at the park while I try to get a few referrals by myself?"

Now he considered. "Va bene." He smiled and I had to turn away. Elder Cooper was only slightly above average in looks, about 5'8" with ash blond hair, but somehow, the longer I knew him, the more attractive he became. Exactly the opposite of my reaction to Elder Walker. I'd thought the senior zone leader was surprisingly good-looking when I first came to the district, but the longer I shared an apartment with him, the less attractive he became. It seemed odd that just knowing a person could change the way I interpreted their physical attributes. A physical shape seemed absolute. A scientific fact. But somehow it wasn't.

I looked over again at my companion as he struggled to knot his tie. He had a nose that turned slightly to the left just at the tip, either a riveting grin or a painful frown, and gray eyes I could look into forever. If I wasn't trying to make it to the Celestial Kingdom.

I'd probably better start rereading *The Miracle of Forgiveness* again. It was one of only two Church books I owned in Italian.

We hurried out of the apartment as soon as the closing prayer at the end of Devotional had been given. "You're supposed to have companionship prayer before you leave!" Elder Walker shouted after us, but we were already running down the marble stairs and then out on the street. Breakfast was three hours behind us by this point, and I wanted a piece of caprino from the formaggeria two doors down, or a Bosc pear from the shop next to it, but we didn't have enough money to eat like our neighbors.

I'd saved up all the funds for my mission myself, while Elder Cooper's parents were heavily subsidizing his stay. We walked into the corner bar where we often picked up our milk, and I bought a bottle of Coke for my companion. A luxury, to be sure, but something about the day warranted it. He smiled in exultation with his first sip, and then we made our way to the bus stop, where he savored every last drop until the 36 came around the corner.

Soon, I could see Villa Torlonia coming up, and I rang for the next stop. We pushed past a couple of heavy women blocking the door and stepped off onto the street. A man hurried by in one direction and two women passed us in the other. I breathed in the morning air and closed my eyes. I was in Rome. Me. A nobody from San Jose. I supposed there were plenty of Italians who'd kill to live in California, or anywhere else in the U.S., for that matter, but every day, all I could think was how lucky I was to be in Rome. Walking into the park, my companion and I both immediately relaxed. A little haven in the midst of a huge, bustling city. Life was grand.

Elder Cooper found a bench and sat down, lifting his face to the sun and closing his eyes in ecstasy. It was an expression I'd fantasized about more than once, before I knelt beside my bed and prayed for forgiveness. Now I turned to the other folks in the park and tried to find a target. We couldn't approach women, and most Italian men worked on weekdays. But there was a young man reading a book on a nearby bench. I strolled over.

"Che leggi?" I asked in a friendly manner.

The young man did not appear anxious to reciprocate my warmth. He held up the book, showing me the front cover. *The Bourne Identity: Un nome senza volto.* Looked like some kind of spy thriller. I smiled and nodded, and the man returned to his book.

I supposed that when I first received my call and realized I wasn't being sent someplace like West Virginia, I'd dreamed of international intrigue. Rome. How could it not be exciting? Cities like this were featured in James Bond films. The Red Brigades had kidnapped and killed the prime minister here just a couple of years ago. And some other group had blown up the Bologna train station just last year. Of course, those weren't spy kinds of things, just murder. Berlin would probably have been more thrilling, with more of a chance to interact with real agents, but Rome was plenty good enough.

Only the most exciting thing I'd ever actually done in Italy was go tracting. Over in Rome Three a few months ago, my companion and I had tracted out an apartment building using the citofono outside. The slip of paper inserted next to one button said, "Brigate Rosse." Surely a joke. But we made sure not to press that buzzer.

And once, a portiere had chased us out of his building with a frying pan.

The Shaw Identity: Chased with Cookware.

"Are you enjoying the book?" I asked the young man on the bench reading about spies.

The man slowly turned to look back at me. "Trying to."

"Is there a better time for us to come talk to you about our church?"

The man tore a blank page from the back of the book, wrote his name and address in a scrawl I could barely read, and handed it to me. I thanked him and headed back to the bench where Elder Cooper was sunning himself. "Got one," I said.

He opened his eyes. "Now we can both take a break." He closed his eyes again. Since he couldn't see me, I took the opportunity to stare at his face for a few minutes. So, so beautiful. I wanted to kiss his forehead and his cheeks. I wanted to kiss that damaged nose. And those lips. But he'd no doubt slug me if I tried.

Elder Cooper opened one eye. I quickly turned away.

I fingered the paper in my hand, amazed again at the difference in penmanship between Americans and Italians. If I didn't know up front this was a language I understood, I'd be certain it was written in some other alphabet. Perhaps in code.

And it may as well have been. The man had surely given us a false address. At least half the referrals we took ended up being addresses for people other than the ones we'd stopped on the street, people baffled to find us at their door. Catholics in Italy weren't particularly interested in becoming Mormons.

I'd baptized two people in twenty months, and it wasn't likely I'd baptize any more. Elder Cooper had baptized one so far. Missionary work wasn't only boring and tedious—it was also fairly meaningless. Why couldn't we do something useful? Help tourists cross a busy street, easy once you learned how but difficult for Americans on their first visit. Or pick up dog crap on sidewalks across the city. Or even help clean a church or cathedral.

Whoa, I thought, shaking my head slightly. I'd just had such a strong feeling of déjà vu.

Elder Cooper and I timed our trip back to arrive at the apartment shortly after 1:30, the beginning of our two-hour lunch period. There'd be no dinner period, of course. After we left the apartment again at 3:30 each day, we wouldn't be allowed to return home until 9:30.

We'd spend hours and hours in the blazing sun one day and hours and hours in the pouring rain the next. Or in the freezing cold. Or fog. Or whatever. Day after day after day doing the same exact things over and over and over.

"How many referrals did you get?" Elder Walker shouted from the kitchen when we returned from the park. He was in charge of cooking this week.

"Abbiamo got due," Elder Cooper told him.

"Pick a flippin' language!" Elder Walker returned. "And two isn't nearly enough if you plan to get your *mandatory* fifteen for the week."

Tortellini was ready shortly thereafter, and when everyone had finished, Elder Cooper started washing the dishes. It would be my turn tomorrow. "Let's get some Dual Study," I said, not wanting to waste the time on dishes alone, which wouldn't count in any category on our weekly stat sheet.

"Va bene," said Cooper, "but no scriptures, no colloqui, and definitely no *Miracolo del perdono*!"

"Grammar all right?"

He nodded and we started studying the imperfect subjunctive, which we'd spent less than an hour on in the Missionary Training Center back in Provo. Almost all the missionaries here used it incorrectly. While I appreciated the opportunity to improve my language skills, I knew we were only doing it because Elder Cooper hated anything solely related to his mission.

He had "Anxious Missionary Syndrome," the desire to be done with the whole thing, despite having over a year left to complete. The truth was his attitude was infecting me more and more as well. When I was with him, I wanted to go swimming, something absolutely forbidden while serving, given that the Devil had power over the water. I wanted to go camping in the hills outside the city. I wanted to sit in a theater and see a good movie. Something like

Culo e camicia which I'd seen advertised in posters pasted on dozens of walls across the city.

Any wall could be turned into a billboard covered with movie posters, political announcements, or a call to repeal legalized abortion. No death notices here like down in Napoli, though.

But *Culo e camicia*—I couldn't help but think of Elder Cooper walking around in our bedroom wearing just his shirt, his ass free to admire. Not that such a thing could ever happen since we always wore our garments underneath our suits. But I simply loved that word "culo."

I also liked the word "vaffanculo" which I sometimes used on Elder Walker. He didn't know what it meant, and I loved seeing the fury on his face when I wouldn't tell him. I could never say such a thing in English, of course. But I loved that "fuck you" in Italian used the word "ass."

I stole a glance at Elder Cooper's backside while he leaned over the sink.

How odd, I thought. I'd just had a flash of déjà vu again.

As we waited at the bus stop later, I clapped my hand on my companion's shoulder. "Buddy, now it's my turn. I'm the one who doesn't feel like tracting tonight. Are you up for a little more hooky?"

He smiled. "I'm always pronto for something like quello."

"I'm going to picchiarti in the head if you don't stop that merda." I showed him my fist.

His smiled broadened and he suddenly leaned forward and kissed me on the cheek. Then he pulled back in horror. "Sorry about that," he muttered.

I tried not to show my shock, but my head was suddenly swirling. Was Elder Cooper gay, too? I thought I was the only Mormon in the world who was such a sinner. Non-Mormons, yes. But missionaries?

I'd certainly never met another person like me in the Church. I'd fantasized about it over and over, of course, but it never occurred to me such a fantasy might ever come true. And now to have someone who was my companion turn out to be another finocchio? Was this a dream? I pinched myself.

Perhaps it was a blessing from Heavenly Father. Or a trial of my faith. Whatever was happening, though, it was big.

Damn! There was that déjà vu again. What the hell was going on?

Maybe we should go door to door tonight, after all, force ourselves to be more obedient. But I didn't want to bore myself into righteousness. Almost without exception, I always felt less spiritual after a few hours of tracting, not more. If only we could meet a terrorist and convert him or find a Catholic priest who was secretly a Mason and convert him, even find a family of zingari and baptize them, do something interesting for a change. Then maybe

I could ask Heavenly Father to kill me, and I could go out on a high.

Instead, I directed us to a bookstore I'd seen downtown before, and we each bought a book, *Il giardino segreto* for me and *Guerre stellari* for him. Neither of them written by Italians. It was too far to take the bus back way past Porta Pia to the park, so we found a bench near the Stazione Termini and started reading.

We watched nervously as a huge flock of pigeons flew overhead but we seemed safe enough and luxuriated in an afternoon of relaxation. I'd enjoyed Elder Cooper's company every day even while doing unpleasant missionary work. Maybe *because* the work was unpleasant. But today showed me that it was even more enjoyable being around him when we were doing activities we honestly liked.

I thought of something I wanted to do with him tonight that I was sure we'd both really enjoy.

I bit my lip and turned back to my book. Colin had to try walking again and again before he got any good at it. I thoroughly loved this story and had read it many times as a child. The kids broke the rules and ended up making life better for everyone. It was fun to be reading it now in Italian. But after struggling with the passato remoto for a couple of hours, which no one ever used in normal speech, I needed a break.

"Want to take a walk around the train station?"

We walked inside to the main room, lined with ticket stations along the wall separating the main area from the platforms. The waiting area was always busy, though a good number of people were locals just looking for a place to hang out. One older woman I recognized immediately liked to lift her skirt when businessmen walked past. They'd stop in astonishment and she'd laugh in return. I watched an older man now reach into the pocket of a younger man struggling to get something out of a machine. The younger man never noticed a thing. Practice made perfect.

And now I wasn't sure coming here was the best idea, after all. While I enjoyed feeling worldly, some worldliness was rather ugly. I was about to turn around when two young men in suits stopped a couple of yards from us. They looked to be in their mid-twenties and had dark complexions, maybe from farther south.

Elder Cooper's pale coloring was pleasant enough, but I had to admit, some Italian men had awfully attractive skin. The two men I was staring at each set a medium-sized suitcase at his feet. I so wanted to ask if they were in town on a visit, if they needed a place to stay. Of course, the zone leaders would never permit it, and as easy as it was to lie to myself, I was still quite aware it wasn't hospitality which drove me.

It wasn't that I wanted to have sex with them or anything. If I wasn't going to make love with my favorite companion, I certainly wasn't going to have sex with total strangers.

But that didn't mean they weren't beautiful.

One of the men seemed especially somber and my missionary instincts jumped in again. Maybe I could make this man happy by giving him the gospel. I'd go over and get a referral to make up for my lustful thoughts. I took one step forward and stopped, feeling I'd approached these men somewhere before.

What an odd feeling. Then, shaking the thought out of my mind, I continued over.

"Buona sera," I said, smiling and offering my hand. "Have you ever wondered where you'll go when this life is over?" It was one of our standard approaches. We asked outrageous questions that baited people to answer. Once they had, they were trapped in a conversation.

The men looked at each other nervously, grabbed their suitcases, and hurried out of the station. How curious, I thought. Elder Cooper shrugged and pointed to his book, so we left the building and headed back for our bench. A pigeon flew over and dropped a spot of white right where I'd been sitting. We kept walking.

We walked several blocks until we came to the Pantheon, where we ordered a cheap acqua minerale from a nearby café and sat at an iron table with a stained marble top, sipping while we continued to read in the shade of the ancient building. After only fifteen minutes, though, Elder Cooper cleared his throat. "Elder Shaw," he said, "I think we need to have Companion Inventory."

I looked up in surprise. Inventories were usually saved for times elders were angry with one another and needed to clear the air. "What's up, Anziano?"

Elder Cooper looked at me and took a deep breath. He calmly closed his eyes and then looked at me again. "Don't you ever just want to run away?" he asked.

I frowned. "What do you mean? Leave the mission and go home?"

He shook his head. "I mean, run off to Aquila or Castel Gandolfo or someplace where there aren't any Mormons, mix in with the Italians. Run off and live a normal life."

I couldn't believe I was hearing this. It was something I had in fact fantasized about many times as I was falling asleep in an apartment full of elders, but it wasn't the kind of thing you admitted to another missionary. In my fantasies, I thought of passing myself off as Italian and never talking to another American again. But while we were fluent in terminology related to the Church, we were still amateurs when it came to holding a normal conversation. On the one hand, I could understand the importance of focus, but on the other, I often wondered if the design was to deliberately cripple us.

"Sometimes," I said softly.

Elder Cooper leaned forward across the tiny table, his face only inches from mine, but I didn't pull back. "We could run off together," he whispered. "Get jobs, share an apartment."

"Apartments are expensive," I protested haltingly.

"We could share a one-bedroom." He paused. "Share a bed if we have to."

My heart began beating rapidly, amazed and thrilled and frightened by the conversation. And yet at the same time, I couldn't knock the feeling we'd already had this talk. Perhaps I'd dreamed it. I did still have nocturnal emissions sometimes, more often the past couple of months. But that wasn't really it. Was it?

Such an odd feeling. Dreams so often dissipated within seconds of waking up. I hoped I hadn't forgotten a warning from heaven trying to keep me pure. I stared at my companion, wanting desperately to lean back toward him the remaining few inches and kiss him full on the lips.

Mary Lennox made her own magic.

"Let's go to Piazza Navona," I said, pushing my chair back and standing. "I'll splurge and treat us to dinner." I smiled. "We don't get to eat dinner often enough."

"Is that a yes?" Elder Cooper asked.

I laughed nervously. "We'll talk more later."

When we made it to the square, there were already lots of people milling about. It was still relatively early in the evening, but the tables at the restaurants lining the square were mostly filled. A man juggled fire in one part of the square as locals and tourists watched together in admiration. A young woman in another area sang "Maledetta Primavera" to a group nodding approvingly.

Other people gazed at the churches or at the Fountain of the Four Rivers.

"Hey, look." I put my hand on Elder Cooper's arm. "There are those guys again." I nodded toward the two olive-skinned Italians we'd seen earlier at Termini, now standing near the fountain.

"They're not interested, Elder Shaw," my companion replied.

"I'm not going to do an approach," I assured him. "Just going to say hi." I walked up to the two men with a smile and waved. I wondered for a second if they might be gay, too. Perhaps they could help Cooper and me figure out how to navigate our future.

But instead, Hell unleashed itself in full fury, and we were cast immediately into Outer Darkness.

***

The alarm went off at 6:30 and I stumbled out of bed toward my desk. Back in the MTC, I'd had a top bunk and would jump to the floor so lightly in the morning to turn off my clock that my companion called me "The Cat." These days, I just plodded loudly across the granite floor, pushing my chair out of the way with a loud screech. I could hear Elder Cooper groan from his bed on the other side of the room. Thank heavens we could sleep in till 6:30 now. If we prayed hard enough, maybe we could get Heavenly Father to persuade the mission president to push the time back to 7:00.

I hurried to the bathroom, but I was already too late. With one zone leader in the shower and the other standing before the toilet, I was out of luck. Elder Walker grinned at me sardonically and said, "The Lord blesses those who take the initiative to wake up early."

"Your mother must have told you you were special every single day as you were growing up," I said.

Elder Walker's face hardened, and for a moment, I thought he was going to spray me with the last of his stream. I nodded a pleasant goodbye and went on to the kitchen, where I poured myself some Corn Flakes. They'd never been my favorite cereal, but it was the only option I'd ever found in Italy. There were two entire aisles in the local grocery featuring several dozen different kinds of pasta, but only one single type of cereal was available. Naturally, the most boring kind, leading me to start off every morning day after day after day with soggy flakes.

As I was pouring milk from a fresh triangle onto my cereal, Elder Walker came into the kitchen and bumped up against me. Milk splashed onto the table.

"Sorry," he said coldly.

I used my hand to brush the milk onto the floor.

"What the flip are you doing?"

"It'll be easier for you to mop that way," I said.

"I'm going to report you for insubordination, Elder Shaw."

"Oh, dear, do you think they'll take away my stripes?"

Elder Walker flicked the last bit of milk from the table into my face and stormed out of the kitchen. I wiped the liquid off my eyelid and flicked it onto the floor. A moment later, Elder Cooper staggered into the room moaning. "I need coffee."

I smiled. "Hang in there, buddy. I'll get you a Coke when we leave the apartment."

I gulped down the rest of my cereal and tried to beat Walker to the shower, but just as I was about to climb in, he rushed through the door and pushed me aside. "Ha!" he said triumphantly, pulling the shower curtain closed in front of my face.

I thought of returning to my bedroom and getting started on the morning's studies, but instead I stood right by the shower curtain, humming "Ye Elders of Israel." After a couple of minutes, Elder Walker jerked the curtain back. "And just what do you think you're doing?"

"Killing two birds with one stone," I replied.

"What's that supposed to mean?"

"I'm waiting for my turn. And I'm making sure you don't do anything in the shower I'll have to report later to the president."

"You little—"

"Is it my turn yet?" I started putting one foot over the edge of the tub.

"Get the fuck out of—" Elder Walker clapped a hand over his mouth in horror at a moral lapse too great even for him.

"Did you say something about fucking?" I asked, pointing to his penis, which for some reason had started to grow, probably from all the "dirty" talk. He jumped out of the tub, grabbed his towel, and rushed off to his room. I stepped into the tub and started washing my hair.

I had no idea what had gotten into me. I often thought about doing things like that, but I rarely actually did them. I wasn't sure I even liked this new me or not. I was being exceptionally obnoxious, which was bad, but I wasn't putting up with his crap anymore, which was good. But if you added -9 and +9, you still came out with zero.

During Quiet Hour, I watched Elder Cooper put on his headphones. We were forbidden from listening to anything other than the Mormon Tabernacle Choir, but he'd smuggled some Springsteen and The Cars into the apartment when he was transferred in from Pescara. Elder Walker sometimes did spot checks on Preparation Day, so the only time my companion could listen in peace was during Quiet Hour.

I read several pages of the Book of Mormon, even more boring the seventh time through, and then tapped Cooper on the shoulder when it was time to get ready for Devotional. We made some plans, shared them with the other elders, and sang the closing hymn at the end of our meeting. We ran out of the apartment the second the closing prayer was finished and grabbed a Coke at the corner bar before heading to the bus stop.

As we rode along, my companion looked out the window as usual while I simply focused on him, admiring his profile. You couldn't see the slight turn at the end of his nose from the side. But the truth was, he looked pretty good from any angle.

Several images of him from a variety of angles, unclothed, filled my mind, and I quickly offered up a prayer of repentance.

But now I imagined him kneeling in prayer while I walked up until he opened his eyes and saw my crotch at face level.

A few minutes later, we stepped off the bus at Villa Torlonia. A man hurried past in one direction and two women passed us in the other. I had a brief sensation of déjà vu and then tried to clear my head, breathing deeply to let the fresh air in. With a broad smile, I looked up at the morning sunlight streaming through the leaves. I was in Rome. Even on days when I had to deal with Elder Walker, I was still in Rome.

But why me? Why hadn't Heavenly Father sent me to North Dakota, like he'd sent my cousin?

Elder Cooper found a bench and sat down with a peaceful expression that somehow still excited me. But I had work to do, even if my companion was taking the morning off. I looked about for someone to approach and saw a young man reading a book. I walked over and asked, "Che leggi?" in my friendliest voice.

The man did not seem to recognize my friendliness. He held up the book, showing me the front cover. *The Bourne Identity: Un nome senza volto.* Some kind of spy thriller.

I suddenly felt a pang of longing. My MTC companion had been in Napoli One last November during that huge earthquake which killed three thousand people. My trainer had told me about a time he witnessed a kidnapping in Sardegna. I always wished I could have some type of adventure myself. Not something as awful as those things, of course. I wanted to catch a bomber or shooter and save everyone he was about to kill.

Be the hero I never was as a missionary. The two people I'd baptized so far were already inactive.

Of course, I was probably no good at conversions because Heavenly Father was the one person I couldn't keep a secret from. He knew I fantasized about Elder Cooper. I looked back at him now and nodded. Yep. I'd give up the rest of my life for just one day of complete honesty with this man. You couldn't call down the Holy Spirit with that attitude.

I turned back to the young man reading his book and decided to leave him alone for now. Why in the world did we keep pestering people who clearly had no interest in our message? Someone had once said that a Buddhapest was someone who never stopped talking about Buddhism. So what were Mormon missionaries called? Missioneri?

Agents of blackness.

Well, perhaps that was a bit much. Still, it was hard to face knowing that people thought of you as bad news every time they saw you spreading the "gospel." I wanted to do something useful. Help tourists cross the street perhaps. Or clean up the messes dogs left all over the city sidewalks. Maybe even clean a church.

I frowned, feeling another wave of déjà vu.

Elder Cooper and I relaxed the rest of the morning, strolling through the park and sitting on various benches to get new perspectives on the other folks enjoying their morning. On one bench, Elder Cooper placed his hand so that it lightly rested against mine, just barely touching. I knew any normal guy would move his hand, but I couldn't. It felt too good. After a few minutes, I shifted on the bench, pushing my own hand ever so slightly more against his.

We arrived back at the apartment just after 1:30, Elder Walker demanding from the kitchen to know how many referrals we'd gathered.

"Abbiamo got due!" Elder Cooper yelled back. This appropriately irritated Walker but he still served a delicious meal of tortellini.

When everyone was finished, it was my companion's turn to wash dishes. I ran to my desk to get my faded purple copy of *Italian for Missionaries* and joined him again in the kitchen so we could get in some Dual Study time. We reviewed the imperfect subjunctive. I watched his ass as we studied.

"Anziano," I said later on our way to the bus stop, "do you mind if we don't go tracting tonight? I'm in the mood for more hooky."

"Tu are the piú fun collega I've ever avuto."

I was just about to make some retort about how annoying he could be when suddenly he leaned over and kissed me on the cheek. We stared at each other in shock, and then we both smiled at the same time. I had a sense that I'd known all along Elder Cooper was gay, even before the kiss, even before the touch in the park. Odd, really, but now that we did know for sure...

How was that going to change anything? We were still Mormon.

We headed downtown to a bookstore, where I bought a copy of *Il giardino segreto* and Cooper bought a copy of *Guerre stellari*. I couldn't face going all the way back to the park, so we just found a bench near the Stazione Termini and started reading.

I watched nervously at the hundreds of pigeons flying overhead. I'd had a perfectly good copy of a Book of Mormon in Italian ruined once as we passed the station on our way to an appointment at a nearby pensione. A thousand lire down the drain. I could have bought a gelato with that. Or a piece of pizza bianca.

Elder Cooper and I read in silence, enjoying the simplicity of sitting next to each other. I could get used to this. We could make our own secret garden somewhere. The endless possibilities started filling my mind, and then blood started filling my member, so I reluctantly turned back to my book. After we'd been reading a couple of hours, I felt Elder Cooper's hand brush gently over my hair. Despite enjoying the touch, I jumped in surprise.

"There was a fly on you," my companion explained calmly. He grinned, and I knew he was lying through his teeth.

"Oh!" I returned, gently caressing his hair in return. "You had one, too."

We stared at each other a moment, neither of us knowing what to do next. Finally, I suggested we take a break and head into the station for a few minutes. We walked into the main room, lined with ticket stations along the wall separating the main area from the platforms. I watched an older man as he pickpocketed a younger man trying to get something out of a machine. I frowned, instinctively covering my front pocket where I kept my wallet. An older woman lifted her skirt when a businessman walked by.

Were Elder Cooper and I facing a future of our own degeneracy? Were we just like them now?

My companion put his hand on my arm and, still surprised by male contact, I bolted from the gnashing of teeth that his touch promised. But I ran straight into two other people, attractive young men with dark complexions.

"Uffa! Mi dispiace!" I muttered. I held out my hand. "Anziano Shaw. That's my companion, Anziano Cooper."

One of the men looked as if he was about to say something, and then both grabbed their suitcases and hurried out of the building.

"Are you okay, Elder?" my companion asked.

I laughed. "Other than being an idiot, I think so." I shook my head. "Let's go to the Pantheon and get some acqua minerale."

Elder Cooper nodded. "I have something I want to tell you anyway."

We left the building, and as we passed the bench where we'd been reading earlier, I watched a pigeon fly over and drop a spot of white right where I'd been sitting. I paused for a second, feeling that odd sense of déjà vu again before we continued on.

It was all I could do not to grab Elder Cooper's hand like a teenager heading to the ice cream parlor. We ordered our water and found a seat at an iron table with a marble top. I took a deep sip, enjoying the sensation of slight burning in my throat.

"What did you want to say?" I asked.

Elder Cooper stared at the stained tabletop a moment and then returned his gaze to my face. "Would you still like me if I didn't finish my mission?"

A brief pause. "Yes," I answered.

"Would you still like me if I left the Church?"

A slightly longer pause. "Of course."

Now it was Cooper's turn to pause. "Would you still like yourself if you didn't finish your mission and *you* left the Church?" He was looking down at the tabletop again.

So this was the kind of proposals gay men received, I thought. Not quite as romantic as what I'd dreamed all these years when I allowed myself to hope for the impossible. I reached over and took Elder Cooper's hands.

I felt suddenly disoriented, as if my inner ears were no longer working. Just yesterday, I would have chosen death before letting anyone else on the entire planet know my secret. And today, it almost seemed like a non-issue, as if I'd had this conversation a dozen times already.

Almost. Though I knew saying yes condemned me to an eternity of regret.

But perhaps also to a lifetime of happiness. My family wouldn't be thrilled, but we hardly lived in the days of arranged marriages. I could choose my own mate.

"Only if I get dibs to the right side of the bed," I said.

Elder Cooper looked up at me. "Call me Greg, Eric." He smiled.

"Let's go to Piazza Navona," I said. "I'll treat us to dinner."

When we made it to the square, there were already lots of people milling about. It was still relatively early, but the tables at the restaurants lining the square were mostly filled. A man juggled fire at the far end of the square while a young woman sang "Maledetta Primavera" closer to us. People were sitting near the fountain, gazing at the statue and chatting.

"Ecco." I put my hand on Elder Cooper's arm. "There are those guys again." It was the two olive-skinned Italians from the train station. For a second, I almost thought I knew their names, though I'd clearly never seen them before this afternoon.

"Are you going to spend the evening with me or with strangers?" Elder Cooper said, taking my hand off his arm and clasping it gently.

I laughed. "You have my full attention," I said.

"That's the right answer," he replied. "I might have had to report you to the mission president if you'd said anything else." He stuck his tongue out at me.

I leaned forward and put my mouth around his tongue, and we stood there by the fountain kissing for what seemed an eternity. We found a seat at the restaurant closest to us and were halfway through our meal when the world suddenly exploded around us.

***

The alarm went off at 6:30 and I stumbled out of bed toward my desk, listening to my companion groan on the other side of the room. After pulling up the serranda, I felt pressure in my bladder and hurried to the bathroom, but I was already too late. Elder Walker was urinating like a fountain into the toilet, an expression of triumph on his face. "The Lord blesses those who take the initiative to wake up early," he said.

I couldn't help but laugh. "Say something original once in a while."

Elder Walker's face hardened, and for a moment, I thought he might turn around and pee right on me. I left and walked a few feet down the hall to the kitchen, where I poured some Corn Flakes into a bowl, added some sugar, and then opened a new triangle of milk. That was odd, I thought. Hadn't I just opened a new container yesterday?

Seconds later, I heard Elder Walker come into the kitchen and quickly moved my arm out of his way. Elder Walker bumped into the table and grunted.

"Fool me once," I said.

With a brief snort, he turned around and left the kitchen. I looked back at him and frowned. Elder Cooper joined me a few moments later and I shared my cereal. "Thanks, comp," he said, still only half awake.

"Anything for you, buddy."

He smiled and I so wanted to tousle his hair. Our eyes locked for a moment, and then we both looked away. What an odd tension in the air this morning, I thought.

I left to take a shower, but Elder Walker beat me to it, so I just started my morning studies instead. First was a review of the missionary discussions that we taught our investigators. We used them so rarely that if we didn't review them constantly, we'd forget them. Next came my shower, with only tepid water by this point. I hurried so my companion wouldn't have only cold water left for his turn. Finally, it was Quiet Hour, when even Elder Walker wasn't allowed to talk to us.

After Devotional, Cooper and I hurried out of the apartment, grabbed a Coke at the corner bar, and headed over to the park on Via Nomentana. As we stepped off the 36, a man walked by in one direction while two women passed us in the other. I looked at my companion and frowned.

"What?" he said.

"I guess it's just déjà vu," I replied. But it was an unnerving, unsettling feeling. It passed, though, as soon as we entered the park. I breathed in the morning air and closed my eyes. I was in Rome. Glorious, wonderful Rome. Even Elder Walker couldn't ruin an experience like this. And my companion and I were going to take things easy today. Kind of a half P-Day. A mini-vacation. Those always felt even better on work days. And it seemed I was doing it more and more lately. Perhaps in a few weeks, when the water warmed up a little, we could sneak a swim in Lake Albano. At least make some lifelong memories before we parted for good.

I frowned.

Elder Cooper found a bench and sat down, lifting his face to the sun and closing his eyes in ecstasy. I felt a tingle in my groin as I started thinking about ways I could make him show me that expression in our bedroom after everyone else went to sleep. Those kinds of wicked thoughts usually made me feel guilty, but today they just made me feel a deeper longing. Perhaps I was already "past feeling," as the scriptures said. Gay people always ended up in the gutter, didn't they?

I decided I'd better do at least a little work while Elder Cooper relaxed. I saw a young man on a nearby bench reading a book and walked over to him, giving a little sigh as I braced myself for the interaction. Hadn't I done this a thousand times already in the past twenty months?

No one ever warned new elders that the next two years might be the most boring of their lives. For every one-hour trip through the Coliseum or five-minute ride past the aqueduct, there were six full weeks of missionary drudgery. "Che leggi?" I asked in my friendliest tone.

I could feel the irritation emanating from the man and almost stepped back. He held up the book, showing me the front cover. *The Bourne Identity: Un nome senza volto.* I nodded. I remembered that lots of Italians believed

Mormons were CIA agents. If only it were true, I thought. "Sounds good. I'll put it on my list." I walked off and joined my companion on the bench, confused.

I had an uncanny feeling I'd had that encounter before. And it meant something.

Spies? Or secret agents? Or terrorists? Maybe undercover police? I wasn't sure, but there was something strange about it. I felt a tickling at the back of my brain, an idea or glimmer of something that was about to happen. What was it? Something about a train? Maybe a bomb?

For a brief second, I saw an explosion. Something I'd dreamed about last night. Had I been given a vision of some terrible event about to happen? I struggled to remember but couldn't. Perhaps it was too difficult for Heavenly Father to communicate with someone as degenerate as I was.

I did feel a brief moment of guilt at that realization and then shrugged. I was probably just having a nervous breakdown because all I could think about the past few weeks was running off with Elder Cooper. Being wicked weakened a person's mind.

If I couldn't be a good Mormon, though, maybe I could settle for being a decent person. Perhaps I should spend some time each day helping tourists cross the street. Or picking up dog feces on the sidewalks. Maybe even helping clean a Catholic church.

Flip. I hugged myself, feeling frightened for some unfathomable reason. Elder Cooper opened his eyes. "Stai bene?"

"I…I don't know."

Elder Cooper reached over and hesitantly took my hand. I looked down at our interlocking fingers. How had he known I wouldn't slug him? I squeezed his hand back.

"Something's happening," I said.

Elder Cooper smiled but didn't say anything in response.

We returned to the apartment on Franco Sacchetti just after 1:30, and Elder Walker immediately demanded we tell him how many referrals we'd taken.

"Abbiamo got due," Elder Cooper called back. I looked at him oddly.

Then Walker served us tortellini again. I stared in confusion at the twisted lumps filling my spoon. Two days in a row? Elder Walker always tried to be irritating. If he'd known I loved tortellini, though, he'd have found a different way to annoy me. It was my second favorite Italian meal. Lasagna was the one I saved for truly special occasions, but tortellini was a close second. I ate another mouthful, enjoying the flavor, yet feeling that there was something wrong I couldn't quite put my finger on.

While Elder Cooper washed the dishes, we spent some time reviewing the imperfect subjunctive and then some new vocabulary. Culo, un buco di culo, cazzo, coglioni, capezzolo, sborra, chiavare.

Cooper dropped a dish in the sink, but thankfully, it didn't break. "What the hell do you think you're doing?" he hissed.

"I…I just thought we ought to know all the words for our own body parts," I said. "What if we have to go to the doctor sometime and we can't even describe what's wrong?"

Elder Cooper raised an eyebrow and put one hand on his hip. "And just what problems do you foresee with your nipple?"

I didn't want to tell him I thought he might bite it too hard one day. And that it still might not be hard enough. I felt as if I'd been thinking about how much I loved him, and about sex, and about running away, for ages. We'd only been together nine weeks. Thank goodness we'd just made it past another transfer. We'd be together at least another month.

But I didn't want to be with him another month. I wanted to be with him the rest of my life.

A brief image of flames filled my mind and then disappeared.

What if the rest of my life wasn't very long?

Urgenza, audacia, intrepido.

We left the apartment at 3:30 and headed to a bookstore downtown, where we each bought a book, a ridiculous splurge. Then we made our way to the train station and found a bench outside where we could read in the spring sunshine. I watched as a heavy zingara demanded money from a man who'd just come out of the pensione where we'd taught an impoverished family a few weeks ago.

I stole a glance at the station and then looked up nervously at the hundreds of pigeons flying nearby. I tried to read but couldn't stay focused and kept looking at Termini. As the name suggested, it wasn't really a station but a terminal. It was massive, with thirty-two platforms. I'd been here a dozen times. We sometimes rode the local trains to Velletri and Albano and Frascati on P-Day.

I wanted to live in Frascati with Elder Cooper, maybe get a job at the observatory. I'd be happy as a janitor or portiere as long as I was with Cooper. But was Frascati far enough away from other Mormons to be safe?

It would have to be.

"Let's take a break and go inside for a bit," I said after a while. We went into the main room and watched the bustle of people. One woman stole a small suitcase from another woman without breaking her stride. A man begging for money was ignored by everyone while a woman lifting her skirt received all the attention she wanted. I saw two attractive young men talking seriously to each other and wondered if I should try to get at least one referral for the day.

I started to approach and then stopped myself. Something was wrong. I had a sudden vision of this moment being played over and over and over, as if we were in a sealing room at the temple, with facing mirrors on opposite walls. If I looked in one direction, I saw images of the room going backward indefinitely. If I looked in the other, I saw them stretching ahead for eternity.

But in each of the hundreds of mirrors, I kept seeing the same image again and again and again. A static eternity.

I felt a sudden conviction that these men were the key to my future. "Buona sera," I said, smiling and offering my hand. "Have you ever wondered…" I felt too confused to go on. The men looked at each other nervously. I realized I must seem like someone quite mentally ill. The men grabbed their suitcases and hurried out of the building.

But something wasn't right. Those men had been up to something. Were they going to plant a bomb and leave? That was the kind of thing the Red Brigades did. I thought back to the book in the park this morning. These guys were spies, or agents, or…or something. I knew it with every fiber of my being. I—I had a testimony of it.

"Are you okay, Anziano?"

I turned to Elder Cooper and smiled. "We need to have Companion Inventory," I said. "A long one. Let's go over to the Pantheon."

"Good. I have something I want to talk about, too."

We walked out of the terminal, and as we passed the bench we'd been sitting on earlier, a pigeon flew over and dropped a spot of white right where I'd been sitting. We kept walking.

I bought two glasses of acqua Ferrarelle, the best mineral water available, and we sat at a table with a stained marble top. We each took a sip. Then Elder Cooper said, "What's up?"

I smiled. "I know it's not fair, buddy, since I called the Inventory, but I'd really like you to go first."

He frowned, took another sip, and set his bottle down. "All right," he said. "It's a bit awkward to just come right out and say it. But…" He took a deep breath. "…what do you think about running away with me?"

I nodded. I'd known that was what he was going to suggest. I saw today happening over and over in my mind, each day the same but slightly different. Something momentous had happened. Somehow, Heavenly Father was making me relive this day until I got it right. Had I said yes to Elder Cooper before? Had I said no? I couldn't think what I was supposed to do to correct our course.

"Well? Don't leave me hanging."

"Elder Cooper," I said slowly, "I don't know if you're aware of what's happening."

He frowned. "You're falling in love with me, aren't you? I've been trying my hardest for weeks."

"We're in some kind of time loop. This day is repeating. For all we know, we've lived this day dozens of times already, maybe hundreds." I didn't understand enough science to know if it were possible. Even Joseph Smith never talked about such things. But angels could transport across the galaxy instantly in a beam of light.

Elder Cooper looked at me, still frowning, and then looked about him at the Pantheon and the patrons at the other tables. He turned back to me again.

"Yes," I said, answering his question. I reached forward and took his hand. "I knew you were special the moment you were assigned to Rome Four. In the two months since, we've become exceptionally good friends. And lately, I want to be more than that."

My companion smiled nervously. My words might have been comforting, but I doubted my tone was.

"But today—it's as if today I've become absolutely committed to marrying you. How can that happen in just one day?"

"You want to marry me?"

I nodded. "Well, move in together and start a life with you. Make cannelloni together. Scopare insieme. I love you."

"Then everything is wonderful!" he said, pulling me close and kissing me firmly, prying open my lips. It was my very first kiss. I'd never even kissed a girl before. Feeling Cooper's tongue in my mouth was the most wondrous thing I'd ever experienced, and yet, it felt as if I'd done this a hundred times before. "The stake patriarch was right when he said a mission would change my life!"

I finally leaned back in my chair. "But something's wrong," I went on.

He cocked his head like a dog.

"We're not going to make it past today. We're going to keep living it over and over."

Cooper's brows furrowed. "What's wrong with reliving today? The day you told me you loved me? Could there be a better day than this?" He spread his arms out as if to encompass the world.

"Yes," I said softly. "The day after."

My companion looked at me uncertainly but smiled anyway.

"Come on," I said, standing up. "Let's go have dinner on Piazza Navona. My treat."

We removed our name tags so we could walk along the street holding hands. If anyone looked at us funny, we didn't notice. I peered up at the architecture of each building we passed, smiled at the Vespas whizzing past, smelled the city air. Perhaps we'd done this a hundred times as well but holding hands with the man I loved felt like something that could never be boring.

The Mormon doctrine of eternal marriage, one of the foundational principles of the Church, had always seemed a bit daunting. I didn't want to marry a woman, but even assuming I did, did I really want to be with anyone at all for two million years? For three trillion? For fifty-five gazillion?

Looking at Elder Cooper, I realized I did.

"Greg," I said, "you should start calling me Eric."

"Are we leaving tonight, Eric?"

"We'll pack what we need and head out around five in the morning in our P-Day clothes before the others get up. Go to Stazione Termini and catch a train to Frascati. We'll figure out what to do from there." I wondered how many times we'd made these plans, wondered what was going to happen to stop them and send us through the loop yet again.

I remembered asking my bishop back home how eternity was possible. I could almost understand the future never ending, but I could never wrap my head around infinity going into the past. Didn't it have to start at some point? Even if it did, though, what existed before? And if there were an infinite number of years behind us, how did we ever finally reach the present?

My bishop had smiled benevolently and said, "Eternity is a ring. A gold wedding band that has no beginning and no end."

A loop, I realized now. All time was a loop. Some loops were bigger and some were smaller, but it was all measured in loops. Somehow, our love had trapped us in a very tiny loop. Perhaps this was our punishment for choosing apostasy and wickedness, to keep reliving the day we made our most sinful decision. Maybe we weren't even actually alive anymore but already in Outer Darkness, living out our condemnation throughout infinity.

As if holding Greg's hand every day could ever feel like punishment. Even eternity in Hell couldn't truly be bad, if Greg and I were there together.

So what power did God really have over us?

It was early evening, but there were already lots of people milling about. The tables at the restaurants lining the square were mostly filled, but I could wait for hours if necessary to celebrate our betrothal. Greg pointed to a man juggling fire, and I heard a woman singing "Maledetta Primavera" in a clear, beautiful voice.

Cursed springtime.

"Hey, look." I put my hand on Greg's arm. "There are those guys again." I nodded toward the two olive-skinned men we'd seen earlier at Termini, now standing near the fountain.

"You're not going to ask them the Golden Questions, are you?" Greg said wearily.

I suddenly felt as if all the air had been squeezed out of me.

I knew.

"Are you all right, Eric?" He shook his head slowly, a tiny smile on his lips. "Using your real name all the time is going to take some getting used to." He put his hand on my back and repeated his question, serious again.

"It's them," I whispered.

"You already said that."

"No," I explained carefully, "they're bombers. They're not tourists looking for a hotel. Those suitcases are bombs."

"Eric."

"For pity's sake, how many days have I known this?" I wanted to slap myself.

"If that's true," Greg said slowly, "what are we going to do? What did you do before? Eric…"

I looked at the men, and looked at Greg, and looked at the people all around us. What if the loop didn't repeat again? What if this was my last chance to get it right? I wondered how many chances anyone ever had, for any of the hundred monumental decisions we all had to make throughout our lives.

Sometimes, we only got one.

What hadn't I tried before? Maybe we should simply turn and run. Maybe the next time around, I'd understand what was happening in time to call the police. Perhaps fifty loops from now, I'd figure out something even better.

My heart was pounding, but all I could think about was why Heavenly Father hadn't just let Greg and me die the first time we were killed. We'd have still been virgins, still have been committed to the gospel instead of each other. We might still have made it to the Celestial Kingdom. There was no merciful reason to let us survive, time after time after time.

Greg squeezed my hand and I suddenly felt safe.

I looked again at the two men with their suitcases. Maybe the explosion about to come somehow split the fabric of time. Maybe similar loops developed every time a plane crashed or a volcano blew.

Perhaps hundreds of disasters over the years had already been prevented and no one was the wiser. Except the lone person at the scene who'd mysteriously been chosen to act.

It was like trying to understand why Heavenly Father had commanded Nephi to kill an unarmed, defenseless man.

Oh, my God, I suddenly realized. *He didn't.*

How long had I known that?

"Love has to be stronger than hate," I said.

"Huh?"

I almost laughed, my profound understanding of the universe merely a repetition of what every wise person throughout the millennia had already stated over and over.

"Stai bene, Eric?"

"I remember something."

Greg looked at me expectantly.

"Their names are Luca and Gianni," I said. "I remember." At some point, I must have gotten a few sentences into a conversation. Remarkable given their apparent skittishness. But I'd obviously still said the wrong thing sooner or later. I looked at the men talking quietly to each other. There was something…something I needed to figure out that I'd missed every other time. I'd already suspected they were gay, but…

"Hurry up," Greg urged. "They can set those bombs off any minute." Sweet how he believed me without any evidence whatsoever. Was that faith?

I shook my head. "The Red Brigades don't blow themselves up unless they have to. These guys are here to blow everybody up."

"Please say something that doesn't make me feel even worse every time you open your mouth."

I pulled him close and hugged him. "Perhaps you should move farther away."

"Are you kidding me?"

I looked at the two men again, wondering what it took to help someone choose life over death. What had it taken me?

"Gianni!" I shouted. "Luca!" I gave the friendliest wave I could muster, showing a big smile. I nudged Greg.

"Ciao, Gianni!" Greg shouted. "Ciao, Luca!"

The two men frowned.

Don't approach them, I told myself. Don't spook them. But how could I possibly shout what I needed to say, with two dozen other people listening to every word?

"Questo uomo ed io siamo diventati amanti oggi!" I shouted. This man and I became lovers today. Shouted out like the "good news" from missionaries of old on street corners. "I know you guys are in love, too." I had no idea how I knew that, but I just went with it, whether it was intuition, knowledge, or a desperate guess. "We have a *lot* to talk about."

The two men turned to each other in confusion, and then stared at the others around us who looking back at them with amusement. They looked as if they wanted to run.

"Abbiate fede," I said, waving them toward us. "Let's order some lasagna." I grabbed Greg's hand and held it high for them to see. We had a life full of repetition ahead of us. Making love night after night. Going to work day after day. Watching TV, taking walks, cooking dinner, washing clothes, being bored, being excited, a whole lifetime of sameness and ever so slight difference. A lifetime of loops before an eternity of them.

I almost laughed, thinking of the first time I heard "Sunrise, Sunset." And the second time. And the third.

If this doesn't work, I prayed quietly, please, Heavenly Father, give us just one more chance to fall in love again.

The two men near the Four Rivers still looked confused and worried, perhaps even embarrassed, but they nodded to each other hesitantly and, holding tightly onto their suitcases, started walking toward us.

Books by Johnny Townsend

Thanks for reading! If you enjoyed this book, could you please take a few minutes to write a review online? Reviews are helpful both to me as an author and to other readers, so we'd all sincerely appreciate your writing one! And if you did enjoy the book, here are some others I've written you might want to look up:

Mormon Underwear

A Gay Mormon Missionary in Pompeii

Mormon Misfits

Sexual Solidarity

Out of the Missionary's Closet

The Golem of Rabbi Loew

Gay Gaslighting

The Mysterious Madness of Mormons

Going-Out-of-Religion Sale

Marginal Mormons

Sins of the Saints

Gayrabian Nights

Invasion of the Spirit Snatchers

Escape from Zion

A Mormon Motive for Murder

Breaking the Promise of the Promised Land

I Will, Through the Veil

Am I My Planet's Keeper?

Have Your Cum and Eat It, Too

Strangers with Benefits

Wake Up and Smell the Missionaries

Kinky Quilts

Racism by Proxy

Orgy at the STD Clinic

An Eternity of Mirrors

Please Evacuate

Please Evacuate Again

Recommended Daily Humanity

The Camper Killings

Inferno in the French Quarter: The UpStairs Lounge Fire

Latter-Gay Saints: An Anthology of Gay Mormon Fiction (co-editor)

Wondering what some of those other books are about? Read on!

Invasion of the Spirit Snatchers

During the Apocalypse, a group of Mormon survivors in Hurricane, Utah gather in the home of the Relief Society president, telling stories to pass the time as they ration their food storage and await the Second Coming. But this is no ordinary group of Mormons— or perhaps it is. They are the faithful, feminist, gay, apostate, and repentant, all working together to help each other through the darkest days any of them have yet seen.

Gayrabian Nights

Gayrabian Nights is a twist on the well-known classic, *1001 Arabian Nights*, in which Scheherazade, under the threat of death if she ceases to captivate King Shahryar's attention, enchants him through a series of mysterious, adventurous, and romantic tales.

In this variation, a male escort, invited to the hotel room of a closeted, homophobic Mormon senator, learns that the man is poised to vote on a piece of anti-gay legislation the following morning. To prevent him from sleeping, so that the exhausted senator will miss casting his vote on the Senate floor, the escort entertains him with stories of homophobia, celibacy, mixed orientation marriages, reparative therapy, coming out, first love, gay marriage, and long-term successful gay relationships.

The escort crafts the stories to give the senator a crash course in gay culture and sensibilities, hoping to bring the man closer to accepting his own sexual orientation.

Inferno in the French Quarter: The UpStairs Lounge Fire

On Gay Pride Day in 1973, someone set the entrance to a French Quarter gay bar on fire. In the terrible inferno that followed, thirty-two people lost their lives, including a third of the local congregation of the Metropolitan Community Church, their pastor burning to death halfway out a second-story window as he tried to claw his way to freedom.

A mother who'd gone to the bar with her two gay sons died alongside them. A man who'd helped his friend escape first was found dead near the fire escape. Two children waited outside a movie theater across town for a father and stepfather who would never pick them up. During this era of rampant homophobia, several families refused to claim the bodies, and many churches refused to bury the dead.

Author Johnny Townsend pored through old records and tracked down survivors of the fire as well as relatives and friends of those killed to compile this fascinating account of a forgotten moment in gay history.

This second edition on the 50th anniversary of the fire includes additional research, photographs, and information not available previously.

A Gay Mormon Missionary in Pompeii

What is a gay Mormon missionary doing in Italy? He is trying to save his own soul as well as the souls of others. In these tales chronicling the two-year mission of Robert Anderson, we see a young man tormented by his inability to be the man the Church says he should be. In addition to his personal hell, Anderson faces a major earthquake, organized crime, a serious bus accident, and much more. He copes with horrendous mission leaders and his own suicidal tendencies. But one day, he meets another missionary who loves him, and his world changes forever.

The Golem of Rabbi Loew

Jacob and Esau Cohen are the closest of brothers. In fact, they're lovers. A doctor tries to combine canine genes with those of Jews, to improve their chances of surviving a hostile world. A Talmudic scholar dates an escort. A scientist tries to develop the "God spot" in the brains of his patients in order to create a messiah. The Golem of Prague is really Rabbi Loew's secret lover. While some of the Jews in Townsend's book are Orthodox, this collection of Jewish stories most certainly is not.

Am I My Planet's Keeper?

Global Warming. Climate Change. Climate Crisis. Climate Emergency. Whatever label we use, we are facing one of the greatest challenges to the survival of life as we know it.

But while addressing greenhouse gases is perhaps our most urgent need, it's not our only task. We must also address toxic waste, pollution, habitat destruction, and our other contributions to the world's sixth mass extinction event.

In order to do that, we must simultaneously address the unmet human needs that keep us distracted from deeper engagement in stabilizing our climate: moderating economic inequality, guaranteeing healthcare to all, and ensuring education for everyone.

And to accomplish *that*, we must unite to combat the monied forces that use fear, prejudice, and misinformation to manipulate us.

It's a daunting task. But success is our only option.

Wake Up and Smell the Missionaries

Two Mormon missionaries in Italy discover they share the same rare ability—both can emit pheromones on demand. At first, they playfully compete in the hills of Frascati to see who can tempt "investigators" most. But soon they're targeting each other non-stop.

Can two immature young men learn to control their "superpower" to live a normal life…and develop genuine love? Even as their relationship is threatened by the attentions of another man?

They seem just on the verge of success when a massive earthquake leaves them trapped under the rubble of their apartment in Castellammare.

With night falling and temperatures dropping, can they dig themselves out in time to save themselves? And will their injuries destroy the ability that brought them together in the first place?

Orgy at the STD Clinic

Todd Tillotson is struggling to move on after his husband is killed in a hit and run attack a year earlier during a Black Lives Matter protest in Seattle.

In this novel set entirely on public transportation, we watch as Todd, isolated throughout the pandemic, battles desperation in his attempt to safely reconnect with the world.

Will he find love again, even casual friendship, or will he simply end up another crazy old man on the bus?

Things don't look good until a man whose face he can't even see sits down beside him despite the raging variants.

And asks him a question that will change his life.

Please Evacuate

A gay, partygoing New Yorker unconcerned about the future or the unsustainability of capitalism is hit by a truck and thrust into a straight man's body half a continent away. As Hunter tries to figure out what's happening, he's caught up in another disaster, a wildfire sweeping through a Colorado community, the flames overtaking him and several schoolchildren as they flee.

When he awakens, Hunter finds himself in the body of yet another man, this time in northern Italy, a former missionary about to marry a young Mormon woman. Still piecing together this new reality, and beginning to embrace his latest identity, Hunter fights for his life in a devastating flash flood along with his wife *and* his new husband.

He's an aging worker in drought-stricken Texas, a nurse at an assisted living facility in the direct path of a hurricane, an advocate for the unhoused during a freak Seattle blizzard.

We watch as Hunter is plunged into life after life, finally recognizing the futility of only looking out for #1 and understanding the part he must play in addressing the global climate crisis…if he ever gets another chance.

Recommended Daily Humanity

A checklist of human rights must include basic housing, universal healthcare, equitable funding for public schools, and tuition-free college and vocational training.

In addition to the basics, though, we need much more to fully thrive. Subsidized childcare, universal pre-K, a universal basic income, subsidized high-speed internet, net neutrality, fare-free public transit (plus *more* public transit), and medically assisted death for the terminally ill who want it.

None of this will matter, though, if we neglect to address the rapidly worsening climate crisis.

Sound expensive? It is.

But not as expensive as refusing to implement these changes. The cost of climate disasters each year has grown to staggering figures. And the cost of social and political upheaval from not meeting the needs of suffering workers, families, and individuals may surpass even that.

It's best we understand that the vast sums required to enact meaningful change are an investment which will pay off not only in some indeterminate future but in fact almost immediately. And without these adjustments to our lifestyles and values, there may very well not be a future capable of sustaining freedom and democracy…or even civilization itself.

The Camper Killings

When a homeless man is found murdered a few blocks from Morgan Beylerian's house in south Seattle, everyone seems to consider the body just so much additional trash to be cleared from the neighborhood. But Morgan liked the guy. They used to chat when Morgan brought Nick groceries once a week.

And the brutal way the man was killed reminds Morgan of their shared Mormon heritage, back when the faithful agreed to have their throats slit if they ever revealed temple secrets.

Did Nick's former wife take action when her ex-husband refused to grant a temple divorce? Did his murder have something to do with the public accusations that brought an end to his promising career?

Morgan does his best to investigate when no one else seems to care, but it isn't easy as a man living paycheck to paycheck himself, only able to pursue his investigation via public transit.

As he continues his search for the killer, Morgan's friends withdraw and his husband threatens to leave. When another homeless man is killed and Morgan is accused of the crime, things look even bleaker.

But his troubles aren't over yet.

Will Morgan find the killer before the killer finds him?

Please Evacuate Again

As Craig and Toby struggle to keep their faltering marriage alive, the climate crisis intrudes, part of a threesome in their relationship.

Craig wants to take drastic action but Toby just wants to live his life as best he can before climate breakdown escalates.

"You fight for your life by any means necessary," Craig insists. "If someone breaks into your house, you pull out a baseball bat or a gun. When there's a mass shooting, you run, hide, or fight back."

But when it involves global warming? And fossil fuel industries buying politicians who protect carbon emissions at the cost of human lives?

Craig wonders if a letter to the editor is effective. If blocking traffic at a rally once or twice a year is enough.

Toby threatens to leave him if does anything stupid. And to report him to the authorities.

But Craig feels he'll need to commit violence one way or another, either by condoning the status quo or by doing whatever he can to fight those who keep destabilizing the climate. So he joins a group of eco activists whose efforts are far more extreme than even he had expected.

Will Craig survive the violent police crackdown on protesters?

Will his relationship with Toby survive the additional stress of betrayal?

And will either of them survive the new wildfire that's just started at the edge of town?

Gay Gaslighting

Family members and religious leaders often invoke "love" as their justification for making the lives of LGBTQ folks difficult. But we've learned how to nurture one another.

In these tales from the author of *Mormon Underwear* and *Gayrabian Nights*, a gay man invites two young Mormon missionaries to watch movies on their day off, offering R-rated and eventually X-rated films for their edification. A man receives a substantial inheritance…on the condition he leave his husband. A customer service rep at a Suicide Center established under a new theocracy "assists" those condemned of homosexuality kill themselves.

A bishop is murdered by one of his congregants for being too "liberal." A lonely wife discovers that her husband of twenty-six years is gay. Two missionaries try to interest men at an adult video store in the LDS Church. Parents tell their son he's ugly from the time they first suspect he's gay, hoping he'll be afraid to date once he becomes an adult.

As the fight to remain free of theocracy intensifies, it's important to understand what we're up against and prepare for the political—and emotional—battles ahead. One way is by telling stories oppressors don't want us to hear.

Sexual Solidarity

"Gay Ex-Mormons Unite!" In these tales by a former Mormon missionary, a polygamist in 1855 Utah is ordered to take a fourth wife, when all he really wants is to be with another man. A Victorian enthusiast has a startling sexual revelation to make at his monthly Society meeting. A gay Mormon hires a hit man in a desperate bid to stop himself from breaking the Law of Chastity.

A Relief Society president is trapped on a plane next to a gay man flaunting his sexuality. The Three Nephites seek counseling to deal with their sexual frustrations since their wives aren't immortal as they are. A worthy gay man becomes a ministering angel in the afterlife. A Mormon missionary in Italy moves in with a man he's been teaching.

Gay men don't always have lots in common, but most of us understand religious bigotry and will enjoy reading some of the many ways we've learned not only to cope but also find *"Sexual Solidarity"* with one another.

Escape from Zion

In these short stories by ex-Mormon author Johnny Townsend, parents hire men to pose as the Three Nephites to teach their children the Book of Mormon is true. A shy single woman meets the man of her dreams at an endoscopy party.

An anti-Mormon mob threatens a church outing. A deceased sinner plots to break out of Spirit Prison. Aliens visiting the UN reveal that God really does live on the planet Kolob. Mormons survive the zombie apocalypse because of their two-year supply of food. A young couple desperately try to escape after America becomes a theocracy.

Another fun collection from the author of *Recommended Daily Humanity* and *Please Evacuate*.

Kinky Quilts

Since patchwork quilts are usually displayed in bedrooms where couples engage in sex, why are there so few quilt designs for folks who want a bit of sexual energy in these intimate spaces?

The original designs in this volume range from simple to intermediate, and with over 250 to choose from, even beginner quilters will find patterns tempting enough to get started.

In *Kinky Quilts*, Johnny Townsend has collected his best designs from *Quilting Beyond the Rainbow*, *Gay Sleeping Arrangements*, and *Queer Quilting*, to offer fun, sexy quilts for men who love men.

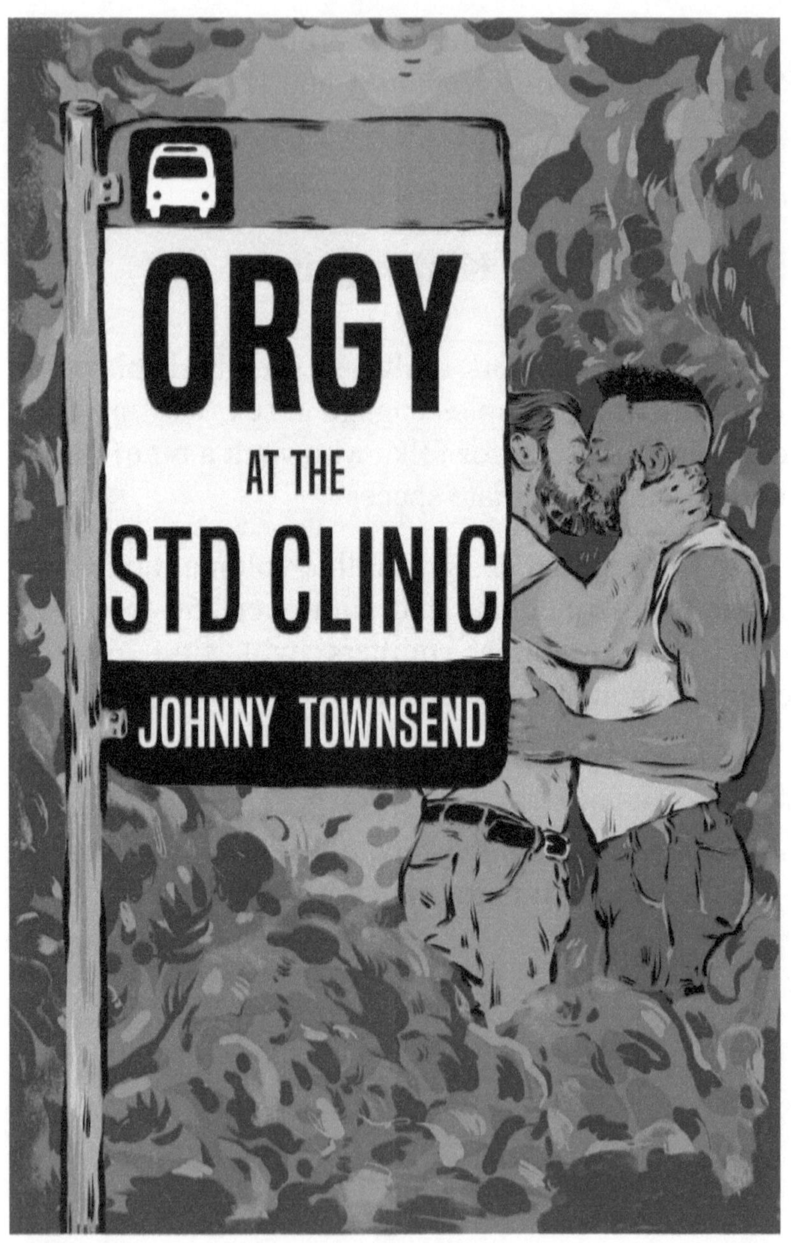
ORGY
AT THE
STD CLINIC
JOHNNY TOWNSEND

HAVE
YOUR CUM
AND
EAT IT, TOO
JOHNNY TOWNSEND

What Readers Have Said

Townsend's stories are "a gay *Portnoy's Complaint* of Mormonism. Salacious, sweet, sad, insightful, insulting, religiously ethnic, quirky-faithful, and funny."

D. Michael Quinn, author of *The Mormon Hierarchy: Origins of Power*

"Told from a believably conversational first-person perspective, [*A Gay Mormon Missionary in Pompeii*'s] novelistic focus on Anderson's journey to thoughtful self-acceptance allows for greater character development than often seen in short stories, which makes this well-paced work rich and satisfying, and one of Townsend's strongest. An extremely important contribution to the field of Mormon fiction." Named to Kirkus Reviews' Best of 2011.

Kirkus Reviews

"The thirteen stories in *Mormon Underwear* capture this struggle [between Mormonism and homosexuality] with humor, sadness, insight, and sometimes shocking details....*Mormon Underwear* provides compelling stories, literally from the inside-out."

Niki D'Andrea, *Phoenix New Times*

"Townsend's lively writing style and engaging characters [in *Zombies for Jesus*] make for stories which force us to wake up, smell the (prohibited) coffee, and review our attitudes with regard to reading dogma so doggedly. These are tales which revel in the individual tics and quirks which make us human, Mormon or not, gay or not..."

A.J. Kirby, *The Short Review*

"The Rift," from *A Gay Mormon Missionary in Pompeii*, is a "fascinating tale of an untenable situation...a *tour de force*."

David Lenson, editor, *The Massachusetts Review*

"Pronouncing the Apostrophe," from *The Golem of Rabbi Loew*, is "quiet and revealing, an intriguing tale..."

Sima Rabinowitz, Literary Magazine Review, *NewPages.com*

The Circumcision of God is "a collection of short stories that consider the imperfect, silenced majority of Mormons, who may in fact be [the Church's] best hope....[The book leaves] readers regretting the church's willingness to marginalize those who best exemplify its ideals: those who love fiercely despite all obstacles, who brave challenges at great personal risk and who always choose the hard, higher road."

Kirkus Reviews

In *Mormon Fairy Tales*, Johnny Townsend displays "both a wicked sense of irony and a deep well of compassion."

Kel Munger, *Sacramento News and Review*

Zombies for Jesus is "eerie, erotic, and magical."

Publishers Weekly

"While [Townsend's] many touching vignettes draw deeply from Mormon mythology, history, spirituality and culture, [*Mormon Fairy Tales*] is neither a gaudy act of proselytism nor angry protest literature from an ex-believer. Like all good fiction, his stories are simply about the joys, the hopes and the sorrows of people."

Kirkus Reviews

In *Inferno in the French Quarter,* "author Johnny Townsend restores this tragic event [the UpStairs Lounge fire] to its proper place in LGBT history and reminds us that the victims of the blaze were not just 'statistics,' but real people with real lives, families, and friends."

Jesse Monteagudo, *The Bilerico Project*

In *Inferno in the French Quarter*, "Townsend's heart-rending descriptions of the victims…seem to [make them] come alive once more."

Kit Van Cleave, *OutSmart Magazine*

Marginal Mormons is "an irreverent, honest look at life outside the mainstream Mormon Church….Throughout his musings on sin and forgiveness, Townsend beautifully demonstrates his characters' internal, perhaps irreconcilable struggles….Rather than anger and disdain, he offers an honest portrayal of people searching for meaning and community in their lives, regardless of their life choices or secrets." Named to Kirkus Reviews' Best of 2012.

Kirkus Reviews

The stories in *The Mormon Victorian Society* "register the new openness and confidence of gay life in the age of same-sex marriage….What hasn't changed is Townsend's wry, conversational prose, his subtle evocations of character and social dynamics, and his deadpan humor. His warm empathy still glows in this intimate yet clear-eyed engagement with Mormon theology and folkways. Funny, shrewd and finely wrought dissections of the awkward contradictions—and surprising harmonies—between conscience and desire." Named to Kirkus Reviews' Best of 2013.

Kirkus Reviews

"This collection of short stories [*The Mormon Victorian Society*] featuring gay Mormon characters slammed [me] in the face from the first page, wrestled my heart and mind to the floor, and left me panting and wanting more by the end. Johnny Townsend has created so many memorable characters in such few pages. I went weeks thinking about this book. It truly touched me."

Tom Webb, *A Bear on Books*

Dragons of the Book of Mormon is an "entertaining collection….Townsend's prose is sharp, clear, and easy to read, and his characters are well rendered…"

Publishers Weekly

"The pre-eminent documenter of alternative Mormon lifestyles…Townsend has a deep understanding of his characters, and his limpid prose, dry humor and well-grounded (occasionally magical) realism make their spiritual conundrums both compelling and entertaining. [*Dragons of the Book of Mormon* is] [a]nother of Townsend's critical but affectionate and absorbing tours of Mormon discontent." Named to Kirkus Reviews' Best of 2014.

Kirkus Reviews

In *Gayrabian Nights*, "Townsend's prose is always limpid and evocative, and…he finds real drama and emotional depth in the most ordinary of lives."

Kirkus Reviews

Gayrabian Nights is a "complex revelation of how seriously soul damaging the denial of the true self can be."

Ryan Rhodes, author of *Free Electricity*

Gayrabian Nights "was easily the most original book I've read all year. Funny, touching, topical, and thoroughly enjoyable."

Rainbow Awards

Lying for the Lord is "one of the most gripping books that I've picked up for quite a while. I love the author's writing style, alternately cynical, humorous, biting, scathing, poignant, and touching…. This is the third book of his that I've read, and all are equally engaging. These are stories that need to be told, and the author does it in just the right way."

Heidi Alsop, *Ex-Mormon Foundation Board Member*

In *Lying for the Lord*, Townsend "gets under the skin of his characters to reveal their complexity and conflicts....shrewd, evocative [and] wryly humorous."

Kirkus Reviews

In *Missionaries Make the Best Companions*, "the author treats the clash between religious dogma and liberal humanism with vivid realism, sly humor, and subtle feeling as his characters try to figure out their true missions in life. Another of Townsend's rich dissections of Mormon failures and uncertainties..." Named to Kirkus Reviews' Best of 2015.

Kirkus Reviews

In *Invasion of the Spirit Snatchers*, "Townsend, a confident and practiced storyteller, skewers the hypocrisies and eccentricities of his characters with precision and affection. The outlandish framing narrative is the most consistent source of shock and humor, but the stories do much to ground the reader in the world—or former world—of the characters....A funny, charming tale about a group of Mormons facing the end of the world."

Kirkus Reviews

"Townsend's collection [*The Washing of Brains*] once again displays his limpid, naturalistic prose, skillful narrative chops, and his subtle insights into psychology...Well-crafted dispatches on the clash between religion and self-fulfillment..."

Kirkus Reviews

"While the author is generally at his best when working as a satirist, there are some fine, understated touches in these tales [*The Last Days Linger*] that will likely affect readers in subtle ways....readers should come away impressed by the deep empathy he shows for all his characters—even the homophobic ones."

Kirkus Reviews

"Written in a conversational style that often uses stories and personal anecdotes to reveal larger truths, this immensely approachable book [*Racism by Proxy*] skillfully serves its intended audience of White readers grappling with complex questions regarding race, history, and identity. The author's frequent references to the Church of Jesus Christ of Latter-day Saints may be too niche for readers unfamiliar with its idiosyncrasies, but Townsend generally strikes a perfect balance of humor, introspection, and reasoned arguments that will engage even skeptical readers."

Kirkus Reviews

Orgy at the STD Clinic portrays "an all-too real scenario that Townsend skewers to wincingly accurate proportions...[with] instant classic moments courtesy of his punchy, sassy, sexy lead character..."

Jim Piechota, *Bay Area Reporter*

Orgy at the STD Clinic is "…a triumph of humane sensibility. A richly textured saga that brilliantly captures the fraying social fabric of contemporary life."

Kirkus Reviews